PERIL
IN THE
POOL HOUSE

PERIL

IN THE

POOL HOUSE

A Chesapeake Bay Mystery

Judy L. Murray

LEVEL
BEST BOOKS

Author Photo Credit: Malgorzata Baker Photography

First edition

ISBN: 978-1-68512-415-1

Cover art by Level Best Designs

This book was professionally typeset on Reedsy.
Find out more at reedsy.com

To my readers who know there is a sleuth within each one of us.

"Do you really want to rake up the past? Who knows what we may find?"

—Miss Jane Marple, Sleeping Murder

Praise for Judy L Murray and Her Chesapeake Bay Mystery Series

"A master of mystery suspense, Judy L Murray is an author to watch… Plenty of red herrings, well-plotted mysteries, and a couple of hints of romance will keep the reader guessing. With a confident voice, the author has created an indelible heroine and a dazzling cast of supporting characters that are as original and vibrant as the protagonist."—PenCraft Awards First Place Winner Review

"The grand opening of Captain's Watch Bed and Breakfast in one of Chesapeake Bay's historic mansions, is ruined when the body of Kerry Lightner, a high-powered political campaign manager, is found in the pool house with fishing shears in her back. Is the killer a rival politician, an ex-lover, a jealous co-worker, or the ghost of missing harbor pilot Isaac Hollowell? When state senate candidate and B&B owner Eliot Davies becomes the prime suspect, his friend real estate agent-turned-amateur-investigator Helen Morrisey and her Detection Club of fictional women sleuths vow to solve the case—even if it means the end of Helen's romance with Detective Joe McAlister. *Peril in the Pool House*, the third in Judy L. Murray's award-winning Chesapeake Bay Mystery Series is smart, fast-paced, beautifully written, and utterly charming. Five stars!"—Connie Berry, *USA Today* bestselling author of the Kate Hamilton Mysteries

"Cozy mystery fans will delight in following Maryland realtor Helen Morrisey as she solves a double murder with the assistance of the vintage de-tectives populating her imagination."—*Lucy Burdette, USA Today* bestselling author of the Key West Food Critics Mysteries

"A clever and well-plotted mystery, Judy L Murray's latest Chesapeake Bay Mystery, *Peril in the Pool House*, is as appealing as the town where it's set. When a candidate for state senate is suspected of murdering his difficult new campaign manager Helen agrees to help clear his name, only to learn that this murder echoes a fifty-year-old scandal involving Davies' grandfather. Fans of this series will not be disappointed."—Lori Robbins, award-winning author of the On Pointe Mysteries

"A gruesome discovery turns a Maryland realtor into a sleuth in Murray's series-starting mystery. *Murder in the Master*...with plenty of romance, surprises, and a climax that's quite the cliffhanger. ...A strong debut whodunit with a memorable main character."—*Kirkus Reviews*

"Five out of Five! A Contender for Top Read 2022! Brilliant! Judy Murray has another hit with the second book in her Chesapeake Bay Mystery Series...A compelling investigation, fascinating details, secrets and motives revealed, ins and outs of the real estate biz, family gatherings, and a bit of welcomed romance (maybe even triangular)... The ending, a key element of any mystery, had the right amount of peril and a surprise, yet satisfying, arrest."—*Kings River Life Magazine*

"Love this series! Compelling page-turning whodunits. I found myself staying up past my bedtime just to get in an extra chapter or two—the sign of a great book. But it is the cast of characters that gives this series its multi-layered appeal. In this installment, their personalities are even more revealed. I find the recurring characters in this book three-dimensional and charming."—Lori Roberts Herbst, award-winning author of the Callie Cassidy Mysteries

"A taunt whodunit. I read Judy L Murray's first book in the series, *Murder in the Master. Killer in the Kitchen* is every bit as powerful...Murray layers lots of suspects. Love the setting in the Chesapeake Bay area, which Murray knows well. Strong characters and conflicting egos really make the plot sizzle. Well-written, and a great addition. I highly recommend it."—Susan Van Kirk, author of the Endurance and Art Center Mysteries

Chapter One

Real Estate Rule #3: It's the rare buyer who wants to buy a haunted house.

"Why are you acting so restless?" Joe McAlister leaned over Helen Morrisey and whispered in her ear.

"Not sure. Something about tonight just doesn't sit right with me. Maybe it's the mix of locals with all these high-powered political types. I feel like there's something in the wind." Helen's large green eyes traveled across the crowded Victorian's huge foyer. Captain's Watch Bed and Breakfast at the top of the Chesapeake Bay was ready for business, and the entire town of Port Anne, Maryland, was looking over the infamous house during its grand opening.

"You're giving me a complex. I'm supposed to be the professional detective."

"Maybe you're desensitized by all your cases." She fluttered her eyelashes at him.

"Very funny. You need to shut down those famous sleuths bouncing around in your head and enjoy the evening." He sipped his bourbon on the rocks.

"You're right. This is supposed to be a victory lap for Alison and Eliot."

"And you. They couldn't have saved this house without you."

Helen looked up at the tall ex-Marine. "Thanks for your loyalty. I'm just so relieved to see this house restored rather than torn down. It was a close call." She accepted a glass of Cabernet from a meandering server.

"So, what's the problem tonight?"

"With Eliot running for state senator, their guests make strange bedfellows. Do you see that little old man over there dropping appetizers into his breast pocket?"

Joe raised dark eyebrows. "Yes."

"After twenty-six years in the real estate business, I've learned a lot about people. He's wearing worn-out Sperry Topsiders, a thread-bare winter coat on an April night, and a wool baseball cap. You might assume he's down and out." She tipped her head toward the opposite side of the house. "See that size four redhead standing in the living room chatting with Ronnie Mann, Eliot's assistant campaign manager? She's got a five-thousand-dollar Louis Vuitton handbag on her arm. It's not a knockoff from Canal Street. She's wearing a Hermes scarf. Her haircut and highlights cost a mint, likely done at a Rittenhouse Square salon in Philadelphia."

"What's your point? Other than I'm glad that's not you."

"That man could very likely own a boatload of stock in pharmaceuticals, and she might not be able to afford her one-bedroom apartment, no less the new Tesla I saw her park as I arrived."

Joe choked on an ice cube. The lines at his eyes crinkled. "That's ridiculous."

She offered up a coy smile, her voice lilting. "Just saying."

"I think you need some air. Let's walk down to the docks and see the house from the water."

They headed out a side door and squeezed between a row of parked cars. Wincing, Helen made her way down the narrow stone walkway in her four-inch stilettos. They were not her Realtor favorites for walking a property, a pair of well-worn, mud-coated red Hunter Wellies.

"Ugh, these shoes are a killer. I feel like M.C. Beaton's Agatha Raisin, in pain because my fifty-four-year-old ego won't give up trying to look chic."

"They look great from here. I like them. Are you Nora Charles tonight? You're very swishy."

"Swishy? That's a new description. Actually, I did invite Nora tonight.

She loves a big party and a martini, or three." She laughed.

They reached the end of the path and the start of two docks jutting out into the water.

Turning their backs to the bay, they faced the looming three-story with its square widow's watch capping the steep slate roofline. Helen held her short dark hair out of her eyes and sighed in satisfaction. Given her obsession with salvaging old buildings, she was as excited about this official unveiling as its new owners.

From ground to attic, the blue-grey paint on the historic house's scalloped shingles glistened. Its trim was bright white. The long wraparound porch facing the water was dotted with white and blue Adirondack chairs and deep cushioned white rockers. A large American flag claimed its expected senior position on a thirty-foot flagpole, with a Maryland state flag below. They snapped in the crisp April breeze. A glossy classic mahogany six-passenger runabout, serving as water taxi, bumped, bumped, bumped against the pilings to her right. An incoming high tide on the bay sloshed over the pier.

To the north and closer to the house sat the original pool house with matching gingerbread, roof, and turret, a charming miniature. Its double doors were flung open, displaying an array of antique buoys, fishing gear, and two sets of worn wooden oars. Heavy, striped canvas drapes hung on large stainless-steel rings along one wall. Steps away, a long rectangular pool reflected an orange ball as the sun slowly slipped down over the western shore into the water. Scattered about the pool's edges, four large teal umbrellas flapped softly in the evening air.

The house had stood empty since the previous owner passed away twelve years ago, and its size and neglected condition intimidated most buyers. Helen showed the property all too often. Port Anne, like many old sea towns, didn't always appreciate its heritage until it was too late. A vocal supporter of the grand old lady during town hall meetings, she'd been determined to counter any talk of it being demolished. Once lost, like others before it, its history would be lost forever. It had been an uphill battle, and some people in town didn't appreciate her determination to save the mansion. Given that a main road through town was named after the past owner, Spencer

Davies, their disinterest surprised her.

When Alison and Eliot Davies approached her about turning the rambling house into a B&B, she was ecstatic. Once she learned Eliot's grandfather was the captain and owner in 1947, she knew this couple was the ideal match.

Ten months later, after working day and night, the Davies were ready for its big reveal. Helen thought tying the event into Eliot's state senate race was a brilliant move. The Port Anne historical enthusiasts were looking forward to a tour. The nay-sayers were here to predict an eventual shipwreck. Everyone knew the Davies had sunk every nickel they had into Captain's Watch.

Joe touched her arm and led the way back up the slight incline. Helen paused to peek into the pool house, smelling of fresh paint and varnish. She'd been entranced by this little cottage since she first saw it. The eighteen by twenty-foot interior, covered in shiplap, was white-washed, its walls decorated with original tools and nick-nacks. A row of white and khaki striped bathing towels draped over four iron cleats. Two fishing poles, a yellowed cotton net, antique shears, and four bright orange life jackets hung on one wall. An old wire crab cage, topped with a square scrap of gleaming teak, served as a small drinks table between two refurbished wicker chairs. A couple empty drink glasses had been left behind by guests. A faded wooden sign with the weather-worn words *Eastern Shore Piloting Services, Inc.* in green script was nailed onto the rear wall over a long wooden desk scarred from use. It was all so Chesapeake charming.

"Mom! Come join us!" Her son, Shawn, called out from the large rear porch and gestured toward the house. As she and Joe reached him, he handed her a fluted glass of champagne. "This is Lacey." He touched the pretty young woman on his arm. "Lacey, this is my mother, Helen Morrisey."

Lacey's light brown eyes met Helen's as she offered her a slender hand. "Nice to meet you, Mrs. Morrisey. I've certainly heard a lot about you. Congratulations on the grand opening." She flashed a wide, confident smile.

Helen protested. "I was only their advocate. The Davies' perseverance is what made this day possible."

"Lacey, this is Joe McAlister." Shawn tilted his head at Joe. "I was afraid you weren't going to make it."

"And miss your mother's favorite cause? Besides, I don't like to skip a good time." Joe offered a strong hand to Lacey, then Shawn. "Great to see you. It's been a little while."

"I believe you're the police detective who moved out of Baltimore homicide. I keep hearing about you," said Lacey.

"That sounds ominous," he responded. "I'd like to think my name isn't always in connection to crime."

Shawn rolled his eyes. "My mother tends to intrude on his investigations."

"I think intrude is saying it kindly. More like barge." Joe raised an eyebrow at Helen. "The past few months, she seems to have taken a hiatus, for which I'm grateful."

Helen protested. "I've never barged. I'd call them coincidences."

"She's delusional," Shawn piped in.

Joe blinked at Helen. "You said you and your friend, Agatha Christie's Jane Marple, don't believe in coincidences."

"I'm amazed," Helen declared, tapping his arm. "Did you all hear him? I've got him quoting one of my Detection Club sleuths."

She gave a cautious side glance at her son and back to his date. Shawn rarely disclosed his dating activity to his mother. Unless his twin sister, Lizzie, filled her in on his romances, she was usually kept in the complete dark. Darned frustrating. Not that Lizzie said much about her boyfriend, Jason. Helen was waiting for an engagement announcement which seemed to be slow in coming.

"Tell me about this Detection Club? Is it something friends can join?" asked Lacey. Shawn choked on an ice cube.

Helen laughed. "I'm embarrassing my son. My Detection Club is strictly in my head." She tapped her temple. "I've been a mystery story lover since I was a kid. My house is chocked with them. A couple years ago, after my husband Andy died, I decided I should use my favorite women sleuths whenever I needed help making personal decisions. Kind of my own private consultants. They each have their own individual quirks, but they're very smart."

"Who are they?"

"Jane Marple, Nora Charles, Agatha Raisin, Jessica Fletcher, and Nancy Drew. Sometimes Trixie Belden." Helen ticked them off on her fingers.

"I love that," laughed Lacey.

"You haven't tried to live with them." The detective rocked on his heels. "On that note, I'm heading for another drink. Can I get anyone a refill?"

"Mom's other obsession is fixing up old houses," Shawn said. "It's one reason she's here tonight."

"Alison and Eliot put lots of elbow grease into this venture. Shawn's dad, Andy, would have been thrilled to see their results," Helen said. She swore she felt Andy's pat of approval on her shoulder. Gone almost five years now, she still missed him. "I'm afraid Shawn and his sister were indoctrinated at a very early age. Andy and I spent our weekends swinging hammers, not golf clubs. Have you seen his rowhouse in Fell's Point?"

"I have," Lacey replied. "Beautiful."

Shawn chuckled. "I showed her the before photos."

"Your parents' passion rubbed off," Lacey grinned at him. "I'm afraid I would have considered the place a lost cause. It was disgusting."

"Agreed. Literally one of the ugliest houses in Baltimore County. The first few months, I swore he slept in a HazMat suit. I wondered how he managed to put on a suit for court every morning." Helen's face brightened. "Lizzie's here. Have you met Shawn's twin?"

"No, but I've heard a lot about her. I've watched her on-air hosting for ShopTV. She knows how to capture her audience."

Shawn gestured at the eye-catching blonde working her way between guests to join them. More than one man followed her progress across the room. Her pale green linen dress fell just above her knees, and a soft yellow wrap draped her bare shoulders. Her mother noticed Jason's absence again and wondered if it was a sign.

"Hello! I'm Lizzie, Shawn's other half." Lizzie gave her brother a quick kiss on the cheek. Her bright blue eyes, which matched her brother's, grazed over Lacey. She squeezed her mother's arm. "Isn't this exciting? I can't believe what Alison and Eliot accomplished in such a short amount of time.

They must have worked twenty-four-seven."

"I've only driven by," Shawn replied. "How bad was it? Given what I went through to make my little place livable, this was a huge project."

Helen raised her eyes to the coffered ceiling and plaster cornices. "Everything you see was damaged by water, mold, or vandals. They were lucky the stained-glass windows survived. If they couldn't restore what was here, they had to track down period replacements. I think they pawed through salvage yards from Philadelphia to Baltimore and every old barn on the Chesapeake Eastern Shore."

Shawn looked about with appreciation. "I'm sure you provided your list of favorite sources. How did they finance the repairs? It's not easy to get a mortgage on an abandoned property."

"I pointed them in the direction of James Corcoran, the director of the historical society. James helped them apply for special funding," Helen replied. "The designation encouraged a mortgage company I trust to fund the rest."

"How's Eliot handling all this in the midst of his campaign? Pretty ambitious," Shawn commented.

Lizzie spoke up. "I want to know when you're running. You're a Baltimore district attorney. You probably follow campaigns closer than anyone. What are his chances? Primary elections are only a few months away."

Her brother ignored her attempt to steer him into a debate on his own candidacy. "Why don't you ask him yourself?"

A tall, hefty man in his early forties clapped an enthusiastic hand on Shawn's shoulder. "Hi, Morrisey family! I'm so glad you all could join us tonight. What do you think of Captain's Watch? Think we'll attract lots of visitors?" He paused and took a swig of a Corona Light. "Lord knows, we better, or Helen will have to unload this albatross on another gullible buyer."

"Don't lay that guilt on me," Helen protested. "It was your grandfather's ghost who convinced you."

Eliot grimaced. "Let's hope his spirit remains out of sight. I'm not so sure he'd attract guests or scare them away. Alison swears she's heard midnight footsteps."

"I wouldn't worry. From the portraits in your library, he looked pretty charming," Helen said.

Lizzie lifted her chin. "There's a ghost?"

A captain's bell clanged from the large front hall. Eliot spotted his wife's wave.

"I'll tell you later," Helen murmured in her ear.

Chapter Two

Eliot joined Alison on the first tread of the foyer's massive oak staircase. A lighted newel post figure of Lady Liberty glowed at the base. Small candlelight bulbs from wall sconces flickered against the dark polished paneling.

"Everyone, thank you for coming!" Alison's sweet voice carried over the chatter. "We'd like to say a few words to commemorate this evening."

Eliot cleared his throat. "As some of you know, this house was built in 1898. My grandfather, Spencer Davies, purchased it in 1947. He was a professional barge pilot all his life. He loved the water. In fact, he added the widow's watch to see the comings and goings of ships on the bay. My father was born here. I grew up here. My mother continued to live in this house until she moved to Virginia to be with her family. After she sold Captain's Watch, it fell on very lean years. About a year ago, Alison and I had the opportunity to move back home to Kent County and approached Helen Morrisey from Safe Harbor Realty. She championed our interest in saving this house." He lifted his glass in her direction. "Thank you, Helen."

"Sarah, Alison's mother, and owner of Howard Travel, who many of you have known for years, was our guiding light when deciding which services would attract guests. She's been invaluable. Thank you, Sarah." A tiny, salt-and-pepper-haired woman in a navy cocktail dress and gold hoops returned his affectionate smile.

"We would like to thank James Corcoran from the Port Anne Historical Society for directing us to special financing and the town of Port Anne for approving our conversion of this amazing house into a B&B."

He stretched his neck to look over the guests. "We'd also like to thank County Commissioner Diane Gleason for coming tonight. She helped smooth the process to save this house. Commissioner Gleason has also been a champion of efforts to improve the condition of our precious Chesapeake waterways. I hope to be working closely with her in the future. Please give her a big hand."

All eyes turned to a full-figured tall woman in a tailored black jacket, silk scarf, and lightly streaked gray hair pulled up in a thick knot. She stepped forward and responded with a wave.

He placed an arm across his wife's shoulders and pulled her close. "Six weeks ago, I announced my candidacy for state senator. Having grown up on the Chesapeake, I know how important the quality of our water is to the livelihood and daily life here in Maryland. Alison and I are looking forward to contributing to this community for many, many years to come. The bay's water has improved over recent years. However, in my opinion not quickly enough. As your state senator, I'll be committed to more rigid testing, expanding clean water programs, and enforcing fines against corporate offenders who continue to ignore regulations. Please join us in a toast! May you send us lots of guests and votes from near and far!"

With a mix of laughter and hear, hears, the gathering lifted their glasses.

Helen spotted Eliot coming back their way.

"You've got most of three counties attending tonight," she exclaimed.

He ran his hand through his short beard. "Isn't this terrific? We even have some first-time B & B guests. They'll be our first victims." He pointed to a sandy-haired, stocky man in a dress shirt and khakis, with a small woman with gray, bobbed hair.

"Who's the woman talking with Alison and Diane Gleason? She's very distinctive."

Eliot clenched his teeth. "That's my new campaign manager, Kerry Lightner. She arrived six weeks ago and is staying with us. She just ran a big Illinois governor's race, and they won by a landslide. She's a bit of a controller but with a lot of connections." His smile faded. "We're feeling our way." He lifted a hand and waved her toward them.

10

Kerry, dressed in a tight cream and white knit dress with smooth brown hair brushing her shoulders, stepped into their circle. "Nice to meet you all. Exciting night." Her sharp eyes gave their little group a cursory inspection.

"Certainly is. We understand you're in charge of Eliot's campaign. Congratulations. What made you interested in working in Kent County?"

"I heard about Eliot's ideas. I've always wanted to work with someone committed to improving environmental funding for the Chesapeake. At this stage in my career, I can choose what interests me." Kerry made a little arrogant toss of her head.

"Lucky you," Helen murmured.

Lizzie exchanged glances with her mother. "Are you from the area?"

Eliot gulped down his drink. "Let's not press her too hard. We've got a lot of work ahead of us. The incumbent will be a tough competitor."

"I'm not worried," Kerry said. "Besides, we'll have reason to work together long after this campaign."

"Did I hear Diane Gleason considered running for state senator?" asked Lizzie.

"We've never discussed it. Perhaps she changed her mind," Kerry replied.

"Have you worked with the commissioner in the past?" Helen asked.

"We've crossed paths. She has alliances that could help Eliot with his 'Clean Up the Bay' pledge at the statewide level." Kerry made a dismissive tap on Helen's arm. "I hope you'll excuse me. I'll catch you all later. I need to work the room." She flashed a smile and turned away.

"I worked a few campaigns when I was fresh out of law school," Shawn commented as he watched Kerry greet another group. "It takes a special breed to last in her business." They listened to her in full glad-handing mode, complimenting the house while interjecting her boss's name with enthusiasm.

"Beware of a wolf in sheep's clothing," Helen remarked under her breath. Eliot's face paled. She wondered why.

"Is that Ronnie Mann making the rounds," Shawn asked. "He graduated from Port Anne a few years ahead of us."

Eliot's voice dropped. "Ronnie's been with me since the preliminary campaign stage. He's a hard worker, but when Kerry approached me, I asked him to step down. It's been a little awkward."

"Choosing is a hard decision." Joe stepped closer. "Any regrets?"

Eliot didn't respond and waved Ronnie over. "Everyone, I'd like you to meet Ronnie Mann, my right-hand and communications director." He patted him on the shoulder.

Medium build, with a neatly pressed suit and striped tie, Ronnie made the rounds of handshakes. "I hope a few of you will volunteer your help for our campaign. These next six months will fly. Every day matters."

"Now that the B&B is open for business, I'll need to find a new local project," Helen spoke up.

"Ronnie," Eliot said. "There's no one better to work your phone campaign than Helen."

The younger man raised his left hand and rubbed a closely shaved head. His gold watch glinted in the candlelight. "I'll be sure to remember. Great to meet you."

"Who was the heavy man in the dark suit Diane was talking with during your introductions?" Lizzie asked. "He looks vaguely familiar."

"That's Craig Olsoff, CEO of Olsoff Marine Technology. Diane introduced me," Eliot explained. "You've seen him on the news. OMT provides water quality testing across the country. I worked with his company as a chemical engineer just out of college. Terrific guy. His company has agreed to a hefty campaign donation."

Helen tipped her head toward a small, round-faced man in a wrinkled brown suit. He was heaping his plate at the buffet. "Eliot, there's James Corcoran, head of the county historical society. He looks like he's enjoying himself, and that's unusual."

"He's been very helpful, but his inspections were nerve-wracking," Eliot sighed. "We had to be sure every repair met his requirements down to the last inch to earn the county's approval. He reserved our largest guest room for tonight at our expense. Says he wants to enjoy the fruits of his labor."

Helen laughed. "Sounds true to form. He'll probably sneak a dessert up to his room when no one's looking. Then again, I would too."

"Mom," hissed Lizzie. "He might hear you."

"Do you know him?" Shawn asked.

"Your dad and I worked with him over the years. He likes to impress everyone with big words."

"I think he relishes his role of supreme expert for the county," Eliot laughed. He spotted his wife flagging him over. "I've got to help Alison. Have a good time."

Helen and Diane Gleason caught each other's eye. Diane pressed her way toward their group.

"Hi!" Diane reached around and gave her a big hug. "Congratulations. House looks gorgeous."

"Thanks to people like you who helped us get the zoning exception," Helen said, lifting her glass in a toast to her friend. "Meet my family." She turned and introduced Lizzie and Shawn.

Diane offered her hand. "All these years, and we've never met. It's a pleasure."

"Let me introduce you to Detective McAlister from the Sheriff's Office," said Helen.

"It's Joe." They shook hands. "Helen tells me if there's anything important going on, you're involved."

"I try, although I can't always work my magic." The commissioner's eyes traveled over to Eliot at the bar.

"Mom talks about you all the time," Lizzie responded. "I gather you've put up with her at every county planning meeting possible. I don't envy dealing with my mother."

The commissioner's eyes sparkled. "She's relentless when she's fighting for a cause."

"Not unlike you. That's why we get along so well." Helen turned to the group. "When Eliot and Alison said they wanted to buy back Captain's Watch and convert it into a B&B, I went to Diane and asked for her support. She was on board in seconds." The two women's eyes met.

"Did you know your mother and I dueled for leads in our high school plays?" asked Diane.

13

"I never realized," Shawn responded.

"It was great fun," Diane said. "When you're seventeen, you think you'll be heading to Hollywood. I met your father soon after they were married. They were working on your old house in town."

"We were young and foolish, and Diane was just getting entrenched in local politics," Helen said.

Diane chuckled. "Little did I know we'd become attached at the hip."

"You're wearing the scarf I gave you."

"Love it. Reminds me of my birthday dinner. It's my good luck charm." She sighed, casting her eyes around the room.

"I know you're disappointed the party chose Eliot as their candidate."

Diane gave a little shrug. "That's politics. I'll focus on my own agenda for the county."

"I realize I'm being selfish, but I wasn't looking forward to you leaving the local scene. We need you here," Helen said.

"Thanks, I appreciate that," Diane sighed. "Wish I could stay longer tonight. You were going to show me the little pool house and the docks. Now I've got a planning meeting for the Five Star event at seven," she sighed.

"Don't worry," Helen grinned. "I know where they hang a key. We'll do it another time."

Diane gave Helen a quick kiss on the cheek. "Great to meet you all." She turned to chat with another group of guests as she worked herself toward the door.

Shawn leaned in. "Mom, I didn't realize Diane was supposed to be the next state senate candidate?"

Helen nodded, her voice lowering. "She seemed to be heir apparent, and she deserved the chance. From what she told me, Eliot approached their party's committee about an endorsement soon after they bought Captain's Watch, and the committee decided to switch horses. She and I discussed it over a lot of wine. I respect Diane very much, but I think the committee was dazzled with him being the younger candidate."

Lizzie made a little frown. "I love Eliot too, but that's a shame."

"I give her credit. She took their decision like a champ, and I'm proud of her for it." Helen said. She looked about. "I think I'll say hello to James Corcoran. And Sarah Howard." She edged her way around some visitors, stopping to chat with a past client.

"James, nice to see you tonight." Helen touched his elbow. "Thank you for helping Eliot and Alison. Are you excited to see Captain's Watch restored?"

The historian offered a self-satisfied smirk. "I am. It's been a bit of a challenge educating them on the right way to go about the process. Too often, people think rehabbing is the same as a restoration. If I remember, you and your husband made a few choices I wouldn't have made."

Helen's eyes narrowed. "Unfortunately, finances and practicality can get in the way of being a hundred percent historically accurate. Insulation and central air do have their advantages. Are you pleased?"

"Overall, yes." He took another bite of a mini crab cake. "Do I wish they could have maintained the house as a private home? Yes, I do." He made a dramatic sigh of resignation.

"Seems to me you've had your own personal house project. Didn't you buy an old cottage off Deer Lane a few years ago? Are your renovations finished?"

"Well," he blustered. "My house requires a much more exacting protocol. It calls for a great deal of analysis before I actually employ contractors."

Helen mentally rolled her eyes at his word choices. "I didn't realize your house had such a complicated history. Tell me, do you know anything about the ghost stories that seem to haunt Captain's Watch? They're floating around town again. Alison saw lights in the pool house last night."

"Ghost stories!" James' florid face paled, annoyance in his tone. "I don't think I'd attribute any substantive validity to them. There's always a few townspeople who like to spread idiotic rumors. I hope you're not one of them." He glared.

"No, but the Nancy Drew in me finds the idea of spirits in the tower room very intriguing."

"Humph. Given your reputation for blundering into local crimes, I'm not surprised."

She started to respond, then clamped down on her tongue. "Good chatting with you too, James." She stepped aside, leaving him alone in the crowded room, and saw Sarah Howard nearby.

"Congratulations. Come join us. I want you to meet Joe McAlister." She gave Joe a little signal. "Joe, this is Alison's mother, Sarah Howard. She built Howard Travel. When she retired a year ago, Alison took over."

Sarah's smile was warm, her voice soft. "Joe, the detective, right? So glad you came. Let's hope our guests don't get too rowdy, and you have to rein them in."

"Looks like a friendly crowd. I'm not worried," he smiled, the wrinkles at his eyes coming out.

Sarah glanced over Helen's shoulder. "I was hoping to catch Diane."

"She may have already left. She has a Five Star event meeting tonight."

Sarah made a little frown. "I'm on the same committee. I've been so busy helping Alison I've neglected them."

"Could you do me a favor?" Joe interjected. "I'm trying to get Helen to take a vacation with me. Any suggestions on how I can convince her?"

Sarah looked over her drink glass at Helen. "I know we can come up with some wonderful choices. Alison's been buried with all this B&B stuff. Have you spoken to Jill Sullivan? We hired her to replace Alison when she took over my role. She's been a godsend. Why don't I have her call you?"

"That would be great, although she'll need to work on Helen. I'll go anywhere."

"She does have a reputation for being a workaholic."

"Joe's not any better," Helen protested.

"I'm ready when you are," Joe said. He lifted a hand at another guest. "Excuse me, I need to say hello to someone."

Sarah regarded her friend. "I'm happy to see you two making some plans together."

"He's been suggesting a trip for months. I'm trying to keep an open mind, especially if there's good food involved."

"That we can promise you. Sounds like Joe's hoping for a vacation that includes more than just food."

"I know. I keep dragging my feet. It's a big decision for me."

Sarah grasped Helen's wrists and gave them a shake. "Andy would approve. I'm sure your kids would too. You deserve good company."

Helen inhaled. "Have Jill call me."

Chapter Three

At about eight o'clock, Helen invited Joe to take a quick tour of the house.

"Come see all the improvements." She led him upstairs and through the guest rooms, each rich with color reflecting the Chesapeake theme. Fresh white terry robes lay across each bed. Scented soaps and plush towels accented the refinished marble bathtubs. "I think Alison learned all these details from her mother. Sarah traveled the world for her business. She knows what picky clients want." She opened a set of glass French doors and led him onto a second-floor balcony overlooking the bay.

A setting sun cast a soft glow over the darkening water. Joe leaned over the rail. "Quite the view from here. Looks like someone's sitting down at the docks."

"Wait until you see the view from the widow's watch."

"What? You mean there's access?"

Helen's face lit up. "Absolutely. Follow me."

She wound along the second-floor hall to the staircase and another set of stairs to the third floor, and four more guest rooms. A fifth door was closed. Helen turned the knob. Eight narrow wooden stairs reached straight up, almost like a ladder.

Helen stopped and pulled off her heels. "Blast Agatha for suggesting these! I should have known better." Joe chuckled again.

At the top, they entered a low-pitched attic lined with bits of abandoned furniture, boxes, and cardboard cartons rimming the room. Rough-sawn rafters pitched just above their heads. Toward the bay side, two short steps led to a narrow unpainted door. "Come," she signaled. They stepped into a tiny room with window glass on all four sides. The temperature had to be ten degrees warmer than the guest floor below. Two old-fashioned wooden folding chairs faced the water and horizon in the dim light.

"What do you think of this?" She said, her voice a child's at Christmas.

Joe turned round and round. "Fantastic. How did you know about this room?"

She put her hands on her hips. "I am a Realtor, after all. It's my job to know."

He stood at a window sill and stared down. "That's a long, long way down. I'm surprised you like it up here. You're afraid of heights."

She inhaled. "This is different. It's enclosed. Still, this view can be a little unnerving. I wouldn't want to be up here in a storm."

"Is Ferry Point directly across? It has to be six miles of water from here to there. I can see a barge coming up the bay beyond Osprey Point."

"It must be heading north to the C&D Canal," Helen commented. "Looks like a Japanese car carrier. See the letters across their bow? In a few hours, the ship will be out of the bay and into the Delaware River toward Philadelphia."

"I'm always amazed at how huge they are," Joe said. "That one's probably a thousand feet long."

"They remind me of silent whales slipping through the water when I pass one in my sailboat. They're pretty intimidating. What I don't understand is how they create so little wake for their size."

She spun around the room. "Looks like we weren't the only ones here." She pointed at the footprints left in the coating of dust on the bare wooden floors. "Did you know this house is supposed to be haunted?"

The detective's head picked up. "What?"

"Yes, it's true."

"Is this another of your sleuths' ideas?"

She ignored him. "It goes back to Eliot's grandfather, Captain Davies, and his work partner, Isaac Hollowell. They made a good living piloting barges in and out of Maryland harbors. Ship captains from around the world don't know the varying depths of the bay well enough to avoid going aground. They need local pilots to get their cargo safely through the channels. Most of these ships are five or six stories high. They're metal icebergs."

"How much do they draw?"

"Could be as much as forty feet. Some channels on the Chesapeake are only fifty. Harbor pilots navigate carriers through the water as if they're threading a needle. If one goes aground, it's a disaster for their shipping company, suppliers, everyone affected by the supply chain. Could be a commercial builder expecting steel parts or factory waste being sent to a landfill. And heaven forbid going aground causes an oil spill."

"Didn't a carrier ship get stuck in Baltimore Inner Harbor last year?"

"It was a disaster. Took the Coast Guard four weeks to help dislodge the ship from the sand below. They had to unload thousands of pounds of cargo. Cost millions. Seemed like the entire country followed the news."

Joe stood, his arms across his chest, and watched the sun dropping toward the water. He turned. "What's Davies and Hollowell's piloting business have to do with a ghost?" He sounded doubtful.

"The story is Isaac loved to go night fishing. He left one Sunday in the summer of 1967 and never returned. His little skiff washed ashore a few days later. They never found his body. People say they've spotted his spirit watching the bay from this room. I'd swear I saw an image flash across these windows earlier today."

"You would say that." Joe pulled Helen close. "You don't think the flash could have been sun reflecting on the glass?"

"Must you be so logical?" She wrapped her arms around his neck. "I admit, the only member of my Detection Club who ran across ghosts was Nancy Drew. My guess, you never read *The Whispering Statue,* one of my favorites. She found out it was a clever trick."

"Glad to hear you haven't lost your mind completely. I never made the connection, but is Davies Road named after the captain?"

"It was. He was a part of Port Anne's Town Council for years and did a lot to help the town grow after World War II." Laughter ebbed and flowed from the pool edge below. "Think we should get back to the party? It has to be winding down." Helen scanned the lawn. The pool house doors were closed, and its lanterns glowed from within. Pool water reflected the moon lighting up the bay. They watched as two youngsters chased each other across the grass and down toward the docks.

Suddenly, an earsplitting cry and a crash of dishes cut through the party chatter below.

"Help! Help! Someone help!"

Helen pressed her hands to the tower's window glass. "Who's shouting? That sounds like Alison!"

Joe gripped the sill. "What's happened?"

"I don't know. Do you think she's hurt?" Helen's eyes widened. "Look! She's in the doorway of the pool house!" She picked up her heels, turned, and started down the narrow stairway in her bare feet. Reaching the main stairs on the third floor, she rounded the banister with Joe racing down the main stairs right behind her. They ran through the big house, dodging guests, and out onto the terrace. She stopped and jammed her heels back on. They tore across the lawn, pushing past a cluster of people encircling the pool edge.

Helen halted in the doorway. "Alison, are you hurt?" She squeezed her shoulder. Alison wailed, turning to expose her blood-spattered hands covering her face.

They stepped around her and jerked to a stop. The motionless body of Eliot's campaign manager, Kerry, was stretched across the bluestone floor. A set of large, wooden-handled scissors jutted from a wound between her shoulder blades. A rivulet of blood trickled across her dress. Her face was turned to the side, stark and colorless in the moonlight, with her arms splayed out to her sides. Broken shards of glass and dishes were scattered across the victim and Alison's feet.

Helen took in the shocked expressions of everyone gathered at the pool house entrance behind her. Why would someone kill this woman? How could this happen?

Joe leaped into official law enforcement mode. He pulled his badge from his jacket vest pocket and flashed it above his head at the stunned crowd.

"Everyone! Everyone! Listen up! I'm Detective Joe McAllister from the Kent County Sheriff's Office! I need your attention. You need to step back but remain here. Do not, I repeat, do not leave the property." His calm, no contest deep voice told them he was now in charge. There was no doubt. Pulling out his cell phone, he hit one digit. Within three rings, the voice of his partner, Rick Lauer, came across the call.

"Joe. Didn't expect to hear from you on a Sunday night," he joked. "Helen send you home early?"

Joe cut him off. "Not quite. I'm at the Captain's Watch B&B party on Blue Point Road, Port Anne. A woman's been stabbed. I need medics here and a crime scene squad STAT. I need enough deputies to control the guests and keep them from leaving."

Rick's tone shifted into emergency mode. "On our way." He clicked off.

"What's going on?" Eliot's voice traveled over everyone's heads as he broke through the group. Shawn and Lizzie were right behind him. "Where's Alison?" He stopped short at the sight of his wife covered in blood, and the body sprawled on the floor. "My God! It's Kerry!" He reached for his wife, his eyes wide and frantic. Alison folded into his arms, sobbing.

Helen touched Joe's arm. "Shall I ask Shawn and Lizzie to move everyone inside?"

Joe nodded. "Move them into the main hall. They might as well get comfortable. This is going to be a long night."

Shawn, long experienced in studying crime scenes, spoke up. "Joe, I suggest we put Eliot and Alison in a separate room."

"Good idea."

Eliot planted his feet. "You can't believe we know anything about this, can you?" Eliot's face flushed bright red.

"The faster we collect the facts, the better for you," Shawn said, gripping his friend's shoulder.

Joe studied the couple. The blood from Alison's hands was smeared on Eliot's shirt. "Let's stay calm. Lizzie, can you take them into the library and stay with them? They are not to speak to anyone other than a deputy."

Lizzie nodded, her face pale white against her cocktail dress.

He stepped closer and spoke in her ear. "I don't want them discussing this with anyone or even each other. Try to keep their conversation to a minimum. Don't let them change their clothes or wash their hands."

She blinked her understanding. Turning, she touched Alison's elbow and started to steer them across the patio. Eliot flashed a frustrated glare at Joe. He ignored him.

Joe turned and wagged his finger at Helen. "I know you want to stay here. Do not move. Don't touch anything. Don't talk to anyone, or I'll banish you to the house."

Helen started to speak up. She bit her lip. She wasn't good at taking orders, and he knew it. But she knew this was not the time to protest. She'd been here before.

* * *

A shriek of sirens cut through the woods, growing closer as emergency vehicles sped south from the center of Port Anne four miles away and wound their way toward Osprey Point peninsula. The sound of grinding brakes reverberated as they made the turnoff to Blue Point Road and the Port Anne River side of the bay. Helen knew these roads in her sleep and could hear the squads slowing as the road narrowed to one lane, passing large year-round mansions intermingled with empty cottages still waiting for their summer visitors.

"Coming through. Coming through." Two medics sprinted their way along the pool's edge, lugging heavy equipment on their shoulders. Helen recognized the athletic build and light brown hair of Joe's partner, Rick Lauer, right behind them.

Joe flashed his badge at them. "Step carefully. This is a crime scene."

They nodded, dropping to their knees aside the victim. In seconds, they were checking vitals. The older man sat back on his heels. "Detective, she's gone. I'm sorry. There's nothing we can do here."

"I understand. Thanks for confirming. A coroner should be here any minute."

"Is there anything more you need from us?"

"No, sorry to pull you into this, but it's procedure." The younger medic closed up her bag and backed away from the victim.

Joe looked at Rick. "Can you give us shoe covers? I wasn't planning on a murder investigation tonight."

Rick pulled a fistful from his pocket. "We'll need a list of everyone here and if anyone heard or saw anything unusual. I'll start assigning deputies to guests and start interviews."

"Won't be easy. There were at least sixty people walking around the property when this happened. If they don't want to get involved, they'll try to wander off."

Rick turned to a deputy. "Make sure all driveways are blocked. Tell the valets to hold all cars. I don't want anyone leaving." He started toward the house.

"Anything look different from earlier today?" Joe asked Helen.

Helen studied the room, her eyes traveling from one corner to the other. She pointed at the crab cage coffee table. "The two wine glasses that were here are gone, but that was easily two hours ago. Waitstaff might have cleared them."

"Anything else?"

She stepped gingerly over to one corner and pushed the striped canvas drapes back a few inches. "I hadn't noticed these two paint cans at the back door. Doesn't surprise me. I was too busy admiring the staging when I peeked in earlier." She kneeled down at a quart container of boat varnish. "Looks like someone might have tipped this over." She touched a shiny puddle on the floor and sniffed her fingers. "Andy and I used plenty of varnish over the years. It dries slowly." She looked up at Joe and Shawn. "This is still sticky."

"Any idea where these scissors came from?" Joe pointed to the blades jutting from Kerry's body. His eyes scanned the pool house.

Helen pointed. "I saw them hanging on that hook when we walked by together."

"You remember them?" Joe said.

"They're antique. By the way, they aren't called scissors. They're fishing shears. This pair is old, probably made in the forties. Fishing shears are still used all the time. You'll see them in anglers' tool kits."

"My dad had a pair," Shawn interjected. "Used them for gutting fish. Mom is right about the age. Those have wooden handles. The newer ones are vinyl coated. If these shears were grabbed off the wall, I wonder if this attack wasn't planned."

Helen's eyes met Joe's. "An argument that escalated?"

Joe nodded. "Sure looks like a possibility." He reached for the back door. "Locked."

"Wonder if it was always locked," Shawn said. "The killer could have slipped out and locked it behind them."

Footsteps crunched along the path. A short, round man in a white bunny suit and carrying a medical bag stepped through the doorway with two women in their protective gear behind him.

Joe offered his hand. "Ed, I was hoping you were on call. This is Helen Morrisey. You met during the Barto case. This is her son and a D.A. from Baltimore, Shawn Morrisey. They were here attending the grand opening."

Ed and Helen exchanged nods. "My forensics team," he gestured as they set down their equipment. He snapped on latex gloves and shoe covers before he approached the victim. His eyes traveled from Kerry's head to her heels.

"Rather a gruesome way to end a party," Ed commented, shaking his head.

"Joe, I'll go up to the house and give Rick a hand if he wants it," Shawn said. Joe nodded.

One deputy pulled out a camera and began circling the body, snapping close-ups of the bloodied shears and the entry wound.

"Any signs of struggle? Did she fight back?" Joe motioned toward Kerry's outstretched hands.

The coroner leaned over and examined her fingernails. "I don't see any marks around her neck or scratches on her hands. She has a bruise on her right cheek, most likely from her fall. We might find more indications under her fingernails, but none of them are broken." He put his face close to the stab wound. With careful, steady hands, he removed the scissors and placed them in a clear bag. Helen averted her eyes.

"The shears are heavy, and the blade is thin and long. Hopefully, we'll pick up the killer's DNA."

"That's if a dozen people haven't handled them before the party." Joe stepped slowly around the victim. "I don't see any indications of multiple strikes, do you?"

"Not yet. I only see one tear. Whoever stabbed her knew where to make a direct hit into the center of her back or was just very lucky. Then they released the scissors. I'll have more to report for you early tomorrow morning." He signaled to his technicians to continue their collection efforts.

Helen stepped forward. "Doctor, is there anything that indicates she knew her killer? Or that she was surprised?"

"That's for Joe to determine."

"Of course. It seems odd for someone who feels threatened to turn their back on the attacker."

Joe ran his hands through his dark hair and grimaced. "I agree, Nancy Drew. Let's leave Ed's team to their work." He paused. "Wait. I want to circle around the back of the building before I talk with the Davies." He reached into an open bag of equipment and pulled out a heavy silver Maglite. He ran the beam around the edge of the white door trim. "When was this painted? It smells fresh."

"It was one of the last buildings painted. I remember Alison telling me they weren't sure if the contractors would finish in time for tonight. When I peeked in this afternoon, the contractor was finishing up, probably about three o'clock. Why?"

"Stay here. Don't touch anything." He turned the rear door knob. It was locked. He flipped the inside knob lock and stepped outside, running his light around the outside perimeter. Frowning, he started to take photo shots of the wooden disk encircling the lock. "There's a few imprints in the fresh paint."

"Could have been the painters," Helen said. "There should be a key tucked over the door frame."

Joe reached up and ran his fingers across the doorway. "Nothing. Gone."

They looked at each other.

"I think the killer used it."

Joe grimaced. "Probably thought they'd prevent anyone from seeing them leave."

"So where's the key?"

He flashed his light across the undergrowth. "Tossed. We'll never find it in all these woods."

He signaled to one of the squad members. "This paint is tacky. Make sure you check all the moldings inside and out. Keep an eye out for a key to the back door."

Joe turned to Helen. "Time to interview the Davies."

Chapter Four

At quarter after seven Monday morning, Helen was pacing her living room, dressed in a baggy fleece, her hair messy and caught up in a clip. Her cell rang. She recognized the phone number. Sarah Howard.

"Helen? I hope I didn't call you too early." The woman's voice quivered.

"No, not at all. I'm on my second cup of coffee. Can't say I slept much last night. I imagine you didn't either."

Sarah took a deep breath. "I'm calling because Alison won't. I think they're in trouble."

Helen stopped pacing. "What's happened?"

"The police talked to them until well after midnight. This morning, they got a call to come into the Sheriff's Office for another interview at two. Eliot called his attorney. I told them they need someone like you."

"Me? I'm not sure if I can help. I'm certainly not a criminal attorney. Have the police accused them of anything?"

"Not yet, but I can feel it coming. Can you talk with them?"

Helen hesitated. "The last thing the detective in charge wants is a nosy real estate agent getting involved."

"I don't care. You have a reputation for digging up the truth. For not giving up. This murder at Captain's Watch could destroy them, even if they're not accused. It could ruin their business and Eliot's chances of getting elected. Please." Sarah sniffled. "We need someone who knows us personally and won't jump to conclusions."

"Joe McAlister is a very experienced investigator. He worked Baltimore

28

City murder cases for a lot of years. He won't take the easier route just to close a case."

"I realize you respect him, but I don't know him like you do. How can I be sure he'll consider every possibility? If this involved Lizzie, would you be frightened?"

"Of course, I would. Do Alison and Eliot want me involved? Sounds like it's your idea."

"I discussed it with Alison. She agrees with me. You've got good people instincts. People trust you. It's why you're good at what you do."

"And Eliot?"

"Sometimes children don't always take our advice when they should. He'll come around."

Helen's eyes roved across the wall-to-wall bookshelves crammed with her collection of detective stories as she mulled over her options. She dreaded Joe's reaction if she intruded into his investigation.

"Let me think about this. I'll call you back." Helen clicked off.

She ran her hands across the shelves to the sleuths she depended on most for advice. Jane Marple was her quiet, clever elder. Her fluffy, reserved appearance helped her stay incognito while she observed the people around her. Jessica Fletcher had business-like savvy and a sharp eye for detail. She was methodical. Nora Charles brought her nineteen-thirties flair, quick wit, and humor. Agatha Raisin was impetuous, her heart vulnerable. Like Helen, she put her foot in her mouth all too often. Unintimated, youthful Nancy Drew and Trixie Belden defied authority. All of them were committed to seeking the truth. Was it time for her personal Detection Club to reconvene?

She sighed and picked up her phone. "What time do you want me?"

She heard Sarah exhale. "Can you be here no later than noon?"

"See you there." Helen tossed her phone onto the couch. "Well, ladies," she groaned out loud. "You better wake up and join me. Looks like we're in for a long day."

* * *

A bright blue 'Open' banner floated in the morning breeze over the yellow and white Victorian housing Safe Harbor Realty on Water Street in the center of Port Anne. Helen pushed open the wide, solid oak door a little before nine. A brass captain's bell above the front door clanged cheerfully over her head. Their receptionist gave her a friendly little finger wave. She returned the signal and headed down the hall toward her office. Safe Harbor was her second family. Her personal assistant, Tammi, a phone pressed against her ear with one hand and a pen in the other, raised her head as she passed.

Helen tossed her orange leather tote on the floor beneath her broad old-fashioned wooden desk and flicked on a desk lamp. She looked up when Tammi tapped on the doorway.

"Sounds like I picked the wrong night to pass up a party to watch *Frozen* with three six-year-olds." Tammi's usually wild black wiry hair was braided into neat cornrow braids. Today, her earrings, always her comment on the season and her attitude, sparkled with rhinestones set into large round yellow sunflowers.

Helen sat back in her leather chair and lamented. "I'm guessing you had a much better night's sleep than I did. Talk about a beautiful night turning into *The Amityville Horror*. A true nightmare. By the time Joe and Rick allowed guests to leave, it was after eleven. I'll bet the Sheriff's Office crime scene techs turned the house upside down until dawn."

"Have you read the *Kent Whig* news?"

"Do I want to?" Helen turned to her laptop and inputted the words Eliot Davies campaign manager. The screen blew up with coverage.

Tammi pointed with long yellow-tipped fingernails. "This murder might have happened in little Port Anne, but with Eliot's election coming up, it's national news. Look at this."

"Brutal murder of Davies staffer," Helen read. "Kent County Sheriff's Office is investigating the murder of Kerry Lightner, campaign manager for Eliot Davies, candidate for Maryland state senator, during a grand opening and campaign launch Sunday in Port Anne. Lightner, credited for pulling Senator Maureen Fenton across the finish line last year, took over the reins of Davies' campaign six weeks ago."

Helen ran her index finger down the screen. "Her interest in running this campaign was unexpected and created a stir throughout the political arena. In a recent interview, Lightner said she hoped to further his pledge to provide more clean water initiatives for the bay." She clicked open a Philadelphia television website. Photos of Davies, Lightner, and Captain's Watch filled the screen. "Phew. I guess we can't be shocked at the attention. It's a gruesome murder linked to politics. Adding a spooky-looking Victorian guarantees this case turns into a tinderbox."

"More like an explosion." Tammi settled into a deep chair across from her. "Have you heard from Joe since last night?"

"Nope. Which doesn't surprise me. You know very well he'll try to steer me away from this if he can."

"I'll bet he can't believe this happened in the middle of a party, no less one given by your clients. Did he accuse you of deliberately creating a crime scene?" She made a rueful smile.

"That's not even funny. We've actually had a reasonably normal eight or nine months together." She hesitated. "Well, not *together*. Dating. We're dating."

"I thought you were planning a vacation."

"He is. I'm deliberating." She opened a desk drawer and pawed around, coming out with three red Twizzlers. "Want one?"

Tammi waved them away. "At nine in the morning? No, thank you."

Helen shrugged and bit off the top of one. "Breakfast."

"Your friend, Miss Marple, would be appalled at your choice."

"When the village of Port Anne has a place where I can buy fresh buttered scones, I'll be happy to change my habit."

"You need to check out Chesapeake Bay Café," Tammi said. "Speaking of habits, are you reactivating your Detection Club? They must be itching to solve this murder."

"My sleuths offer advice to me on all kinds of issues. It's not *always* centered around crimes."

"So you say." Tammi pointed at her phone calendar. "As your personal drill sergeant and close friend, we need to go over your schedule before you're side-tracked into a new case."

"I am not being side-tracked," Helen huffed. "Give me twenty minutes to make a few calls. I need to leave here about eleven forty-five."

"You have an appointment I don't know about?"

"Alison's mother, Sarah Howard, called me. I'm meeting them at their house at noon."

"Ahh, huh. And you're not involved?" Her assistant's brows drew together. Her sunflowers swung to and from as she closed Helen's door behind her with a snap. Helen could hear her laughing out in the hall.

* * *

Captain's Watch was no longer the cheerful, welcoming Chesapeake inn she'd approached yesterday afternoon. Two police cars were positioned across the U-shaped drive leading to the front door. A deputy stopped her as she pulled to the side and parked.

"Can I help you, Ma'am? This area is restricted today." He touched his hat.

"Hello, Deputy. I'm Helen Morrisey, a friend of the family. The Davies are expecting me."

"Let me check with them." The deputy left her standing on the front porch. A moment later, he opened the door and signaled her forward. The house was eerily quiet compared to last night's chaos. After recording her name and contact information on a clipboard, he pointed her toward the library off the hall.

Sarah spotted her in the doorway and rushed forward. The two women hugged. "Thank you for coming. I was afraid you might change your mind."

"Not a chance." Helen turned to an ashen-faced Alison, dressed in grey sweats and an oversized sweater. She was enveloped by a wing chair tucked into a corner. She offered up a weak welcome, her eyes encircled in dark shadows and the rims red.

"Alison, I hope you don't mind. Your mother asked me to come. She felt I could help." Helen pulled up a chair and reached for her hand.

The younger woman leaned toward her. "Thank you. I don't know how you can, but I'm glad you came," she whispered, glancing toward the door. "Eliot's on the phone again with our attorney." A tear trickled down her cheek. "Helen, why in the world would someone kill Kerry? Who would do this? She's barely been in town a month or two, and it's obvious Detective McAlister suspects one of us."

"It's much too early to believe that." Helen searched her face. "You found Kerry. You had her blood on your hands and clothes. The police are forced to start with you. Are you willing to tell me how you walked in on her?" She stroked Alison's brown hair off her cheek.

"Sorry." She gulped tears, then inhaled. "I'm so tired, I'm numb. We haven't slept more than a couple hours."

"It's a terrible thing to go through. Tell me, why were you in the pool house?"

"I decided to take a tray of desserts to everyone outside. I made the rounds along the pool, then I walked over to the pool house. The doors were closed, but our lanterns were on. At first, I thought it was locked, which didn't make sense to me. I pushed again and a chair behind the door fell over. That's when I saw Kerry lying on the floor. I was so shocked, I dropped the tray and screamed."

"How did you get blood on your hands?"

"I thought she might still be alive, so I leaned over and touched her back. I was frantic. I didn't know what to do. I ran to the door and shouted." Alison's voice trembled. "Then, I knelt down and reached for one of her hands. The stone floor was slippery with her blood. I stepped in it." She shuddered. "Broken glasses and food were all over the floor, and I cut my hands, getting back up. I tried to wipe my hands on my dress."

"Did anyone see you go in?"

"I have no idea. Everyone at the pool was busy talking and eating."

"Did anyone pass you as you entered?" Helen asked.

"No."

"There's a little rear door beside the storage closet," Helen said. "Could a guest use it to enter?"

33

"I don't know why. I hung striped canvas drapes along that wall. It's hard to see." Alison explained.

"It was locked last night from the outside. Did you lock it?"

Alison frowned. "I can't tell you. The painters finished late that afternoon. I ran in, straightened up the seating, and left out the front."

"How long were you alone with her?"

"It felt like ages, but I couldn't have been inside more than a minute or two. Now I know what people mean when they say, 'time stood still.'"

"Is there anyone you think Kerry might meet in private? Anyone she didn't get along with? Had business with?"

"I don't know." Alison hugged herself. "Eliot worked with her. I didn't. I met her when she first joined us. We gave her a guest room here, but she worked from his campaign headquarters, and we rarely ran into each other. I can't imagine she was in town long enough to make any enemies. He's making a list of people she dealt with for the detectives."

Helen's eyes met Sarah's.

The library door cracked open. Eliot, with a day-old beard and matted hair, stuck his head into the room and offered them a tense little nod. "Alison, we can shower. Come upstairs with me. Helen, can you stay here and wait? Sarah, maybe you can make us all something to eat."

Sarah looked grateful to be useful. "Of course. I hope you're not upset I asked Helen to meet with us."

He made a half-hearted smile at Helen. "I'm not sure how she'll help, but she knows the locals better than anyone." Eliot signaled for his wife's hand and ushered her upstairs.

Helen followed Sarah into the big kitchen. Her cell rang. It was Joe. She took a deep breath.

"Hi."

Joe cut right to the chase. "Are you at Captain's Watch?" His voice was edgy.

"Yes. Yes, I am. When did you leave here last night?"

"Don't try to steer our conversation. Why are you there?"

"Sarah Howard called me early this morning and asked me to come.

34

Alison and Eliot are upstairs showering, and then we're going to make them something to eat. Is that a problem?"

He took a deep breath. "Helen, I'm meeting them this afternoon to review their statements. They have an attorney. What in the world do you think you can provide them?"

"Encouragement? I've known them for years. Alison, Lizzie, and Shawn go way back to high school. They want to talk this out with someone they know." Helen held back the word 'trust' as she paced across the kitchen. "Do you know anything new that could help them?"

"It's not my job to help them. It's my job to find out who killed Kerry Lightner."

"I understand. Can you tell me if you've ever dealt with their attorney before?"

He hesitated, then measured his words. "I have not. I understand he was working with Eliot on the legal side of his campaign."

"Is he a criminal attorney?" she asked.

"I don't know."

"I googled his name this morning. He doesn't have any experience with criminal defense."

"Sounds like you already knew the answer to your own question." He sounded more and more annoyed. "What are you suggesting?"

Helen inhaled and mentally straightened her shoulders. Time to take a Jessica Fletcher stance, she thought. "I'm suggesting they need to have a criminal attorney like Shawn arranged for Susan during the Capelli case."

Silence. She waited, chewing her tongue and forcing herself to count to ten. "You're not saying anything. Are those wheels turning? Or steam coming out of your ears?"

"Both. I'm never going to suggest a specific attorney. That's out of line. But I agree, Eliot's attorney is probably in over his head. I'll leave it at that."

"Gotcha. I'll give them my opinion."

"As I'm sure you will. You usually do."

She tried to lighten the tone. "Does this mean your plan for a vacation with me this fall is canceled?"

He grunted. "I don't know. I guess a trip depends upon whether you can keep your chums from poking around where they don't belong. Going by myself is looking more and more appealing. I'll talk to you later." He clicked off.

"It sounds as if Detective McAlister isn't very happy with you." Sarah handed Helen an iced tea.

"No, he definitely is not. Our relationship ebbs and flows like the tide, depending upon whether I'm involved in a case he's working. Truthfully, I can't blame him. The state attorney almost took him off the Roberto Barto murder because I kept snooping."

"I'm sorry I made your relationship difficult for you." Her friend attempted a weak smile.

"Don't worry. I seem to be very good at making our relationship difficult all by myself."

Sarah pulled out a kitchen chair and wearily sat down. "According to Lizzie, you cracked two cases."

Helen waved her away. "I may have helped. Joe doesn't miss much."

"Why were you discussing Eliot's attorney? Do you know something we should know?" The tap of footsteps interrupted them.

Sarah got up and kissed her daughter. "You two look much, much better. Come sit down. We've got hot soup and ham and cheese on rye."

Eliot looked more like himself except for the strain around his eyes. "Thanks, we haven't eaten in hours." He took a big bite of his sandwich and swallowed. "It sounded as if you were discussing our attorney. Why?"

Helen hesitated. "It's an observation. I thought, as good as he may be handling your campaign issues, his bio doesn't show a lot of success with criminal matters. Attorneys all have their specialties. I wouldn't want a corporate attorney handling a child custody hearing."

"Do you have someone to suggest?" Sarah put down her soup spoon.

"When my real estate partner needed a defense attorney, Shawn convinced Ben Horowitz from Baltimore to handle her case. He's very, very good. And caring."

"I was hoping we wouldn't need to escalate this in the press by bringing in a big gun," Eliot said.

Helen put her hand on her chin, her eyes directed at Eliot and Alison.

Alison spoke up. "You don't think this situation is going to go away quickly, do you?"

"I don't. I'm sorry. I understand you may hate giving the press more to chew. But the quickest way to redirect some of this attention is with a skilled criminal attorney. They can deflect it with the right questions. My advice, hire someone who has experience talking to the press and facing a judge in a criminal court."

Alison grabbed her husband's hand. "Right now, I'm suspect number one. You're next."

"It's absurd." Eliot pushed his empty bowl aside. "How do we reach this Ben Horowitz?"

Helen pulled her cell from her bag. "I'll call Shawn. He can get to him more quickly than any of us." She hit Shawn's name on her speed dial list. The call went into his voicemail. "Don't worry. He always calls me back as soon as he can."

Three minutes later, Shawn called. "Mom, I'm walking into court. What do you need?"

She handed her phone to Eliot. Shawn's voice was muffled.

"Yeah. It's been rough," said Eliot. "We're going into the Sheriff's Office to meet with Detective McAlister this afternoon. Your mother tells me we need to replace our attorney with Ben Horowitz. Can you talk to him? I know it's short notice." A few mumbles later, they hung up.

He inhaled, then exhaled. "Shawn's tracking him down."

Chapter Five

The village was awash not just in spring rain but network news stations and local reporters. Calli's Tomes and Treasures and Bright and Sassy Boutique gave them plenty of colorful contrast against a brutal stabbing in an historic B&B. Helen jockeyed her navy-blue Mini into a parking space between two WJAZ lettered television station vans three blocks down from Jean's Coffee Pot. She didn't care about the walk. She needed the fresh air to help sort through her conversation with Eliot and Alison and was desperate for a caffeine fix. *Just what I need*, she thought. *More nerves.*

A line for orders started at the green wooden door and wound its way through the shop. Every seat at three tiny square tables lining the rear wall was filled. She tapped out a few email responses from clients on her cell before reaching the high wooden counter. A litany of coffee flavors and choices filled a wall-length chalkboard behind Jean and her helper.

The plump, gray-haired woman dressed in a dandelion-yellow cotton apron greeted her with a broad smile. "I was hoping I'd see you today. This place has been a madhouse since I opened at six am. It's never like this at two."

"Apparently, murder is good for local business. I wish I could say the same for Eliot and Alison Davies. Hear anything interesting?"

Jean's signature plastic coffee pot pins danced across her chest. Her silver coffee pot charms jangled at her wrist. "I've already had your Joe here. Why? You planning on jumping into this investigation?" Her eyes twinkled.

"First of all, he's not *my* Joe. Second, I'm only asking because the Howards are old friends." Helen bit down on a cranberry muffin she'd pulled out from beneath the glass.

Jean handed her a steaming latte. "I've heard all kinds of rumors this morning. Someone said Kerry was a bear. And that's not the first 'b' word people used. The campaign staff was unhappy when Ronnie Mann was replaced, and she took over. He was the local boy, and she was pretty insufferable, always bragging about the bigger campaigns she'd run."

"If this was such a step-down, I don't understand why she took the job."

"They said she wanted to return to her Chesapeake roots."

Helen made a face. "I heard that too. Hear anything else?"

"The incumbent. Some people say his staffers aren't heartbroken to see Eliot and Alison splashed all over the press. Doesn't leave much time for them to campaign."

Helen scooped up her coffees and set them into a brown paper tray. "Their time for campaigning is the least of their problems."

"You missed James Corcoran from the historical society. He was especially interesting."

"What elaborate story did he have to tell today?"

Jean leaned over the counter and whispered into Helen's ear. "He said he overheard an argument between Eliot and Kerry Lightner last night."

Helen set her tray back on the counter. The coffee sloshed over the lids. "No! Did he tell the police?"

Jean nodded. "He met with them earlier today." She raised her eyebrows. "He's feeling very important."

"That's not the news I wanted to hear. Keep your ears to the ground. You're one of my town sleuths, and I'm depending on you."

Jean rolled her eyes. "Get out of here. I've got customers in need of their caffeine."

* * *

She slipped through the front door of Safe Harbor as a client was leaving.

"Brought you an afternoon reinforcement." She handed Tammi her favorite caramel latte and an apple muffin. "It'll help tide you over until dinner."

"God bless you. Exactly what my head needs, and my hips do not." Her assistant followed her into her office and plopped herself down.

Helen set down her cup. "Anything happening that could make us a living?"

"I want you to listen to this voicemail. It came in this afternoon." Tammi clicked open the speaker on her phone. A high-pitched, nervous voice started. "Hello, my name is Britany Bowers. I'm trying to reach Helen Morrisey. I've read about her in the *Kent Whig* and want to talk to her about selling my house. I live in the Jamestown development. My number is 410-555-2368."

"What's so strange about this call? It's good news."

"You know I always check public records and social media to find out a little more about clients." Tammi stood up and clicked across Helen's open laptop, inputting Britany Bowers in the Facebook search bar. She pointed.

Helen leaned closer and examined the seller's expression. "Uh-oh. She might be a problem."

The image featured a gangly woman with reddish-brown hair in a long sweater, standing behind a sale sign stuck in the grass with a two-story colonial in the background.

Helen read aloud. "For sale by Scorned Wife. Adulterers and Bimbo Girlfriends need not apply. SeeMyGreatHouse.com Call 410-555-2368." She clicked open the website link. Up popped a slew of house and community pictures.

"What do you think?"

"I think we'll be working with a bitter, vengeful woman. She certainly is resourceful."

"Do you want to ignore her?"

Helen studied the face on the screen. "Not yet. I'll call her. It's not the first time we've been stuck in the middle of a nasty divorce."

"And we often regret it."

"Let's not judge too soon. We've helped families get through some tough times." She waved Tammi away, gulped down more coffee, and picked up her cell.

"Britany? This is Helen Morrisey from Safe Harbor Realty. I'm returning your call."

* * *

A little after five, Helen decided to head home to Osprey Point. She called in for a Margarita pizza at Tella's. She and Agatha Raisin may be opposites on the subject of men, but they matched culinary skills. Take-out crab soup and Herr's Old Bay flavored chips were their answer to cooking. Microwave was Agatha's middle name. The only cookbooks in Helen's house were gifts from her daughter. How was Lizzie such an amazing cook? She certainly didn't inherit any talent from her mother. At Leaver's Liquors, she treated herself to her favorite bottle of Sauvignon Blanc. Was it a bad sign when the clerk knew her name, she mused. 'Don't be silly,' piped up Nora, her card-carrying partier.

Glancing down at the pizza on the seat of her Mini, she felt a bit sorry for herself. Eating a pie alone was kind of depressing. And fattening. Joe hadn't returned her call, and Helen knew she wasn't at the top of his list tonight. "Can I blame him?" she said out loud.

Lizzie checked in as she wound her way through the six miles of Osprey Point State Park out to her peninsula.

"Hi, any news on Alison and Eliot? I heard you met with them today." She sounded worried.

"News travels fast. The last I heard, Shawn got them in touch with Ben Horowitz. I don't know much more."

"That was smart thinking. Where are you now?"

"I'm on my way home and about to lose cell service through the park."

"Anything from Joe?"

"Not a word. I'm trying not to feel ignored. He's swamped. My getting the Davies to switch attorneys complicated his day even more."

"Mom, you did what you had to do. He knows that. I've got to run. I'm about to go on air in a few minutes. Talk later."

"Good luck with your show."

Her A-frame house, perched high on a cliff south of Buoy Two where the bay met the Port Anne River, gave her a view of the water stretching for miles. The woods below her deck led down to her dock. It's what got her to pull up stakes and leave her family's rambling Victorian after Andy died. It was a tough decision for her and the kids, but the right choice. It marked a new chapter, if a lonely one. She wasn't quite sure how to turn the page. She might never.

Trixie and Watson greeted her at the front door, wrapping themselves around her legs and meowing for dinner. "Well, at least someone loves me," Helen exclaimed as she tossed her laptop on the kitchen counter and served up their dinner. She turned on her oven to reheat her pizza and kicked off her shoes on the way to her bedroom.

Bundled in pajamas and a robe, she walked out onto her deck and gazed across the bay. She shivered. Sunday's weather during the grand opening had been a brief taste of spring. This evening the temperature had reverted to a last gasp of winter. The wind was up, whipping waves into white caps like a recalcitrant child determined to stay put. Her cell rang. She pulled her sliders shut behind her and reached for the phone. Joe.

"Hello, I'm surprised you're calling me. You have to be toast."

"I'm operating on about four hours sleep. Pulling into my drive in Far Hill now. But I knew darn well you wondered if Ben showed up for the Davies. Rick and I delayed their interview to give him time to drive up from Baltimore."

"Thank you. How'd their meeting go?" Helen started walking a circle around her living room. Trixie and Watson followed her with their eyes.

"As much as I was annoyed that you interceded, dealing with an attorney who knows the ropes of a criminal proceeding actually made my job easier. The Davies seemed encouraged to see him take charge."

"Good. Any closer to knowing who may have killed Kerry?"

"You sure don't waste time holding back on questions or opinions. I've got a few ideas, but this case is too new yet. We're running background checks on Eliot's list of people Kerry knew in town."

"You have Jessica Fletcher's sympathy. She says it's hard to find what you're looking for when you don't know what it is."

"Let's keep Jessica's opinions out of this. If Alison's innocent, she was definitely in the wrong place at the wrong time. Ben might be skilled, but he can't change the facts as of now. Alison's fingerprints were on the shears. Smeared, but there. The coroner's report says the splatter marks of blood on her clothes could easily be from the stabbing, not because she tried to wipe her hands clean like she claims. That's not good news."

"She's not a murderer," Helen said stubbornly.

"I'm inclined to agree with you. Her profile doesn't fit."

"Anyone see Kerry go into the pool house before her?"

"No one noticed, which doesn't surprise me. Most of the guests seemed to be gathered on the dock side of the pool near the outside bar. According to Alison, the front door was jammed. You and I know someone locked the rear door from the outside with a key. It's an old lock. You have to use a key. I tested it."

"Do you think the killer came and went from the rear door?"

"It's the only way they could jam a chair under the front door knob first."

"They'd have to know where the key was hidden," Helen said.

"Owners are stupid. Everyone hides a spare key over a doorway or under a nearby rock. Done every day."

"Huh. You're right. I keep one for my garage in one of those magnetic key boxes."

"Let me guess; it's on the side of the house under an electrical box."

"Don't be so annoying." She sighed.

"We dusted for prints. Eliot's are all over the fresh paint along the doorknob."

"He's the owner. Wouldn't you expect them?"

"Not on top of fresh paint applied that afternoon. Rick's trying to locate the contractor to confirm the time they finished. He's on a camping trip in upstate New York, no cell service. We've got a state trooper tracking down our wilderness man." He paused. "There's been another development. James Corcoran overheard an argument between Eliot and Kerry during the party.

In his opinion, it was pretty heated."

"I wondered if you were going to tell me. I heard about the argument at Jean's. What did James say?"

"You sure get around," Joe growled. "James told me he only heard part of it. They were both shouting. Something about how he wasn't 'willing to do it'. James didn't know what he was referring to, but Kerry told Eliot he had twenty-four hours to decide, or she'd go to the police. That he owed her."

"Did you ask Eliot about it?"

"He said it wasn't an argument. They were discussing the campaign. Then he clammed up. He's got first place on my suspect list." Joe grunted. "Let's talk more tomorrow. Do you want to meet for dinner? Prime and Claw? Six?"

"I'd like that. I'll make a reservation. Port Anne is jammed with all those out-of-town reporters. Go get some sleep."

"Thanks. Do me a favor. Try to have some patience."

"Patience isn't one of my strong points. Ask Agatha."

* * *

Helen settled into a corner of her couch with Trixie and Watson curled next to her. A text from Sarah popped across her phone screen.

Thank you for sending us Ben. We're grateful.

She sipped on her Cabernet. Why were Eliot and Kerry arguing? Why would a stranger in town be killed? Who hated her that much? Was the killer a stranger to Port Anne too? Or someone local who considered her a new threat? Tossing the rest of her wine into the sink, she turned off the lights and crawled into bed.

Three in the morning and she was awake and roaming the house in the dark. The wind was howling, buffeting her little cliff house and forcing the chill in through the edges of the floor-to-ceiling plates of glass. Stumbling around in her kitchen, she unearthed her Red Rose teabags, a habit from her mother. Neither of them had ever been sound sleepers. Watson and Trixie ambled into the room, hoping for a middle-of-the-night snack.

"You realize, Watson, you're easily twice the size you were when I found you at the county shelter. The brown and white tabby turned his head and blinked with wide yellow-green eyes. He lifted his white milk face to say, 'And your point?'

Tonight, she missed Andy keenly. She still had those sudden clutches to her heart, an open sore, slow to heal. Joe had been a welcome addition to her life since they met about two years ago, and she wondered why he was this patient. When it came to a serious relationship, she was the queen of avoidance. Did she really want to go Jessica Fletcher's route, widowed and single forever? All business, no romance?

Nerves stretched, she pulled out a legal pad and started making a list of suspects, like the ones she made for clients evaluating a house. Across the top, she wrote in big, bold, black letters, *Who killed Kerry Lightner?* Under the question, she wrote *Motive plus Opportunity equals Murder.* She drew three columns. The first column said *Suspects.* She wrote the words *Pro* and *Con* above the second and third. She moaned at the blank lines. 'Come on, ladies. I need inspiration.' Disgusted, she pushed the list aside. She'd hit Joe with it at dinner later. Poor guy.

Nancy Drew whispered in her ear. 'He's lucky he's got you in his corner.' Agatha nodded in agreement.

'Enough, everyone. You're very biased.'

For a second time, she crawled back into bed and nudged her furry companions aside with her cold feet.

* * *

"Helen!"

Just as she clicked her Mini's key fob in Safe Harbor's parking lot Tuesday morning, she heard her name.

Jill Sullivan from Howard Travel scurried towards her. "I'm glad I caught you." She dug out a lemon-yellow pocket folder with the blue Howard Travel insignia. "I promised Sarah I'd get a few travel ideas together for you and Joe to consider. Thought you might want to start with these. You can't beat the Caribbean, especially since I hear you're a sailor."

Surprised, Helen slowly reached out for the packet. "I can't say I'm thinking of trips right now. How are Alison and Sarah? I imagine the agency is quiet." Annoyed, she studied the younger woman. Is she really this insensitive, she asked herself.

"Oh. Well, yes. They asked me to take up the slack. Sarah's come out of retirement to fill in for Alison until the police sort all this out."

"They have to be overwhelmed. No guests, a mortgage, the campaign. I'm sure they appreciate your efforts at the agency."

"I'm trying my best to keep the business afloat," Jill said, her tone stiff.

Helen leaned against her car door. "Do you have any idea who might want Kerry dead? Did you deal with her at all?"

"I barely knew her. We worked together because she funneled all of Eliot's travel arrangements for campaign stops through us. Plus, a few trips to D.C. to meet their contributors. It was all strictly business." She avoided Helen's eyes. Helen wondered why.

"Did you work with Ronnie Mann before she replaced him?"

"I did. Coordinating with him was a lot easier."

"Is he back in lead position now that Kerry's gone?"

Jill's lips puckered. "I haven't asked."

Helen tucked the folder under her arm. "It's a mess. If you hear anything useful, I hope you'll speak up. I appreciate the information." Her voice told Jill otherwise.

Jill gave her a disappointed look and trotted back down the street. Digging her cold hands deep into her pockets, Helen watched her confident stroll down the sidewalk.

Was Jill a little too indifferent to her boss's problems? Or am I reading too much into her reaction? With all that's gone wrong, the Davies must be relieved the agency was still functioning. They needed the income. Still, Jill's lack of concern bothered her. There's something that she's not telling us.

* * *

At about one o'clock, she leaned over Tammi's shoulder.

"What do you know about ghosts?"

Tammi's head jerked up. Today, her earrings were bright red cardinals. "Why are you asking me? Why are you asking at all? I've never known you to be into paranormal."

Helen laughed. "I'm afraid my mystical interests match Kayla's. *Frozen* is as far as I go. I read a new headline this morning about the murder. The reporter latched onto old rumors that Captain's Watch was haunted. It's in the 'Around Town' section. Take a look."

Tammi tapped onto her PC screen. "That sounds creepy." She read, "Has the Captain's Watch ghost returned to haunt Eliot Davies? Kent County Sheriff's Office is seeking witnesses to the brutal Sunday murder of Davies' campaign manager Kerry Lightner during the grand opening of his restored B&B. Once owned by Davies' grandfather, Davies repurchased the property last year. Isaac Hollowell, Captain Davies's partner, disappeared in a squall off Osprey Point in 1967. Locals claim his spirit has been sighted looking out to sea from the watch tower. Police questioned the current state senator's staff regarding their interactions with Lightner before her death. He issued a press statement expressing condolences and described his relationship with Davies as a friendly political rivalry."

I'll bet, Helen thought, and Jane Marple seconded.

Tammi studied Helen's face. "What do you think?"

"I'm thinking the press is looking for every possible angle to feed the public's curiosity."

"You would think a murder in a pool house would be enough."

"They want to add fuel to the fire. I should do a little research on both campaign staffs and this ghost rumor."

Her assistant wriggled her brow. "I would think the police would be too smart to fall for a ghost story."

"I agree. I'm having a hard time caring about a cold case from the 1960s. On the other hand, I'm convinced there's something odd about Kerry leaving a bigger campaign to take up this local one. Now, we've got ghosts. It just doesn't make sense to me or my Detection Club squad." Helen's eyes twinkled.

"I knew it!" Tammi tossed down a pen. Her cardinals took flight. "I knew you'd get them involved!"

"Shush," Helen whispered, a finger to her lips. "Where do you think I can find some background on Kerry I won't find in the news?"

"Start with Alison and Eliot. They hired her."

"You're right. I was too soft on them yesterday." She tapped her phone for Eliot and got voicemail. "Eliot, this is Helen. We need to discuss Kerry and how she came to join you. Call me. Thanks."

She opened her calendar. "Wonder what more I can find out in the meantime."

"What about Shawn? After all, he is a D.A."

Helen frowned. "You're right. He must know the inside story. Unfortunately, he's a pro at stonewalling his mother. It's the whole confidentiality thing."

"If you want information on Hollowell and the watch tower ghost, you could check with Calli at Tomes and Treasures. She carries a bunch of local books about Eastern Shore, Maryland history. I'll bet she's got stories about haunted places."

"You are the best, my personal Google." Helen grinned and grabbed her tote. "Be back in a couple hours. Oh, by the way. I'm meeting our scorned client, Britany Bowers, at her house tomorrow at ten."

Tammi's cardinals danced in protest as she jotted the appointment into her calendar.

About one o'clock, Helen tossed her laptop into her car and reached for the ignition button. She stopped. Tapping her fingers on the steering wheel, she tossed out a question to her squad. 'Who in town would know more about local and state politics than anyone else?'

She gazed down busy little Water Street. Yesterday's news crews seemed a little less prevalent. They were probably indulging in The Blue Crab's homemade crab cakes. Her writer sleuth Jessica spoke up. '*Kent Whig's* one of the oldest newspapers in the country. Who's their star reporter? No one better to help you than a news hound.'

Helen smiled to herself. 'Thanks, Jess. I know exactly who to call.'

A nasally receptionist's voice picked up her ring. *"Kent Whig Newspaper. How can I help you?"*

"I'd like to talk with Maggie Dyer. How do I reach her?"

'Maggie is out on assignment. She'll be in soon. Can I have her call you?"

"Thank you. I'm Helen Morrisey. I'll give you my cell number."

"Does she know what this concerns?"

"No. I want to talk to her about the Kerry Lightner murder."

"Gotcha." Her voice rose an octave. Eight minutes later, her cell rang.

"This is Maggie Dyer. I assume this is Helen Morrisey from Safe Harbor Realty."

"It is. I'm surprised you know."

"The throaty monotone voice issued a little chuckle. "Your reputation precedes you."

"Really? That might be concerning. I certainly know your name. You seem to cover almost every news story in the county. I read your 'Around Town' feature every time."

"Been in this business a lot of years. 'Around Town' posts are my readers' favorite." She paused. "Your message said this concerned the Lightner murder. What do you have for me?"

"Not a lot, but I do have some ideas. I need your insight on local politics. Could you meet me at Prime and Claw tonight about six?"

The reporter hesitated for a second. "Yup. See you there."

* * *

Helen texted Joe. **Call me.**

Tied up. Problem with dinner?

An FYI, bringing a guest.

Who?

A *Kent Whig* reporter.

I don't give unplanned interviews.

Consider this reconnaissance.

Says who?

Jessica Fletcher.

Damn her.

Helen returned a smiley face wearing a disguise.

Chapter Six

Prime and Claw Oyster Bar on Water Street was jammed. In the late 1800s, the two-story wooden building served as one of Port Anne's original taverns. Old-timers, grateful for a place to tell tales, were known to drop off duck, geese, and rockfish in a bucket outside the owner's door as thank-yous.

Helen squeezed past a string of bar stools, her eyes traveling around the room. A polished brass rail ran the length of the U-shaped bar. A mosaic of old rings from glasses never quite disappeared. They'd become part of the bar's history. A blackboard sketched out the specials for each day. Tuesday's was steamed shrimp in Old Bay. In the winter, anyone could overhear the thread of embellished sailing trips. With spring here, boaters in windbreakers stopped for a local ale, Maryland crab chowder, great steaks, and an excuse to talk about de-winterizing boats and getting them off the hard. No one seemed to mind the stale smell of smoking from years past except Helen.

She spotted Joe leaning on the far end of the bar, chatting with a skinny guy with a huge purple Mohawk that added another six inches of height and a hefty older man wearing a worn Raven's cap. The Raven's man raised his brow and tipped his head toward Helen. Joe picked up his beer and signaled goodbye to them.

"Hi there. They wanted to know if I was waiting for the good-looking woman at the door."

"Oh, yes? And you said?"

Joe took in her shiny dark hair and green eyes. "I said, 'of course'. I've got a booth in the corner. Are you hungry?"

"Silly question."

A server handed them menus and took Helen's request for a New Zealand Sauvignon Blanc. She shed her jacket.

"By the way, Ed says hello," Joe said.

"He does? That's nice of him."

"I personally am having a problem with dating someone who runs across the county coroner almost as often as I do. And knows him on a first-name basis."

She chuckled. "Let's not exaggerate."

"I wish I were."

Helen ignored him. "Well, any news?"

Joe pushed his beer aside. "Not good if you're talking about Alison or Eliot Davies. Not one person saw someone in the pool house with Kerry. The blood on the scene only implicates Alison. The argument overheard by James and fingerprints on the rear door implicate Eliot, big time." He stopped.

"You didn't tell me where they argued. In the pool house?"

"No. James said he went upstairs to his guest room on the second floor to drop off his jacket. He could hear them in the adjoining guest room where Kerry stayed. It went on for about ten minutes. Then Eliot came out, slamming the door behind him, and she followed a few minutes later."

Helen smirked. "I can picture James trying to listen."

"And you wouldn't?"

She shrugged. "Okay, agreed. What does Eliot have to say?"

"He clammed up. Said it was strictly business. There's something he's not telling me." Joe glanced toward the entrance. "Is that the reporter we're meeting?"

Barely five feet tall with sandy-colored short hair and wire-rimmed glasses, a woman peered across the bar. A nylon backpack was strung over her left shoulder.

"I've never met her. Only heard about her." Helen gave her a wave.

"How did you talk me into this?" Joe grimaced, standing up and straightening his tie.

"Because she knows everything about politics in this county, maybe the state."

Helen stood up and extended her hand. "Maggie, thanks so much for coming. This is Detective Joe McAlister. Joe, this is *Kent Whig's* longtime reporter, Maggie Dyer."

The detective had at least fourteen inches on the slight woman. Maggie was tight-mouthed and unintimidated. "Wouldn't be any good at my job if I weren't curious. One-on-one time with the law can be valuable." She took a seat next to Helen. "Meeting you, with your reputation for poking into police business, puts the icing on the cake."

Joe cleared his throat. "What can we get you to drink? We're about to order dinner."

"I'm still on the clock. Have a township commissioner's meeting at seven. I'll take you up on a Corona. Might make the meeting a little more bearable."

Helen laughed. "I've been to my share. They're like watching paint dry, interspersed with a few contentious moments, usually angry neighbors."

"Even those get predictable after a while. The phrase 'tabled for future discussion' is a phrase I'd be happy to never use again under my byline."

"It'll be written on your tombstone," Helen joked.

Maggie's light eyes traveled between her two hosts. "What did you want to discuss?"

Helen took a deep breath. Joe's shoulders stiffened.

"It's my idea. I convinced Joe to listen in," Helen said.

Maggie pulled out a plain five by eight wire bound notepad and pen from her bag.

"We're wondering if you know anything about Kerry Lightner and how she came to Eliot's campaign?" Helen started. "Everyone says she was whip-smart at winning elections. What do you think really drew her here? She had to have a half dozen candidates clamoring for her to work for them, so why'd she pick his?" Helen sat and waited.

The wizened-looking reporter chuckled. "You're giving me more credit than I deserve. Until her murder, I didn't have much reason to pay any attention."

Joe shifted the beer in front of him. "How do we get more inside background on her? The info not on the record books."

"I assume you searched her family history. I could make some calls to reporter buddies in Annapolis and D.C. Maybe someone will open up."

"Here's my question," Helen added. "Is there any chance she came as an operative for someone on the opposite political aisle?"

"Are you suggesting she was a plant for another campaign?"

"I have absolutely no idea. Tossing the idea onto the table."

Maggie sipped her beer and contemplated. "If I find out something that affects this investigation, what do I get in return? I'd want to be the one to break the story."

Joe clasped his large hands together. "This conversation is strictly off the record. If you find out something important and hold back, that's obstruction."

Maggie only shrugged. She was no cub reporter.

Helen turned to Joe. "Can we agree Maggie gets the news lead first?"

The detective's brown eyes regarded the reporter. "When I knew you were meeting with us tonight, I did a background check on you. I've been told you're a straight shooter, for a reporter."

"Reluctant praise," Maggie said. "I'm sure you realize I did the same on you."

"As I expected." Joe's mouth twitched in appreciation. "Let's agree that if you dig out any details that help me, I'll remember. This investigation is too new for any worthwhile conclusions based on facts."

"It can't be good for Eliot Davies." Her eyes slid to Helen. "I also did a little more digging into you."

"Me? Why would you be interested in me?"

"Seems like you've gotten far more involved in your real estate clients' problems than the usual agent. I've been told you take no prisoners when it comes to helping people who've been wronged. You've been involved in two murder investigations in the past eighteen months or so."

Helen threw up her hands in protest. "I'd call them strictly an effort to protect my clients."

Maggie raised her brows. "Seems to be a habit." She studied Helen and Joe. "I'm sensing a vibe here. If you two have a thing going personally, fine by me. I couldn't care less. I do wonder how a former Baltimore homicide detective deals with your...." She pointed at two words scribbled on her pad with a stubby index finger. "Detection Club. What's that about?"

Helen squirmed. "Lots of people use private consultants. Professionals have reference libraries. My Detection Club is mine. Amateur detectives, especially women, give me great advice, not just on a murder case but life in general. If I were a health scientist, I'd refer to JoAnn Manson or Virginia Lee. If it were physics, Marie Curie."

"That's a unique approach to solving murders. I may have to find time to start reading mysteries. Who are they?"

Helen's face turned pink. "Off the record?"

Joe laughed. "Don't look to me to explain. I used to wonder if you were deranged. Now, I'm positive."

"Thanks a lot." Helen retorted. "Jane Marple, Nancy Drew, Nora Charles, Jessica Fletcher, and Agatha Raisin. Sometimes Trixie Belden." She ticked them off on her fingers. "They're my core squad."

"You are a very interesting woman." Maggie finished her Corona and set the bottle down.

"Yes, she is," Joe grinned as he glanced at Helen.

"Is the word 'interesting' code for odd?" Helen picked up a menu. "Now that my disorders have been identified, can we order dinner? I haven't eaten in hours."

Joe tipped his head toward her. "Eating is often her biggest priority."

Maggie smiled, then rose, slinging her backpack onto her shoulder. "Thanks for the beer and the invite, but I need to get to my town meeting. I'll keep you posted if I find anything." She gave them a brief wave and headed toward the front door.

They placed their order. "What do you think of her?" asked Helen.

"It's her job to keep her ear to the ground and given her track record, she's an expert. Be careful what you say to her. She might be an asset. Or she'll try to use us. I'll end up being the headline on the front page, and my boss will want to kick me to the street. Lucky for you, I'm at a stage in my career where I don't worry about the press very much."

"Are you talking about Scott Harris?"

"He *is* our State's Attorney."

She groaned. "His ego is bigger than the Capital Building. A stud in his own mind. Do you know he called me again a few weeks ago? Wanted to meet for dinner. I told him I was going out of town."

Joe's eyes snapped. His jaw clenched. "Let's get back to suspects."

She dug around inside her tote. Out came her Safe Harbor business card stapled to a folder marked "Jordan Plot Plan" in thick black marker. She set the folder aside and searched again. She pulled out a piece of folded yellow legal paper, smoothed out the creases, and slid it across the table.

He moaned.

Helen gritted her teeth. "It's my *Pro Con Suspect List.*"

"Who helped you?"

"You *know* who. My Detection Club. We worked through the night. Just for you." She shot him an over-the-top sweet smile and batted her dark eyelashes.

The detective tried not to grin. "Let's hear it."

Helen handed him a wide black pen. "Start with Alison."

Joe encircled Alison's name twice. He wrote under *Pro* 'claimed to find murder victim.' 'Had Kerry's blood on her.' He dropped the pen.

"That's it?"

"That's a pretty big *it.*" He defended.

"What's her motive?" she asked.

"Maybe she was jealous."

"Jealous about what?"

"Kerry was attractive. Maybe she was hitting on Eliot, and he showed interest? If word got out, Alison would look like the lame wife, embarrassed in front of her entire world. Wouldn't be the first time. This crime has revenge written all over it."

Helen's eyes narrowed. "Wow. You say I've got a wild imagination. You have no proof of an affair."

He raised an eyebrow. "We're working on that."

"Next?"

"Eliot. Maybe he and Kerry had an affair, and she threatened to tell Alison."

Helen smirked. "Even if they were having an affair, why would Kerry tell Alison before his election? Talk about fireworks. She'd be out of a job."

"She was calling his bluff. Eliot knows the public isn't fond of cheating husbands running for office. Never a good image. He decided he wanted to keep her quiet."

She scoffed. "There's no sign of another woman. Besides, how would he go into the pool house without anyone noticing?"

"Someone did. During a party, it's not that hard." Joe flipped Helen's *Pro Con* list over. He sketched a rudimentary diagram of the Captain's Watch property. "Here's the front drive and the walkway along the side of the house leading to the pool." He inserted three rectangles, marking them 'main house,' 'pool,' and 'pool house.' "Eliot knows where their security cameras are positioned. He could have circled around the side of the pool house closest to the woods to avoid them. He sneaks through the rear door, then out. He knows Alison is walking around the pool area, offering more drinks. She finds Kerry, starts screaming, and he rejoins his guests in the yard."

"You need a motive stronger than a make-believe girlfriend."

"Here's another. Eliot and Kerry had a big argument. Loud enough for James to overhear from his guest room."

"He probably used a glass against his bedroom wall."

Joe laughed. "You wouldn't?"

She rolled her eyes. "Okay. You're right. Let's talk about the why. Alison isn't stupid. Either is Eliot."

"I'm telling you, one of them could have lost their temper. Killers have done it before."

Helen scrunched her lips together in disbelief. "I know Alison too well. She stayed for sleepovers with Lizzie all through high school. Shawn took her to his senior prom."

"I've got my squad going through the Davies' and Kerry's emails. And their cell phone records. Given what we have, Eliot's my best bet."

"Aren't you lucky you have a squad helping you with data research? My squad isn't good at it." She stopped, tapping her index finger on her temple. "Actually, that's not true. They're very good at research."

"Your squad, shall I point out again, isn't real."

Helen sniffed. "They're real, not tech-savvy. Who else can we put on this list? Eliot must have an enemy or two. You don't run for office without making a couple."

"Or a lot. Rick and I met with the incumbent and his top staffers. No one from his campaign attended the party. They didn't have much to say other than their condolences. Very smooth. This senator's been in office twelve years. I don't think he has any intention of letting Eliot or any other candidate unseat him," Joe said. "He'd have to have someone working from the inside."

Helen grabbed the pen. "Eliminating Eliot's very successful campaign manager is one way to eliminate competition. I'm adding the incumbent to the list."

Joe pushed his plate to the side. "Rick and I interviewed Eliot's campaign staffers, No one liked her, but we haven't found a reason for them to hate her. Ronnie Mann, the one demoted when Kerry arrived, he's a different story."

"Agree one hundred percent, as much as he seems like a nice guy."

"Kerry had all the high-powered credentials and connections. It was as if Eliot replaced a twenty-foot skiff with a cigarette boat. Ronnie had to be furious."

"I like your boating analogy." Helen underlined Ronnie Mann's name. "Being demoted had to be embarrassing. Ronnie is the local, and with Kerry dead, he's back in the head chair. Any fingerprints on the shears?"

"Lots. But fingerprints on the weapon don't tell us much. The shears were moved during renovations by Eliot, Alison, the painter, cleaning people, even Alison's mother. Smudged, but there, nonetheless. Nowadays, there's latex gloves in any commercial kitchen. Someone could have easily pocketed a pair."

She pushed her dark hair off her forehead. "Was Ronnie on camera?"

"He walked past the pool house about seven-thirty. The cameras didn't film the doorway. They're directed onto the patio and pool."

"So you think we have two strong suspects. Eliot argued, but we don't know why. Ronnie hates his boss for taking his job," Helen said.

Joe's cell rang. He picked it up and frowned. "I've got to go."

Helen snatched back her *Pro Con* list. "There has to be more. My Detection Club is on the case."

Joe sighed. "Stay out of trouble. This killer could strike again."

Chapter Seven

Helen had done her homework on the Bowers house. Built in the early 1800s, the narrow three-story was one of only four to survive the burning of Grace Harbor by the British in 1813. The town, situated on a river which fed into the top of the Chesapeake from Pennsylvania, it drew history buffs and local shoppers into its stores and restaurants, much like Port Anne. At night, southern glints of lights from Grace Harbor winked at her own house on Buoy Two and Osprey Point Lighthouse from across the water.

Wednesday morning, she wove through the village and past The Vineyard, a popular wine bar, triggering memories of her first investigation. Older properties were her favorite, even if marketing them could be a bigger challenge. A house on Lafayette Street like the Bowers' offered a unique charm difficult to recreate in a new one. A tall, narrow French-styled house, it had deep yellow louvered shutters at the door, white painted wood and stucco siding, and keystones over each of the eight street-facing tall windows. Great curb appeal, neatly aligned with other Revolutionary and Victorian houses. Some of Bowers' neighbors were converted into B&Bs much like Captain's Watch. The lots were barely a third of an acre, with separate garages added over the years. According to tax records, the Bowers house had a 1700s smokehouse in the rear they likely used for storage. At ten am, Lafayette Street was quiet.

Helen knew this was a Norman Rockwell neighborhood. Parents would soon be chatting at the corners, waiting to meet school buses. By late afternoon, the sidewalks would be littered with bikes and skateboards. Helen felt badly this young mother was facing the prospect of leaving. Moving was not always a happy conversation.

Britany Bowers opened her front door on her first knock. "Good morning. Thank you for coming." Britany, her hair shoulder length and tucked behind her ears, wore leggings, a grey sweater, and Pumas. She had strong cheekbones and a bright, even smile. She looked like a runner.

Helen stepped through the doorway into a narrow period foyer with ten-foot ceilings and wide moldings. To her left, a neat living room with a fireplace built of local bluestone flanked the far wall. On her right, a chestnut staircase ran along the exterior wall and was peppered with children's photos. Two boys in soccer uniforms kneeled in the grass. A girl, about six, with a missing front tooth and wearing a Brownie uniform, mugged for the camera.

She followed Britany into a fairly new kitchen addition. More pictures, a school calendar, and a crayoned drawing hung from the refrigerator.

"Coffee?"

"Love some. Thank you." Helen plled out a chair. "I gather from a few Facebook posts you need to sell."

Britany flinched. "I'm not surprised you saw my post. I've gotten hundreds of responses from buyers looking for a bargain. I took it down yesterday. A couple of my clients were upset with my post, and two companies threatened to cancel my contracts." She added sugar to her mug. "I run mental health programs for human resource departments. For someone who deals with emotional disorders, exposing my personal problems to the world wasn't one of my best decisions."

"We've all made them." Helen sympathized. "My twins don't mind pointing out my mistakes when they get a chance. Tell me what you actually do. There's no reference to counseling on your Facebook page."

"I use my maiden name with patients and don't usually post personal photos. I don't want them recognizing me. I've learned the hard way charismatic people can be the deadliest, the most disturbed. I've had my life threatened twice while driving patients to hospitals."

"Charismatic people can be adept at deception. I've been fooled too," Helen said. "Did you have any training on how to deal with them in that kind of situation?"

"I've gotten good at calming down patients."

Helen studied her client. "Tell me what's happening now."

Britany grit her teeth. "About seven months ago, my husband Todd left his phone open, and a text popped up. I realized he was seeing someone he was supposed to be training. I guess in today's world, cell phone texts have replaced diaries when it comes to discovering secrets. When I confronted him, he said he wanted a divorce. I was shocked. Ironic for someone like me, trained in recognizing odd behavior." She flushed. "I'm trying to face a future without him."

"It's harder to see problems when you're personally involved. My mother ignored family issues just to keep the peace. I lived it myself. Do you want to stay here or move?"

"I'm wavering. Part of me wants to start over, but this is my kids' world. Their friends, their school. If I can, I'd like to make my husband an offer and hope he'll agree. We're splitting the mortgage payment for now."

"Your first step is an appraisal your attorney can present to your husband," Helen explained.

Britany frowned. "If we were to work out a number, you won't get a commission."

Helen waved a hand. "That's the least of your concerns."

"What if he doesn't trust your appraisal?"

"It could happen. Old houses can be hard to quantify, but I've sold a lot of them, and they actually have a lot of similarities. The biggest variation is their condition. I'm factual, so he'll have a tough time claiming my numbers are skewed to favor you. If he responds with objections, I'll deal with them. How quickly do you want the report?"

"Yesterday?"

"Why did I know you'd say yesterday?" Helen laughed. "I need until Monday. It's a complicated process." Helen picked up her iPad. "Can we start in your living room?" Helen stopped in the doorway. "I'm curious. Why did you call me? There are other real estate agents right here in Grace Harbor."

Her client's cheeks flushed as she pointed at three long rows of classic mysteries. "I heard you were involved in solving the case of a murdered builder. Then I read about the celebrity chef's death on ShopTV. A friend of mine in the neighborhood told me you fought for the zoning change that saved the Davies house. I decided you're not the usual Realtor."

"Hopefully, that's a good thing," Helen smiled. "Did you come to the grand opening Sunday? I don't remember seeing you."

"I wish. My oldest had his first soccer practice of the season, and I had to be there. Todd was working. He's a licensed harbor pilot like Davies and Hollowell. The stories about Captain's Watch being haunted always fascinated us."

Helen's eyes lit up. "Piloting is an unusual career choice."

"Not many people qualify. Piloting goes back generations in Todd's family."

"With Kerry Lightner killed Sunday, the press is perpetuating all kinds of rumors. Do you know anything about Isaac's ghost? I never took them very seriously. Now, I'm beginning to wonder if they're connected to her murder."

Britany's eyes widened. "Isaac disappeared sixty years ago. Police questioned Captain Davies, but they never found anything incriminating. Anglers who drown in the Chesapeake weren't unusual. No one wore life jackets, and even today, people are too careless. Isaac went out in his boat when a squall was predicted. My husband always thought he should have known better with all his experience."

"That's an interesting observation. Do you know if he had family?"

"He was married, and they lived in Grace Harbor. I'm not sure if they had children. She stayed here a year or two after he disappeared, then moved out of state."

"What happened to his share of the business?"

"Haven't any idea."

Helen's cell rang. "It's my assistant, Tammi, checking on me," she explained. "She'll be following up with your paperwork. You'll love her. She has a daughter about the age of yours."

Britany let out a sigh. "I feel better now that we've talked."

"Good. One last question, how do you plan to finance what you owe Todd?"

"I'll need to refinance. It'll be tight, but I have a good job, thank goodness."

"I'll email names of mortgage reps I trust to you."

Britany walked her to the front door. "Thank you." Her eyes teared.

Helen patted her arm. "We'll get you through this. I'm glad you want to stay here if you can. It's a good decision. Take one step at a time."

The young woman nodded. "I'll keep you posted if I hear anything more about your ghost."

Helen gave her a thumbs up.

Chapter Eight

A call came in from Tammi as Helen unlocked her car. "Not sure if you noticed, but Eliot and Alison are trying to reach you."

"I'm just checking my cell now. They each called twice. Lizzie called too. Any idea why?" asked Helen.

"Not at all. How did your meeting go?"

Helen drew in a breath. "All good. Britany's hoping to buy out her husband. We need to put together an appraisal for her by Monday."

"Monday?" Tammi's nails clicked on her keyboard. "That's a lot of work and not a lot of time."

"We'll manage. It's the best scenario for her family. Hopefully, the numbers will work for her. I'll call the Davies on the way to the office."

She dialed Eliot. He picked up on the second ring.

"Helen?"

"I was in a meeting. Has something happened?"

Eliot took a deep breath. "McAlister stopped in to see us this morning. They've gone through all our texts and emails for the last six months."

"Okay. Is there something you're concerned about?"

"He found texts from Kerry to me. McAlister believes he found a motive for me to kill her." He paused. "She was blackmailing me."

"I'm sorry, slow down. What did you say?" Helen jerked her Mini into a driveway and stopped. "Why on earth would she try to blackmail you?"

Eliot spit out the words. "She claimed my grandfather killed her grandfather."

"Are you serious? Who is her grandfather?" Silence. "Eliot? Who is it?"

65

"Isaac Hollowell, his partner."

"You can't be serious."

"I am. Can you come to the house? Can you bring Lizzie?"

"How is Lizzie involved?"

"Alison needs a friend to calm her down. Do you mind?"

"Not at all. Lizzie could be a big help."

Helen glanced at her dashboard. It was a little before noon. "I have to make a quick stop. I'll see you about one-thirty." She pulled out of the drive and into traffic. "Do you have a copy of those texts, or did Joe keep them?"

"We have a printout. The police sent a copy to Ben Horowitz."

"Good. I'll see you soon."

She dialed Joe's cell. He didn't pick up. "Joe, Eliot called me. He says you found texts that implicate him."

* * *

Port Anne, with its one-way in, one-way out main street, was backed up with its usual shoppers and lunch crowd. She texted Tammi.

Hi. Have you eaten lunch? Want to meet at The Wooden Mast? We can review Britany's file.

Her response popped up. **On the phone with Jordan Builders. Love to. Be there in ten.**

Tom, the cook at The Wooden Mast, spotted Helen through the kitchen pass way and gave her a friendly wave. He'd worked at the little corner restaurant since their high school days. She'd heard he'd taken ownership four months ago and was happy for him. Sally, his head server, was at least seventy and had marshaled their staff of teenagers that came and went over the years with an iron fist. Helen remembered what it was like to earn a small tip for a lot of work. It hadn't hurt her or Shawn and Lizzie.

Helen followed Sally to a tiny Formica table at the end of a row flanking the windows. Their decorating motif seldom changed. The lamps made of red, blue, and green artificial stained glass hung from a 1930s white tin ceiling, and a mural by a local artist of Osprey Point Lighthouse covered one wall. Local contractors anxious to eat and run filled a row of round, red leatherette and chrome stools from the fifties running the length of a long counter.

She spotted Tammi at the doorway, squeezing past diners paying their checks at the register. Today, a cluster of coral pebbles dangled from her ears and encircled her neck.

"Hi! This was such a good idea." She flashed bright teeth while she strung an enormous brown leather handbag onto her chair.

"I thought you'd be hungry and needed a break."

The Wooden Mast mainstay was thick cheeseburgers and hot, crispy fries. They arrived in minutes.

Tammi lowered her voice. "Tell me about Britany Bowers. Was she half as bizarre as her Facebook post? I noticed it was taken down."

"She's very nice, normal. Believe it or not, she's a mental health counselor. She admitted she had a temporary meltdown and I get the idea she's heartbroken. She has three kids under the age of ten with their life turned upside down." Helen set down a folder with Bowers written across the tab.

Tammi added ketchup to her burger and passed it to Helen. "Phew. I thought raising Kayla alone was rough. At least I know Marcus is on his last deployment. I'm counting down the months when he gets his assignment at the Navy base here."

"You and Kayla are troopers. Just don't dare tell me his assignment is out of state. I'll have the meltdown."

"I don't say much to her about his return. I don't want to disappoint her if he gets a delay. Marcus has been gone so long, I'm worried we can adjust to being a family again." She picked up the folder. "Do you want me to input your notes into our appraisal forms?"

"Try to find all their tax records, too," Helen said. "I'll search comparables."

"Anything new on Kerry Lightner's murder? I saw two news stations parked outside Eliot's campaign office this morning."

"I'm meeting Alison and Eliot now. Let's say this doesn't look encouraging. Have you heard anything more about Isaac's mysterious disappearance?"

"Just worthless gossip," Tammi said, swallowing a last bite.

"Gossip isn't *always* worthless. It depends upon who initiates it." Helen paid their bill and gave Tom another wave.

"That sounds like one of your Jane Marple-isms."

"You know me too well. Talk to you in the morning" They both took off in opposite directions.

* * *

Captain's Watch didn't have a single car in guest parking. Alison met Helen at their front door. "Lizzie is here. We're in the library. I made coffee." She hesitated. "By the way, we let our chef go. No guests to feed."

Lizzie offered her mother an anxious smile. Eliot took a seat next to Alison.

"I'm not sure this is a good idea. You're dating the detective in charge of this case," he said.

Helen pulled off her jacket and sat down. "That's your decision. I know from experience Joe is smart. He's not interested in arresting the wrong person." She eyed them both. "Could you start at the beginning? How did Kerry convince you she wanted to run your campaign? We all know she could have worked at more lucrative ones."

Eliot dropped his hands down between his knees. "Kerry convinced me she wanted to work with a Chesapeake candidate committed to clean water issues. She introduced me to Craig Olsoff, the CEO of Olsoff Marine Technology. He'd spoken before congressional hearings and fundraised for public support for the bay. Her connections to Craig and other political types was a huge asset. I was excited. I let my ego get in the way of my judgment."

"What did she threaten you with?" Helen asked. Eliot thrust a printout of texts into her hands.

"March 30th. That was a week before she was killed." Helen looked up.

"Keep reading," he said.

"I am the granddaughter of Isaac Hollowell, Spencer Davies's partner." Helen stopped. She sat back against the cushions, her face pale white.

Lizzie made a little gasp.

"Wow. I never saw that coming." Drawing in a breath, she continued. "Your grandfather murdered him and took over their business. I demand four hundred thousand dollars in four equal payments for an inheritance I never received. The first is due Monday, April 9th. You have two choices. One, pay me, and I leave the area immediately after I get you elected. Two, I take my evidence to the police, and your future reputation will be destroyed. No one will elect the grandson of a murderer."

Helen stared up at Eliot. "Now we know why Kerry took your job. She wanted to be part of your inner circle. To pressure you for the money."

He avoided her eyes, his lips pressed together.

"How did Kerry prove she was Isaac's granddaughter?"

"She showed me a genealogy report. I couldn't believe my eyes."

"Did you pay her?" asked Helen.

"When I received the first blackmail note, Kerry and I argued. I made one payment to her from our home equity line. Last Sunday, I told her we couldn't pay her any more. We'd put all our money into the house. She mocked me. She said I had campaign funds, and I could tap into the account."

Alison spoke up. "We knew we could end up in jail if we used those funds. It was out of the question."

"Kerry's threat was eating me up. All our hard work was about to be decimated." Eliot reached for his wife's hand. "Helen, I promise you, I didn't touch that campaign money. The next payment was due the Monday after our grand opening. I didn't know what to do. I could barely look at her at the party," he said, his voice bitter. The room was quiet.

"I understand James Corcoran told the police he overhead you and Kerry arguing Sunday night. He also told Jean at her coffee shop the next day."

Eliot's jaw dropped. He glanced in panic at his wife.

"Now, Joe McAlister has a motive for murder," Lizzie interjected.

"Only if he believes you would kill Kerry to keep this quiet." Helen's eyes drilled Eliot's. Her voice was low and direct. "We want to believe you. Here's my problem. As much as you didn't want to face Kerry's claim that your grandfather killed his partner, why would you give in to her? Why would you not call her bluff? It was sixty years ago."

"I panicked. I shouldn't have, but I did."

"You had no other reason?" Helen was quiet, waiting, then sighed. "If you didn't kill her, who do you think did?"

"I have absolutely no idea. When I told Alison about Kerry's threats, she wanted to go to the police. We decided if the public didn't want to support my election because of her claim, then so be it. I'd bow out."

Alison squeezed his hand, her eyes filling with tears.

"Did you tell Joe all this?"

"Not until he showed the texted threads to me and Ben. He doesn't believe me," Eliot said.

"You can't blame him. Even if you decided to stop paying her, you had to be angry. She extorted you for a hundred thousand dollars. People have lost control for less. That's what Joe is thinking."

Helen got to her feet and studied the formal oil painting of Captain Spencer Davies hanging over the fireplace and a smaller painting of his genteel wife. A small fire in the fireplace crackled. It may have been early spring, but the heat was welcome. She rubbed her arms.

"Let's try to take this from a different angle. What do you know about these ghost rumors? Do you think someone else knew more about Isaac's disappearance? Someone besides Kerry?"

"Mom," Lizzie leaned forward. "Could someone collude with Kerry? Are they behind these stories?"

"Maybe. They might even be our killer. Something may have gone wrong between them." Her mother turned again to the group.

"What did she show you about your grandfather and Isaac that convinced you to pay?"

Eliot dug into his jeans pocket and pulled out a folded note.

Helen and Lizzie examined the sheet. "This looks like a page from a journal," Helen said.

Lizzie read the cryptic notes out loud. "July 15th, 1967, meeting Spencer four pm." She looked up. "Is this the day he disappeared? Is this Isaac's handwriting?"

"Yes, I've seen his handwriting in some of the company books."

"Have you ever seen any other notes about this meeting?" Helen asked.

Eliot and Alison exchanged glances. "We tore down broken plaster and rebuilt walls and ceilings when we restored the house," Alison said. "We never came across anything referring to Isaac's death. Nothing."

"It may be sixty years ago, but even then, newspapers and libraries archived press clippings on microfiche," Helen mused.

"That's public record," Lizzie said. "If there's information that incriminated the captain, why didn't the police pursue it at the time?"

"That's what we have to find out," Helen responded. "We have to comb through anything and everything you have from your family's past. Every ledger, every notebook, every photo."

Eliot stood up and walked to a window. He turned, staring at Helen. "Why is that important?"

Helen grimaced. "I'm not sure, but I don't like loose ends. Right now, we've got someone who drummed up his ghost. There must have been a reason."

"We have boxes of handwritten ledgers for their business in the attic. I meant to ask the historical society if they might want them. I'm glad we didn't."

"What about computer printouts?" asked Lizzie.

Alison shook her head. "Small companies didn't use them before the early 1980s. Howard Travel was one of the first in Port Anne to buy one."

Eliot's cell rang. "Ben...I understand. We'll be there at four." He hung up and looked at Alison. "We have to meet with Joe McAlister. Ben says to be prepared for a long night."

Chapter Nine

Outside Captain's Watch, Lizzie leaned against her mother's coupe. "What shall we do? My heart breaks for them. Look at this parking lot. Not one guest."

"It's tough to sell overnights in a B&B when it's no longer cozy. Now, it's creepy." Her mother fingered the brass key on a set Alison had handed her.

"How are they going to survive this even if they're proven innocent?" Lizzie gazed at the old house.

"Finances are the least of their problems right now."

"With Eliot and Alison not able to campaign, his senate run is dying a quick death. Their life is sinking like the *Titanic*."

Helen rubbed her eyes. "I can't help but wonder if someone else knew about Kerry's blackmailing. I could be completely wrong, but I think Isaac's ghost and Kerry's murder are linked together."

"What's our next step?"

"We'll have to work quickly. My gut tells me an indictment could be only days away. They've got to start searching through family records. I'll head to Safe Harbor. Can you meet me here about five?"

"Sorry, I'm due at ShopTV. I'm on air until seven. I could be here about eight."

"I'll get a head start."

"Mom, I'm afraid to say the words out loud. Is there any chance Eliot did kill Kerry?"

Helen frowned. "Jane would tell you that ordinary people can sometimes do the most astonishing things. Let's pray that's not the case here."

"That doesn't make me feel the least bit better. See you tonight. Love you."

* * *

Unless it was snowing or teeming rain, Calli's Tomes and Treasures had her Port Anne t-shirts, sweatshirts, and banners swinging in the light breeze outside her shop. Locally crafted wooden signs with boating coordinates and colorful handmade jewelry and pottery filled one large window. A bay window displayed a slew of local authors' books on every subject, from Chesapeake Bay-centered mysteries to cookbooks, history, and folklore. Today, it was all the town talk drawing Helen into the shop.

Tall and thin and smartly dressed, Calli started her business on her own at least twenty-five years ago. She had an innate instinct for attracting tourists and out-of-town water lovers. Her assistant, Viv, greeted Helen as she walked through the door. Between the two of them, they knew most of their customers by name. People enjoyed doing business with them.

"Helen! How nice to see you. Have any mysterious cookbooks for us?"

"Hopefully, a murdered chef's edition was a one and only for me," Helen said. "I do have a couple questions for you if you have a few minutes."

Calli's eyes crinkled in anticipation. "What's up?"

Helen gestured at the stack of books centered around Kent County. "Have either of you ever heard about Isaac's spirit walking the tower in Captain's Watch?"

The women exchanged glances.

"That rumor's been floating around Port Anne ever since Isaac Hollowell disappeared off his boat. I was just a kid at the time. Some people say he knew this bay so well, there was no way he'd have drowned." Calli lowered her voice. "A few said Isaac and Spencer weren't getting along."

Viv eyed her boss. "The police never found anything suspicious. The captain was a respected town business leader. Everyone searched for days."

"You were both at the party Sunday. Did you notice anything odd?"

"I had to leave about seven thirty," Calli said. "My granddaughter was expecting me. Val stayed."

"The valet company told Joe they helped ten or twelve cars leave before Alison found Kerry. Did you pass anyone on Blue Point out to the main roads?"

Calli hesitated. "A handful. There were a few that pulled out of the private drives onto Blue Point. I assumed they were neighbors."

"By the way," Val added. "Did you know there's a memorial coffin for Isaac in St. Cecilia's graveyard?" Val asked.

Helen started. "What? I don't understand. How could there be a grave without Isaac's body?"

Calli chuckled. "His coffin is empty. His wife insisted on a memorial, and Spencer Davies paid for the grave. Apparently, the ceremony was quite the town event at the time."

"That's bizarre. How would I recognize it?"

"Look for a tombstone with a chain running around the plot. Isaac's empty coffin is suspended on chains inside the open hole dug for his grave. It's creepy." Calli drew out her hands. "There's stone slabs positioned over the opening, and kids say they hear the chains creaking at night as the coffin sways in the wind."

"Why in the world would his wife want an empty grave?" Helen couldn't help but shiver.

"Years ago, families of sailors lost at sea might memorialize a lost loved one with a coffin that wouldn't touch the ground. There's another grave from the 1800s like Isaac's. It's south of Grace Harbor near the Navy munitions base," added Viv.

"That's incredible. Why do you think there's rumors Captain's Watch is haunted? Until now, I never gave them a thought."

"Only that Isaac's soul never rested, like with most ghost stories," Calli said.

"What happened to his wife?"

"She died not long after he did."

Helen leaned on the countertop. "I need a favor. If you hear anything around town about the Spencer and Isaac, will you call me? I want to know who's stirring up these stories."

"Are you adding us to your detective squad?"

Helen laughed. "You'd be perfect."

Calli gave Helen a wink.

* * *

It was almost four by the time Helen pulled open the door at Safe Harbor Realty.

"Well! I thought you fell into the bay," Tammi said. "What have you and your sleuths been up to?"

"Let's just say this has been a very strange day. Lizzie and I met with the Davies, then I stopped at Calli's. Any chance you've started the Bowers appraisal?"

"I didn't get very far."

"Don't worry. I can't work on the data tonight. I'm going back to the Davies' house and digging through the captain's old files."

"What's happened?"

Helen glanced about the office. "Come." She closed the door behind them. "Joe found texts from Kerry to Eliot. She was blackmailing him."

"For what?"

"She claimed Isaac was her grandfather, and Spencer killed him. She threatened to destroy Eliot's reputation."

"Do you really think people would care what his grandfather might have done years ago?"

Helen shrugged. "Truthfully, no, I don't. I think Eliot isn't telling us the whole story. He paid her a hundred thousand dollars. I can't picture him or Alison killing her because of it. There has to be a bigger scandal Kerry knew reflected on him today. Something that he'd have a hard time shaking off. Something he's convinced is so damaging, he can't let it go public. What that is, we don't know. For Joe, he's got a witness overhearing an argument between Eliot and Kerry, plus Eliot's fingerprints at the rear door. It's Eliot's real motive we're missing."

"Let me guess. You're hoping to find something in the captain's papers proving him innocent."

"I don't know what I'll find, but we need to figure out why these rumors of ghosts were resurrected. If Eliot's innocent, then who wants to plant Kerry's murder on him?"

"Anything new connected to the campaign?"

"Nope. I plan to stop by their headquarters tomorrow and talk to Ronnie Mann."

"Could he have killed Kerry? He won't like it if you're asking too many questions."

"I can't worry about who likes me," Helen shrugged.

"That's something your Detection Club would say. Speaking of liking, what does Joe say about your sleuthing?"

"I haven't spoken to him since early Tuesday. I thought I should give him some space. Besides, this case buys me a little time."

"Time? What do you mean?" Tammi furrowed her eyebrows.

"While we're both trying to solve this, the subject of planning a vacation together is on the back burner."

"You're impossible. You've had some close calls in the past, and he worries about you. So do your kids. Does Shawn know you're sleuthing? Don't expect me to lie for you. If Shawn asks, I'm telling."

Helen waved her away. "The less he knows, the better off I am." She grabbed her laptop and stuffed it into her tote. "See you tomorrow. You need to go home to Kayla and your mom."

"Just be careful."

"I'm running home to change my clothes. Stop worrying. This isn't the first time I've sorted through a musty old attic."

"Alone in the dark?"

"I'm counting on Nancy Drew for courage and a strong flashlight. Besides, Lizzie will be meeting me later. Maybe I should invite Nora Charles and Agatha Raisin along. They can pour me a couple drinks to build up my nerve."

Chapter Ten

By the time Helen turned off Blue Point Road and down the long narrow lane leading to Captain's Watch, it was close to seven pm. The day had been overcast, and the sun reflecting on the bay beyond the big old house was losing its fight with the cloud cover. She parked on the circular drive and turned off the ignition. She pulled her flashlight out of the glove compartment and stepped out of her car. She still had about forty-five minutes of daylight. She glanced across the gravel parking area and along the deep grove of shrubs and trees encircling the property. No one was around.

She inserted a brass key for the front door, its intricate bow-shaped handle giving away its age and turned the lock. After all these years showing property, she'd been in a lot of empty houses. It could be an odd, discomforting sensation walking through someone else's private life when they weren't home. She'd become fairly desensitized, but tonight was different. After the crowd of guests on Sunday, then Kerry's stabbing, Helen couldn't ignore the eerie sense of desertion and silenced joy. Sadness seemed to be taking over. It seeped into her bones.

She inhaled. Setting down her purse at the door, she flipped on the hall lights and cast her eyes from left to right. The formal front parlor with multiple seating areas and the dining room that easily seated sixteen people felt abandoned. The excitement of welcoming visitors had evaporated, and the ten-foot ceilings echoed her footsteps. Helen turned and locked the front door behind her, pocketed the key, and pulled out her cell. She straightened her shoulders and texted Lizzie.

I'm at CW. Call me when you arrive. I'll unlock the front door for you.

The Lady Liberty figure lighting the newel post cast irregular shadows on the oak floors. Flicking on the row of etched glass sconces marching up the staircase wall, she climbed from the first floor to the second with her cell in her jeans pocket and her flashlight in her right hand. The four guest bedrooms ringed the main hall and led to the smaller private hallway for Eliot and Alison's bedroom suite. Winding up the broad stairway again, her hand traced along the oak banister. She swore she felt the cold touch of long-gone owners on the rail. She reached the third floor and more empty rooms, their doors all open but one. Thank God, I'm wearing sneakers, she declared aloud. 'Practical decision. Glad you listened to my advice,' commented Jessica in her ear as she climbed up the narrow, ladder-like last set of steps.

Helen turned on her flashlight and ran the beam across the eaves closest to the entrance. She knew there was an overhead lamp someplace. 'Where the heck are the lights, Nancy?'

Her beam picked up a couple long brass chain pulls. She jerked hard, and three bare bulbs strung together on a black electrical cord turned on, swinging in the air from her touch. Geez, Eliot, couldn't you send an electrician up here? Running her flashlight around the perimeter, she spotted stacks of yellowed cardboard file boxes lining one wall.

The initials for Eastern Shore Piloting Services in black letters were along their sides. Each one had a year inked below them starting in 1948 when the business opened. The last read 1976. Helen pulled one off the stack and sat down on the box. 'This could take forever,' she told her squad. She sifted through the first two.

A ring pierced the silence. Her heart jumped to her throat. "Holy crap," she cried out loud. She picked up her phone. "Lizzie! You just scared the life out of me! Are you here?"

"I'm at the front door. Mom, this is spooky being here all by ourselves," she whispered.

"Tell me about it. I'm in the attic. I'll be right down, after my heart rate drops to something near normal."

Helen padded silently down the stairs. She turned the front door lock and flung open the heavy door. "Hi. Did you lock your car?"

Lizzie nodded. "I'm glad the security lights came on. It's pitch black out here."

"The attic isn't much better. Follow me. It's a hike." Her mother turned and started up the stairs again. "When this is all resolved," she puffed, "I'm going back to jogging Osprey Point trail to the lighthouse every day. I'm out of shape."

Lizzie climbed up the last stairway into the attic. "How'd you even find this? I feel like we're living Nancy's *The Hidden Staircase.*"

"You did agree to be my George for the night."

"I didn't quite realize what I was getting myself into. You actually meant it." Lizzie blinked and stepped back. "Are you telling me all those files are from Eastern Shore Piloting? Are you sure this isn't *The Secret in the Old Attic?*"

Helen chuckled. "If we're lucky, we're living the remake. At least you have your mother's odd sense of humor. I've gone through these four boxes. I thought we'd be more likely to find something around the year Isaac disappeared. Take a look at these notes for 1965 and 1966. Isaac referred to a place called Deale Island. Ever hear of it?" She moved the light over the files.

Lizzie shook her head. "Any maps?"

"Not yet. There's no way we can get through all these tonight. Let's work until eleven. At least we've created a system. We can pick up again tomorrow."

"Can we see the pool house from here?"

"Follow me." Helen pointed at the last few steps to the widow's watch. She opened the creaking door. "It's a cloudy night but you can still make out the lights across the bay to the Navy base."

"Quite a view," Lizzie said. She stopped and pressed her hands against the glass. "Mom, look! There's lights running along the dock."

Helen squinted. "That's not a boat. And they're not dock lights. Someone is wandering around."

"Should we check them out?"

Seconds later, the light went out. "They're gone. Who in the world would be down there at this hour?"

"Maybe it's our ghost."

Helen let out a breath. "More likely the person stirring up the rumors. The question is, why?"

Lizzie's blue eyes widened. "Why are you whispering?"

"Why are you?" Her mother retorted. They both started to laugh, their nerves on high alert.

"Be careful. We might wake up the dead."

"That's not even funny."

"It kind of is," said Lizzie.

Helen's cell rang out. They both jumped a mile. "It's Joe," she groaned.

"Hello… Where am I? I'm with George, I mean Lizzie … Are you asking where specifically?" She rolled her eyes at her daughter. "Well. We're in the Davies' attic, looking through Captain Spencer's old records. Where are you?"…"No, we've been working here a couple hours. Are Eliot and Alison still at the police station?"…"Okay. Can Lizzie and I meet you tomorrow morning for coffee? I have a few bits of information for you"…."We're fine. Stop worrying. See you at Chessie Cafe at nine-thirty."

"What did he say?"

"He doesn't like us being here by ourselves. Eliot and Alison are finished for the night. They're meeting with Ben alone now, and they should be home soon. By Joe's tone, sounds like they're on borrowed time." Helen checked her watch. "Let's try to get done with this next stack before they're back."

Lizzie tucked her blonde hair into a short wisp of ponytail. "I decided to stay with you tonight. I brought a change of clothes."

Helen brushed the dust off her hands onto her jeans. "Good idea."

"How was Joe?"

"Not happy. Least of all with me. I'm on borrowed time too."

A little after eleven, they locked up Captain's Watch and dashed through the dark to their cars. Helen pointed her flashlight at her door handle, then stopped.

"Lizzie, there's something wrong with my car." She ran her light over the Mini's body. "Somone slashed my tires!"

Lizzie gasped and glanced around. "Do you think they're still here?"

"They're long gone. That ghost on the dock is more than a mirage. Someone wants me to stop helping the Davies."

"This was really vindictive. What shall we do?"

"I'll ride back to my house with you and call a tow for tomorrow. Joe will be furious. He warned me."

Chapter Eleven

Chessie Café bustled with coffee drinkers short on time and short on caffeine. The whir of fresh grinders and morning chat greeted Helen and Lizzie at the door. For a little town, Port Anne seemed to keep Jean's Coffee Pot and the café very busy. While Jean specialized in freshly ground coffee to take home, the café concocted homemade pastry from apple pie scones to frosted donuts topped with bacon. Calories welcome.

In a fresh suit and tie, Joe still looked like he was short on sleep. He offered a crooked smile as he stood and pulled out a chair for Helen and Lizzie. "Just arrived. Do you need coffee?"

"Why don't I make this my treat?" Lizzie offered. "Be right back."

Helen studied the detective. "Do I dare ask how your interview with the Davies went?"

He looked away and then to Helen. "They insist Kerry's threat against them had nothing to do with her murder. I've got his fingerprints on the outside of the rear door, a loud argument with Kerry earlier Sunday night, and his hundred-thousand-dollar payment. Frankly, I'm looking for a stronger motive. I'm struggling to believe he would cave in to her blackmail threat because his grandfather might be accused of murdering someone sixty years ago. He must have known she'd never succeed in claiming a portion of his family inheritance."

Helen sat back and studied his face. "I'm questioning the exact same thing. Paying Kerry doesn't make sense."

"What isn't he telling us? What have you heard?"

"Gossip. My sleuths are reminding me gossip can be valuable and vicious. I don't want to discount it." She held up her hand to stop his protest. "I keep asking myself, why would someone want to kill Kerry? Why would they want Eliot or Alison, or both, to take the fall? Are the two questions even related?"

"The easiest answer is one, or both of them, planned to put an end to her blackmail and save their reputation."

"According to them, they planned to go to the police for help. They decided to wait until the B&B grand opening was over," she said.

He rubbed his chin. "Sounds convenient, doesn't it? An 'after we're caught' explanation."

Lizzie placed their mugs in front of them. "Joe, Alison is my long-time friend. The Howard family has had a business in Port Anne for years. We believe them."

"Then why didn't they tell me about Kerry's blackmail when I first interviewed them Sunday night? Why'd they keep it a secret until I found Kerry's threats on Eliot's phone? There's something they're holding back."

Lizzie's hands started to tremble as she lifted her cup.

"It has to be something so damaging, Eliot's sure he'll be handing you a motive for murder." Helen opened her purse and pulled out a sheet of paper.

"Not your *Pro Con* list again." Joe protested.

Helen tapped at the note. "Have you interviewed Ronnie? Jean tells me he resented Kerry big time. We know he benefited from her murder."

"I don't know if I'd consider Jean a great source." Joe set his mug down with a thud. "Are you suggesting we put her under the witness protection program?"

"Yes, Sherlock, *that's* what I'm suggesting." She glared.

"About Ronnie. We've interviewed him twice. We all met him at the party, but there's no sign of him being in the pool house later. He's been polite and calm each time."

"Of course, he's polite to you. He also had a big motive. He got his precious job back," Helen grumbled.

"We're still digging," Joe said.

"What about Kerry's family? I learned yesterday that Isaac's wife lived in Grace Harbor. Maybe Kerry hired someone else to help her blackmail Eliot."

"Mom thinks we need to figure out who's reviving these ghost tales."

Joe pushed back his chair. "Look here, you two chums. People like ghost stories. I can't assign my squad to knock on doors around town, asking who's seen a ghost at the Davies place."

Helen's eyes glinted. "You can't, but we can. As soon as we learn anything, we'll let you know." She glanced at Lizzie then took a deep breath. "Our ghost slashed my tires outside Captain's Watch late last night."

Joe set down his coffee. "What? Why didn't' you call me?" he growled.

"The damage was done. I hitched a ride home with Lizzie."

"You're impossible." He shook his head.

"You're the second person to tell me that this week." She reached up and planted a kiss on his cheek.

Joe uttered a half-hearted scowl. "Call me the next time someone defaces your property. And, when you're not combing through boxes."

* * *

Helen spied Owen's Bait Shop across Water Street as she stepped outside the café. She left a voice mail for Tammi. "I'm just coming out of Chessie Cafe with a latte and chocolate cream donut for you. I need to keep you energized. My car should be in the parking lot by now. Long story. See you in about twenty minutes."

Owen had taken to hanging t-shirts under his narrow overhang, similar to Calli's Tomes and Treasures. Unlike Calli's, his shirts were aimed at reeling in fishing enthusiasts. An oversized cardboard figure of George H. W. Bush stood on the sidewalk, holding a long reel and wearing a cap, next to a sign advertising fishing licenses. A vending machine mirrored a soda machine and dispensed minnows, nightcrawlers, and blood worms. It sat on his sidewalk for his before-dawn customers. I guess you can never get up too early if you plan to fish, she thought.

Port Anne drew hundreds of serious competitors from across the country for tournaments held throughout the year, and Owen's shop attracted anglers like a fish to water. His website posted weather reports for all the rivers and creeks surrounding the bay. Denim blue and khaki shirts, imprinted with giant blue crabs, had sayings like "Keep your mouth shut" across the backs and "Owen's Bait Shop" on their pockets. 'Let's hope that's not his personal philosophy,' Jane said to Helen.

From the outside, the bait shop looked tiny. From inside, it was quadruple the size. The family opened their business in the sixties, about the same time Isaac Hollowell disappeared, and passed it on, generation after generation.

Helen ducked around a wall jammed with fish nets and assorted tackle, all hung neatly on hooks. The entire ceiling from one end to the other was covered with rods of every type and length. An angler's heaven, no doubt.

Owen hadn't aged much since the last time she'd seen him, which had been years, about five foot ten, thinning grey hair and a neatly kept mustache and beard. Strong leather-like hands came from growing up handling a rod. He studied her as she approached his long green Formica counter at the rear of the store. He probably didn't see many women dressed for the office cross his threshold. Visitors wearing waterproof ankle boots with extra traction and sweatshirts with funky fish graphics were far more likely.

He pushed a faded blue and grey plaid flannel up to his elbows. "Can I help you?" His smile hidden under a thick white mustache was the type that didn't show many teeth, but smile lines gathered around his clear light eyes and tan, weathered skin.

She smiled. "I'm Helen Morrisey with Safe Harbor Realty. I live out on Osprey Point. My son stops in for bait when he has the chance." She hesitated. "I've got an odd question for you. Have you heard any rumors about Captain's Watch and a ghost?"

"A ghost?" His eyes widened. He stuck a yellow pencil he held in his hand behind his right ear. "Can't say I hear that question often. You talkin' about Isaac?"

"I am. Eliot Davies' grandparents once owned the house. Eliot and his wife, Alison, bought back Captain's Watch last summer. I'm sure you heard about the murder in their pool house Sunday night. Seems to have stirred up some old rumors."

The shopkeeper crossed his arms and leaned against a freezer chest marked 'chicken necks'. "I was just a youngster. My aunt used to rattle on about the night he disappeared. Every so often, someone will wander in here and ask me how to find his grave. Saint Cecilia's Church is right down this street. You may already know."

"I do. Ever wonder how Isaac died?" Helen studied his face.

"There's plenty of people who drown in the bay because they're not careful." He tsked. "Stupid. Why you askin'?"

"The Davies are good friends of mine. This murder on their property is hitting them hard. Accusations are flying along with the ghost stories. Do you know them?"

"Met Eliot at their party. A little too fancy for me, but I was curious to see what they did with the place. Alison used to come in here with her daddy when she was a little girl. He'd take her fishing. Get the idea Eliot wants to raise more money for the upper bay if he gets elected. That's if he doesn't get tried for murder. Never met the woman killed. Sounds like weren't her kind of store.

"Ever hear if anyone resents his moving back into town?"

"I haven't. Interesting idea, though." He rubbed his short beard.

Helen reached into her wallet. "Could you hang onto my card? Give me a call if you hear anything you think could help us. Old grudges that turn into revenge can destroy people."

He took the card, flipping it from side to side, then pinned the card to a bulletin board behind his register. He studied the text a second time. "Say, you the real estate lady who solves crimes? I've heard of you."

Helen gave a little shrug. "I've heard of you too. Something tells me you like things fair and square. I just want to help the Davies get their lives back." Her smile was tight, frustrated.

He gave her a slow nod. "Tell Alison I remember her and her mother. Give my regards to Sarah."

Helen held out her hand. "Thanks for keeping your ears open."

* * *

Texts filled her phone screen as she stepped outside.

The first was Eliot. **Call me, please!**

The second and third was Sarah. **Alison's in the emergency room!**

Helen halted on the sidewalk to reread the text and banged into a pedestrian walking their dog. "Oh, excuse me." She stared at her phone. What happened?

She dialed Sarah's number. She didn't pick up. Eliot answered on her first ring.

"Helen. I'm at the hospital. Joe McAlister was at our door to do another search. Alison collapsed when she saw him."

"Will she be okay?"

"The ER doctor says she had a panic attack. They're keeping her for a couple hours."

"Do you want me to come? Wait, Sarah's calling."

"She's here with us. I'll tell her I reached you. Did you find anything about Isaac last night?" His voice was low, discouraged.

"Nothing. We sifted through ten boxes."

"I'm worried you'll find something that proves Spencer killed Isaac. It'll make me look even more guilty."

"Paying Kerry a hundred thousand dollars is what makes you look guilty, Eliot. We don't understand why you were so panicked about an event that happened years ago, even if it was your grandfather." Her frustration was loud and clear. "By the way, your ghost is back. Someone was out on the docks last night and then slit my tires."

Eliot went silent.

"What does Ben say?" asked Helen. "Or are you keeping him in the dark too?"

He ignored the question. "He thinks ghost rumors are unrelated to who killed her. What if someone wanted a share of the money I paid her?"

"No one knows," she sighed. "What about Ronnie? Is he at your office now? I'm hoping if I stop in to volunteer, I'll have a chance to talk with him."

"Thanks. I'll go check on Alison."

"Give her my best."

* * *

At about three-thirty in the afternoon, Helen left Safe Harbor and headed out. On the first corner coming into town, a red, white, and blue *Eliot Davies for State Senator* sign couldn't be more obvious. Maryland state flags stirred in the spring breeze from both ends of the building. Helen had been happy to see them choose this spot. For all the busy storefronts on Water Street, this space had been vacant far too long. 'If we don't get this case solved, it'll be empty again,' observed Jessica 'Don't pressure me,' Helen retorted. 'Not everything can be neat and orderly the way you like it.'

The office was bustling. Helen assumed most of the staff were volunteers. She spied Eliot's campaign manager on the phone inside a small, glass-enclosed private office toward the rear. A young woman in a blue Vote for Davies long-sleeved polo stood at the front desk. About five foot five, she had spiky green streaks and long bangs grazing her thin cheeks.

"Can we help you? I'm Pam."

"Nice to meet you. I'm hoping I might be able to help with get-out-the-vote phone calls." Helen gave her a big, enthusiastic smile. "Is Ronnie Mann available?"

"Let me get him." She tapped on the glass and pointed to Helen. He waved.

"Hi." His face brightened in recognition. "Thanks for coming by." He ran his hands across his shaved dome.

"You might not remember, I'm Helen Morrisey. I'm the real estate agent who negotiated Eliot's purchase of Captain's Watch. I want to help his campaign. It can't be easy right now with your candidate not working. How are you doing?"

Ronnie waved her into his office and offered her a seat. "That's only one of our problems. We're being hounded by the press day and night. Our bank of volunteers is shrinking. They're intimidated by the questions they're being asked. Some of them are starting to worry he could have killed Kerry. Who wants to represent a murderer?"

"It's terrible," Helen sympathized.

"We were fine before she arrived six weeks ago. It's this investigation that's the problem."

"I only met her Sunday night. I hear working with her was tough."

Ronnie leaned back in his chair, and his eyes narrowed. "That's being polite."

"You must have an opinion as to who killed her." Helen tilted her head.

He opened his hands in dismay.

"Is there no one who benefited?"

He shifted in his chair. "Are you suggesting I did?"

"Didn't you?" Helen clamped her lips together. Ronnie squirmed.

Pam rapped on the glass again. Ronnie looked up. Helen sensed he welcomed the interruption. She turned around to see a heavy, distinguished man with dark hair standing in the doorway. His light wool suit, with its knife-edged pants, easily cost more than one of her commissions.

"Craig!" Ronnie rose and reached out his hand. "Great to see you. Come in. Do you know Helen Morrisey? She's a friend of Eliot and Alison."

Craig reached out a strong hand. "Helen, nice to meet you. How's Eliot doing? We're all concerned."

Helen turned on the stylish Nora Charles feminine charm. "As are we. If I remember, you're with Olsoff Marine Technology. I've heard so much about your company. Eliot was looking forward to working with you."

"Eliot is a fantastic candidate."

Helen relaxed and crossed her legs. "Please, join us."

The CEO followed her moves. Unbuttoning his suit jacket, he made himself comfortable. "Kerry's murder shocked me to the core. We had high hopes for her candidate. She was a fighter." His chin dropped as he examined her up and down. "Tell me a little more about yourself. Why have we never met?"

Helen took in his shiny, manicured nails and the square-shaped black onyx ring on his right hand. "In little Port Anne? I'm sure you're too busy traveling the country to notice me."

His face smoothed. "I assure you, I would have noticed."

Ronnie interrupted their little love fest. "What brought you in?"

"I'm staying at the Baltimore Four Seasons tonight. Thought I'd drop by for a drink at Prime and Claw. Would either of you like to join me for dinner?" He glanced at Helen.

Ronnie looked surprised and a little disappointed. "I wish I could. I have a committee meeting at six down the street."

Helen's eyes moved from one man to the other. Please, Lord. Give me an excuse to escape. She lowered her eyelashes at the CEO. "I'd love to have dinner, but I'm running late." She paused, adding hastily, "For a client."

Craig's eyes twitched. "Another time?" He tugged at the cuffs of his dress shirt. His cuff links glinted.

"Love to," she purred. "I hope you don't mind my asking. You crossed paths with Kerry more than either of us. Any ideas on who wanted her dead?" Her green eyes grazed his face.

"Well...no. I didn't know Kerry personally. Have the police come up with any possibilities?"

"No," she responded sadly. "Eliot and Alison are under the law's microscope right now."

"I admire your concern, but I'm sure the authorities will clear this up. Why don't you leave Kerry's murder to them?" The warm tone of Craig's voice cooled a degree or two. "I'm sure they're far more experienced in this kind of a problem than the average citizen." He offered her a sympathetic pat with his large, smooth hands, glancing at Ronnie. She tried not to pull back. "Unfortunately, my company's donations may need to be curbed until this killer is caught."

Ronnie tensed, shifting in his seat. The CEO turned to him and raised a hand. "Let's talk about donations later."

Helen deliberately ran her hands through her hair. She twisted the watch on her wrist. 'Time to lighten the mood,' directed Jessica. "I'm glad we had a chance to bump into each other. Hope we meet again." She turned to Ronnie. "Don't forget my offer to help the campaign. I'm right down the street." She uncrossed her legs and tugged on her jacket. "Call me an optimist. I think the police will track down the real killer. Let's hope it's soon."

She turned and, in Nora's flamboyant style, sashayed out of the office.

* * *

As soon as she sank into the seat of her car, she dialed Joe. "Thank goodness you picked up."

His voice quickened. "Are you alright?"

She exhaled. "I'm fine. I was chatting with Ronnie at Eliot's headquarters when the CEO of OMT, Craig Olsoff, walked in. "Another cad. Reminds me of your state's attorney Scott Perry."

"Ahh. The boss of my dreams."

"Umm. I know this is last minute, but do you want to have dinner?"

He hesitated. "I'm actually on my way home. Other than my walker, Rocky's been alone for three days. He needs a run and time with me."

"Of course." She tried not to sound disappointed. "I thought we could talk about the case."

"What if I change my clothes, pick him up, and come to your place?"

Her voice brightened. "Even better. I'll stop at Tella's for some lasagna."

He chuckled. "I guess that's the closest I can get to homemade at your house. I could definitely use a night off. Although with you, it's half a night off."

"Very funny."

* * *

Trixie and Watson meowed their indignation the moment Helen unlocked her front door. She couldn't blame them. Talk about an absentee owner. First things first, treat them to their favorite tuna. Their complaints stopped as soon as dinner was served. Too bad I can't whip up a good meal for myself as quickly.

Twenty minutes later, she was pulling on jeans and a long, pale blue sweater. Her cat squad followed her around as she plumped up a few pillows.

She set a few logs in the floor-to-ceiling stone fireplace dividing the living room from the dining room. Fifteen minutes later, Joe's Explorer crunched on her drive. He tapped on the front door.

"Rocky! How are you, sweet boy? Are you here to visit me?" Helen kneeled down and stroked the big Golden Retriever's ears. His eyes were warm, his muzzle sprinkled with grey. She kissed him on the top of his head while he wiggled all over.

"Wow. Talk about him stealing my thunder. When do I get that kind of a greeting?" He handed her a bottle of Cabernet.

"Sorry. I haven't seen him in a while." She reached up and planted a light kiss on Joe's lips.

"Not quite as enthusiastic, but a start," he muttered.

"I have the lasagna heating up in the oven with Italian bread. Should be ready in a few more minutes."

Joe pawed through a drawer on her island for a corkscrew.

"Not a screw top?"

"Thought we'd treat ourselves with something more special than five-dollar boat wine." Joe spotted her two cats sitting erect, their tails switching like metronomes and wide eyes glaring.

"Don't worry about them," Helen grinned. "They like Rocky. They just want to remind him who's boss." The Golden circled around the island.

"Do we have time to let him stretch his legs?"

"Let's take the stairs down to the lower dock. That's a challenge for anyone, and you won't have to leash him. It'll be good for us too."

They grabbed their jackets and walked onto the deck. Rocky gleefully bounded down the stairs ahead of them. He ran back up to meet them before they were one-third of the way down.

"I'm looking forward to getting *Persuasion* out of dry dock and into the water."

They walked onto her pier while Rocky charged into the woods. They could hear him crashing among the trees, barking at night sounds. A pair of Bald Eagles swooped across the water from a nearby tree to ferret out dinner, their seven-foot wingspans and strong talons visible even in the dark.

Helen sat down, pulled off her sneakers, and dangled her legs in the water. "Water's cold."

Joe sat down next to her. "I can warm you up," he said, wrapping his arms around her. She leaned against him, and they watched the lights twinkle from across the bay. He gave her a long kiss. "Better?"

"Much," Helen smiled in the dark.

Rocky paraded back down the dock and nuzzled Joe's arm.

"Looks like someone is anxious for his dinner." Helen rubbed the dog's ears. "It's been a long time since coffee this morning."

Joe stood up and pulled her to her feet. The three trudged up the stairs.

"Lasagna smells great," Helen said as she pulled open her sliders. She handed Joe a box of matches. "Let's eat in front of the fire."

The detective emptied his pocket, placed his Glock and leather holder onto her mantel, and claimed his glass. Rocky sprawled out in front of the hearth. Trixie and Watson took up perches on each arm of Helen's couch and watched.

Helen handed Joe a filled plate and a cloth napkin. He sank into her couch. "Feels good to put my feet up. I gather you've been traipsing around town."

"How did you know?"

"You're not the only one with a private squad."

She swallowed and reached for her Cabernet. "I wandered into Owen's Bait Shop after our coffee. Figured he knows anglers better than anyone. I asked if he'd heard anything about the Isaac ghost story or Kerry's murder. He wasn't much help and wrote off the rumors. Hopefully, he'll be more tuned in to the next bit of local gossip. Sounded as if he planned to vote for Eliot before the murder. Now, he's not so sure."

"What happened with Ronnie? Anything?" He topped off their glasses.

"I'm trying to figure him out. I don't know if he's a bit of a con man, or he's just a hometown guy anxious to prove himself to the locals."

"What's bothering you?"

"He's wearing a Rolex and makes an effort to flash it around. The watch doesn't match the worn collar on his dress shirt or his car."

"Why not?" Joe added a log to the fire.

"For one, his watch isn't a Rolex. It's a good fake. And he's driving a six-year-old Ford Focus."

"Maybe he's a guy who's not into cars?"

She rolled her eyes. "Every single guy in his early thirties is into cars. Especially if he doesn't own a house yet."

"Maybe he's trying to save his money to buy one. How do you know the Rolex is a fake?"

"The gold is off color, and the logo on the face isn't clear. I may not own one, but with clients in every price range, I notice jewelry."

Joe turned up his shirt cuff and studied his watch on a wide black leather band. "Didn't realize I needed to up my jewelry style."

"You've got more important attributes. Did you look at his financials?"

"Nothing unusual. He's living a little lean, but I don't think most campaigns pay very well. Getting back the lead job with Eliot helped."

"So, you don't deny he benefited from Kerry's death."

"Not at all. He did. Other than Eliot, he's next on my list. So far, I can't find anything at the scene to incriminate him."

"Ronnie got really edgy when I pointed it out to him."

"I'll bet he did." Joe reached for his plate.

"Craig Olsoff from Olsoff Marine Technology walked in. Offered to take me to dinner."

"Oh, did he? Can't say I blame him." He picked up her hand.

"I opted for you or an empty couch. He's cut from the same cloth as your boss. They're both out to impress the ladies. To be fair, Scott is much better looking than this guy."

"Did he say anything about Kerry?"

"He said he admired her commitment to environmental issues and enjoyed working with her. He's reconsidering his company's plans for contributing toward the campaign since Eliot's under investigation."

Joe grunted.

"Have you traced the hundred thousand dollars Eliot paid to Kerry?"

"She dropped forty into her bank account. Where she stashed the rest, we don't know. We searched her guest room at Captain's Watch and her office. Nothing."

"Did you find out anything more linking her grandfather's death to Spencer?"

"No." He reached over and nuzzled her neck. "You smell good. Can we talk about something else? This is supposed to be relaxing."

"I imagine we can." She wrapped her arms around him. "What do you want to talk about?"

Chapter Twelve

The next morning, she jogged the mile-and-a-half trail to the lighthouse. No cell service meant she had time to shut down the mental chaos of the past week. Joe headed for home last night about eleven, and she'd crawled into bed with her two furry roommates.

The sun worked its way across the water, cutting through the morning mist. She reached the historic lighthouse perched on a one-hundred-foot cliff. Crab boats slowly chugged their way past an electronic channel marker. Like farmers, they planted baited cages across the bay and along the Port Anne River flats. Crab buoy technology hadn't advanced much in three hundred years, yet professional crabbers still did their jobs. Hours from now, Helen knew these boats would return to reap their crop. It was a hard way to make a living, and she admired them for it.

She took her favorite spot, leaning against one of the old posts near the lighthouse, and took in the panoramic view. The huge bow of a cargo carrier plunged northwards, sounding a deep horn to a small powerboat and turning north towards the C&D Canal and the Delaware River.

She set her head against the worn concrete and studied the pale blue sky. What are we missing in this case? Who grabbed those shears off the wall and stabbed Kerry? Their rage was uncontrollable. How many people knew there was another exit out of the pool house through the rear door? Or was the killer simply lucky and escaped into the surrounding woods? Who could remain calm enough to circle around the building and rejoin the party afterwards?

Closing her eyes, she let the light breeze chill her face. She shivered and pulled her knit cap down over her ears. Do I know what I'm doing? Probably not. She inhaled the fresh air off the water. Joe's an excellent investigator. I should stop being such a fixer-upper. 'Friends lives are at stake.' Jane chastised. 'Murder is not simple.' 'Learn from those crabbers. Cast a wider net,' Jessica added. Helen swore she could sense Jane tilt her head in agreement.

* * *

Safe Harbor was empty that morning except for a receptionist, one sales associate, and Tammi. She brightened when she saw Helen.

"Let's catch up," Helen suggested, waving her into her office. "I'm sorry you've been abandoned. Anything urgent?"

Tammi tugged a dramatic black and purple shawl around her shoulders. "I need your data to wrap up Britany Bowers' appraisal." She flipped through the file. "I didn't see any photos of the basement or smokehouse. Do you have them?"

Helen tapped her fingers in annoyance. "Darn. I completely forgot." She opened her calendar on her laptop. "I could stop there today and take a few. We can't submit our report without them. I'll work on the comparables now."

"You promise?" Her assistant's eyes narrowed. "You're a little distracted."

Helen grimaced. "I know. I promise. Where are we with the Baywood project? Any updates from our builder?"

"Nothing."

"That's not good," Helen acknowledged. "I'll call Alex Jordan right now. Did he send our signed contract?"

"Not yet. I thought you should ask."

"Absolutely."

"Any news on finding Kerry's killer?"

"Only if you want to accuse one of the Davies." Helen rubbed her temples. "Seen Joe lately?"

"He came by last night. I invited him for takeout. Tella's."

"Thank goodness. I thought you two might not be talking."

Helen's cheeks flushed. "We're talking. It's good."

"You look tired. Did you discuss the case all night, or did you take some time to relax?"

"We did a little of both." Helen struggled to withhold a grin.

Tammi wiggled her brows. "How much relaxing did you two do?"

Helen held up her hands in protest. "Enough. No more details. I sent him home about eleven."

Her assistant made a satisfied smirk. "I guess it's progress. You are excruciatingly slow. Isn't it time you picked up the pace?"

"What pace? Go away." Helen reached for her phone.

Tammi stumped toward the door. "Lord, you're stubborn. That man must be head over heels. I feel sorry for him."

* * *

"Alex, Helen Morrisey. I thought I'd stop by Baywood, and we could review your latest floor plans." She could hear an earth mover and a dump truck grind in the distance.

"Helen!" the builder bellowed. "Sorry, hard to hear you."

Helen shouted back. "I wanted to stop by this afternoon about three."

"I'd like that. I have crews here until then. Come to the office trailer on the south side of Ferry Point."

"Thank you. See you soon."

Her next call was to Britany. "Hi, Helen Morrisey. I need a few more photos of your basement mechanicals and your little smokehouse. Do you mind if I stop by in about an hour?"

"Not a problem." Dishes rattled. "I might be out, but I'll leave my kitchen door open. Help yourself."

"Perfect. Did you contact my mortgage reps yet?" Britany filled her in on her progress. "Good to hear. I'm on my way." Her phone rang as she ended their call.

"Maggie, what's up?" Helen dug around her desk drawer for her Twizzlers stash. She frowned at the package. They were stiff and bent. She picked off a bit of dust and stuck one in her mouth.

"Olsoff Marine Technology withdrew campaign contributions for Eliot Davies' campaign today."

"Really?" Helen stopped chewing. "I can't say I'm very surprised. I bumped into Olsoff at Eliot's office. He stopped by to talk with Ronnie Mann. When I asked what he thought of Kerry's death and Eliot's campaign, he said he was concerned."

Maggie tapped a pen to paper. "He claims his board made the decision."

"No backbone, all gloss. Anything more about Kerry through your media buddies?"

"She was married about six years. Divorced four years. Her maiden name was Hollowell."

"She *is* Isaac's granddaughter. What do you think she was up to, working for Eliot?"

"Can't say."

"Where'd she live the past ten years? Do you know where she went to school?"

"That's an easy one. Graduated from the University of Kansas. Biology fourteen years ago."

"Biology! How'd she migrate to politics?"

"As they say, politics makes strange bedfellows. Get this, her first job was with Olsoff. A couple years later, a Washington think tank recruited her as their in-house environmental expert. Then she started working political campaigns and, practically overnight, started being hired for the top slots. She had a real touch when it came to winning elections."

"Hmmm." Helen dragged out another Twizzler and gnawed. "Sounds like she could have had an inside connection to OMT? Maybe got her candidates to do them a few favors?"

"Or the other way around," Maggie muttered. "Haven't found anything yet. All I've got is a string of articles about OMT and their success in winning contracts. I'll email them to you right now. Hey, I've got to run. Catch you later." She clicked off.

Helen cast her eyes to a crack running across her office ceiling. It was an old house, retrofitted for business and due for another. She picked up her phone.

"Eliot? It's Helen. How's Alison feeling?"

"She's hanging in. We're still digging through those files in the attic. Nothing helpful."

"What do you know about Kerry's personal life?"

"I've seen a couple photos of her and staffers from Craig's company. That's probably how she got him interested in making donations. She had an ex, but I didn't get the idea they spoke any longer."

"Did you know she worked for OMT years ago?"

"No. I guess I was focused on her political skills."

"What's with Ronnie?"

"He called me an hour ago to tell me OMT retracted their donation pledge. That's the third corporation in the state who reneged since Kerry died. This investigation is killing our campaign." He sounded disgusted. "Another week or two of this, and I'll have to withdraw."

"I know it's devastating. Keep searching those files. Can you get me into your headquarters so I can dig through Kerry's? I may as well check yours too. I want to try to trace all your donations."

"Sure. I'll email Ronnie and tell him."

"No, no. Don't do that. Send me an email giving me permission, and I'll take it to Ronnie. I don't want to give him any advance notice."

"Ronnie? You think he's involved in her death?" His voice rose in alarm.

"Jane Marple tells me not to ignore any possibility."

"Jane Marple? Never mind, I won't ask."

"If you're not the killer, then who?"

"Good point." Three minutes later, an email from Eliot arrived in her Google Mail for Ronnie.

* * *

About one-thirty, Helen crossed the Harbor Bridge spanning Kent County from its neighbor towards Grace Harbor. Water flowed from the Susque-hanna Dam, past the town, and into the bay. The April sun seemed stronger today. *Maybe a sign I can turn this case around.* Her phone rang as she slowed toward town and onto Lafayette Street.

"Hi," Joe's squad car handset crackled in the background. "Where are you, and what are you up to?"

"Boy, do you sound suspicious," Helen responded. "As a matter of fact, I'm meeting a handsome attorney at The Vineyard in Grace Harbor. We're reviewing some paperwork."

"Who does paperwork with wine at two o'clock in the afternoon?" A moment of silence. "Do I know this guy? Is it that smooth-talker from Philadelphia?" The detective wasn't doing a good job of hiding his annoyance.

Helen laughed to herself. "I assume you're talking about Peter Askins. You should like him. He helped us when we worked on the Capelli case, remember?"

"He wasn't *that* helpful."

She groaned. "For your information, Pete's diligently working from his condo on Rittenhouse Square."

"How would you know?"

"He happened to text me this morning. Checking in."

"That's nice of him," Joe said sarcastically. "Did you tell him to stay put in Philly?"

"Ah, no, I did not. You should be happy to know I'm about to park in front of a client's house in Grace Harbor. Then, I'm meeting with my client Alex Jordan from Jordan Builders at Ferry Point."

"It's about time you went back to work."

"Let's not be insulting. I can walk and chew Twizzlers at the same time," she declared.

"You've finally admitted to your addiction."

"I'm ignoring you. La, la, la. Why'd you call?"

"Thought you'd be interested to know Diane Gleason is pressing my D.A. for answers on Kerry's murder. She seems anxious to see an arrest. Says she's getting calls from worried citizens concerned a killer is on the loose."

"She probably is. Of course, Scott Harris started breathing down your neck as a result," Helen replied in disgust. "Doesn't your D.A. have another sheriff's office to annoy?"

"You know Scott. If it's big news for the state, he wants to grandstand."

"Not sure I should tell you. Eliot gave me permission to go through Kerry's files at his office."

"Does Ben Horowitz know?"

"I'll tell him afterwards."

"That's not protocol." Joe's radio squawked. "Got to run."

Helen sat in her car and drummed her steering wheel. 'Nancy, do you worry about protocol?' 'Never,' retorted Nancy. 'Exactly right,' Helen declared and reached for the door lever in front of the Bowers.

* * *

The Bowers house was quiet as she walked around the stucco smokehouse. Inside was a pile of gardening tools, a soccer goal net, and three bicycles. The building helped make up for the property lacking a garage. She opened the kitchen door, and a large note in red crayon caught her eye.

"Helen, came across these articles in Derek's desk. Maybe they'll help you. Britany."

She pulled up a chair, sat down, and flipped through them. A headline read "Marine Pilots Assist Trafficking Stops." The second read "Marine Pilots Lead MDE to Toxic Scam." Four more articles referenced marine pilots assisting Coast Guard patrols. Helen tucked them into her bag and headed into the basement. She snapped photos of the furnace and their water purification system and checked the electrical box, then flicked off the lights. Back on the street, she texted the photos to Tammi.

* * *

Four miles beyond historic Ferry Village, the Baywood job sat right on the water. She'd worked on getting this development on the market the last three years. Alex Jordan had a solid reputation for higher-end homes in great locations, and she liked dealing with him. He promised her the out sales, but Helen had learned to never count on a builder's business until the homes went on the market. She'd gotten burned before.

Her little Mini scraped along the dirt road toward the water. Pulling to a stop, she focused on the Chesapeake lapping against the shoreline of Baywood. She'd convinced Alex to save the trees. The upfront costs would pay him back tenfold. The hulk of motionless heavy equipment perched across the hillside reminded her of sleeping tigers waiting to lunge. A red Chevy truck with a Jordan Builders logo on its doors sat alone outside the office trailer. Good timing. Alex wouldn't be distracted by his crew.

She tugged open the trailer's white aluminum door. "Alex?"

He raised his head. His light grey hair touched the collar of his denim shirt and a thin cotton vest. A Jordan Builders logo in black was embroidered on the left. "Good to see you. Thanks for coming out." He gave her a big welcoming smile.

"Of course. I haven't seen the site since you broke ground. Tammi and I are excited to work on your next phase." A drawing at least four feet by five hung along one wall. Lot lines and typography lines swirled through colored rectangles marking each of the thirty-two house locations. "You're fortunate your grading is so gentle." She studied the cut lines. "Do you know when the county will approve this stage?"

He stuck his hands in the pockets of his vest. "We'll be ready for them by early May. It's the health department that's holding me up at this point."

Helen turned. "Why? What's the problem?"

"The water studies are delayed. Until I have the ground water results, I can't finish up my grading." He sounded frustrated.

"Seems odd. You applied months and months ago. Who's doing the testing?"

"OMT. Their regional office is based in Delaware."

"Do you want me to contact them? I just met Craig Olsoff, their CEO, a few days ago. He probably doesn't get involved in day-to-day schedules, but it might be worth a phone call."

The builder's face brightened. "Certainly can't hurt. Thanks for doing that."

"No problem." Helen tilted her head at the renderings on his desk. "Do you want to discuss your model designs?"

Alex rolled out three sheets of drawings. "Absolutely."

* * *

At five o'clock, they locked up the trailer together. She navigated her car back up the truck-rutted road and turned toward Port Anne. Alex followed behind.

Her phone rang. A *Kent Whig* newspaper identification popped up. "Maggie. What's up?"

Her gravelly voice started. "Thought you'd like to know, I found out Ronnie Mann has a girlfriend. Her name is Pam Breen, and she works with him at campaign headquarters. They live together. Apparently, she has a temper."

"Hmmm. That could be interesting. Could be completely innocent, but good to know. I'm stopping in there tomorrow morning."

"Want another tidbit? I'm going to send you a few articles about OMT."

"What's so interesting about them?"

The reporter chuckled. "You're the one with the Detection Club. Take a look and let me know what you think."

"Thanks a lot," Helen protested. Maggie clicked off.

A minute later, four links came into her email. Her eyes ran across the storylines. "Maryland Department of the Environment awards study to testing giant Olsoff Marine Technology." The next read, "New tests show Chesapeake water improving." A photo of a smiling Diane Gleason with a stack of reports was under the caption. Three paragraphs down, the writer attributed the results to OMT. The next headline read, "MDE sets bid deadline." Seven months later, another said "State contract awarded." OMT was the contract winner. Craig Olsoff stated, "We're very pleased to be working with the MDE." Standard blah, blah, blah, Helen thought. Boring stuff.

Jessica spoke up. 'I wonder who lost the contract.' "Good question," Helen replied out loud. She texted Maggie.

Can you get me names of companies who were outbid?

Do my best.

Chapter Thirteen

The next morning, Helen pulled on dark leggings, short black boots, and an olive-green cotton jacket. A silk scarf in greens and browns around her neck was in deference to Jessica, her methodical sleuth. She strolled into Davies Headquarters and spotted Pam dressed in jeans and a cotton V-neck sweater.

"Hi Pam. I'm Helen Morrisey. I stopped in a few days ago to volunteer and met with Ronnie."

"Is he expecting you today?" She picked up a sign-in sheet off her desk.

"No, Eliot asked me to stop by and look through Kerry's files." Helen lilted her voice.

"Really?" Pam raised one eyebrow and regarded Helen up and down. "What are you looking for?"

"He wants me to review her interactions since she joined you."

Pam set down the clipboard. "I'd have to call Ronnie. Why don't you come back?"

Helen reached into her big tote. "Here's an email from Eliot with his instructions. Can you point me to her records?" Her stance told Pam she wasn't leaving.

Pam reluctantly studied the email. "I think you need to come back later." She put her hands on her hips.

"I'm sorry. Is there a problem? You do report to Eliot, don't you?"

The young woman's eyes flared. Helen pretended not to notice. "All our files are against the rear wall. Make sure you return everything to where it belongs."

Helen wove between a handful of desk cubicles. Setting down her tote, she began to pull open drawers. Pam marched into Ronnie's office and slammed the door. Her sharp voice started coming through the glass. A few minutes later, she jammed the phone into its cradle.

"Ronnie will be in shortly," Pam tossed at Helen as she walked past her.

In Jessica's unruffled, authoritative voice, Helen said, "That would be great. I'll keep working." She continued to flip through legal folders. Pam picked up a pack of cigarettes and went out a rear door, banging it behind her. Through the rear window, Helen could see her walk behind the building to the little creek beyond and begin to smoke.

One by one, file by file, she sifted through Kerry's notes. In the fourth drawer down, she found a folder labeled Olsoff Marine Technology. Inside were three pledges for campaign contributions on their stationery, all signed by Craig Olsoff and totaling three hundred fifty thousand dollars. 'I ran a lot of PR campaigns. This is a major contributor,' commented Agatha to Helen. Helen studied the correspondence. Why was OMT so interested in supporting Eliot's campaign, she asked herself.

More folders marked *Contributors* followed. Inside was a list of corporate and business associations endorsing Eliot. The United Warehouse Association, Steelworks of Maryland, and the Chesapeake Bay Newspapers Alliance were the largest. They all seemed logical. Smaller personal donors followed.

Kneeling on the floor, she dug into another drawer. A thick file labeled *Press* was stuffed with clippings and photographs. Darn. Nothing.

The front door opened, and Ronnie marched in. He planted his feet in front of her. "Pam says Eliot wants you to look through Kerry's records. Can I help you?" He offered her a momentary flash of teeth that tightened into a straight line.

"Hi." Helen stood up and leaned against the filing cabinets. Surprised Ronnie's tone was so contentious, she forced a cheerful smile. "Great to see you. I don't need to tell you, of all people, that her murder is destroying his campaign and the B&B. Is there anyone you would suspect?"

"How would I have any idea who might want to kill Kerry? I avoided her every chance I had."

Helen pointed to the Olsoff file. "Did you ever get the idea she had any special connections to Craig Olsoff's company? He certainly has been generous with their donations, not just for Eliot but other campaigns. It's almost as if he's followed her throughout the years."

Ronnie lifted his jaw and glared from lowered eyelids. "I couldn't stand Kerry, but I don't see anything odd about OMT. I'm praying we get this mess straightened out and we can get them back on our donation list. The last think we need is you upsetting him with odd questions."

"Where were you when Kerry was killed?"

"I was down at the docks talking to the mayor. We both ran to the pool house when Alison screamed."

"Where was Pam?"

"She'd gone up to the bar."

"She wasn't with you?"

"Look, you're not the cops, and I don't know why we're having this conversation." Ronnie's voice grew louder.

Helen pursed her lips. "Aren't you anxious to get Eliot cleared? Without him, you and Pam won't have jobs."

"I'm not the police. Do what you have to do." He stalked into his office and slammed the door.

Helen kept looking. She could hear Pam arguing with Ronnie through the plate glass wall, her voice shrill. He waved in Helen's direction, his face red and his teeth gritted. Another hour later, Helen was close to giving up her search. She hesitated. Slowing herself down, she laid out some older photos based on dates of Kerry's previous work. A man and woman, her hand tucked into his arm, stood with a city harbor in the background. Where was this? She paused. That's Kerry with Craig, looking very friendly. Helen recognized the harbor area and Chicago skyline. That's Lake Shore Drive. Enough rich people there to rival Rodeo Drive in Los Angeles. Why were they together? Were they a couple?

She pulled up a chair and sat down. 'Come on, Jessica. This is your kind of discovery. Why were they together in Chicago?' She unearthed Kerry's resume from another drawer. A penciled date on the photograph matched the time she was working for an Illinois governor's campaign. She flipped through more clippings from *The Chicago Tribune* announcing water studies for Lake Michigan. Later, another photo of the grinning governor holding a report in his hands. "We are extremely pleased to see progress in curbing pollution in Lake Michigan. While far from pristine, we're seeing good results from our funding."

She texted Maggie.

What years was Kerry in Chicago? What company completed Lake Michigan water studies for Illinois? Thanks.

Helen hesitated. Why did this seem familiar? She sat up straight. Reaching for the first folder marked Chesapeake Eastern Shore, she took out another photo. Its caption identified Commissioner Diane Fischer and Kerry Lightner with Craig Olsoff positioned in the middle, his arms draped over their shoulders. A sign over their heads said, "Mid-Atlantic Environmental Conference." She laid it next to the one from Chicago. "Snakes and bastards!" She ducked her head, glancing at Ronnie's office and hoping they hadn't heard her use Agatha Raisin's favorite curse."

She walked to the office copier and ran off reprints. Kerry and Craig sure got around. Who did the water studies? Ten bucks, his company. She stopped as she reached for the print button again. Did she spot a trend here? Every clipping showed government funding with positive results. Was OMT that lucky? Good results certainly would encourage more public funding. Her finger hovered over the blinking copier screen while her heart skipped a beat. She needed Diane's opinion, and quickly.

She jammed her copies into her tote, picked up her jacket, and strode into Ronnie's office. "I'm heading off. If you think of anything else that might help Eliot's case, give one of us a call."

Ronnie and his girlfriend gave her a pained look.

"Actually," Ronnie stood up. "This box is stuff I took out of Kerry's desk drawers when I moved back into *my* office. You're welcome to it." He shoved the box into her hands. "I've been kicking it around the last few days."

Helen grasped the carton before it fell to the floor. "Does she have any family interested in her personal things?"

He shrugged. "I don't think anyone is missing her." He cleared his throat. "I mean, anyone is missing her stuff."

"I thought she and Craig Olsoff were kind of cozy. What do you think?"

He gaffed. "Olsoff's strictly business."

Helen put her back to the front door. "I guess I've got my homework for Sunday. Thanks for your help."

* * *

Word was out Monday morning. Kerry's relationship as Isaac's granddaughter flooded the county and across the state. Like water leaking into an old boat, the news couldn't be stopped. Every news channel and paper found the story juicy, including Maggie Dyer. Helen didn't blame her.

Her phone chimed with new texts every few minutes.

Sorry Helen, but I have to run this story. Can't take sides.

Helen dialed Alison.

"I was hoping you'd call," she breathed. "The press got wind that Kerry extorted money from us and that Isaac was her grandfather."

"What does Ben say?"

Alison's voice trembled. "We look bad; there's no avoiding it."

"Did you finish going through the attic files?"

Alison went quiet.

"You found something, didn't you."

"We found some notes in Spencer's handwriting."

Helen inhaled. "What year?"

"1967, the year Isaac disappeared."

"What did they say?"

"Eliot thinks we shouldn't discuss it with you or the police."

"Did you talk to Ben about Spencer's notes?"

"Ben says to sit on them for a few days. In the meantime, he's scheduled a press conference for one o'clock." Alison's voice broke.

* * *

A barrage of television vans plastered with network logos choked the one-way main street from one end of Hollings, the county seat, to the other. Helen squeezed her Mini into a spot behind the administration building next door and passed Diane's black sedan in her assigned commissioner's spot. Someone had keyed her car. Helen grimaced. It looked deliberate. Can't keep all your voters happy, she mused. She continued to weave in between curiosity seekers to reach a better vantage point of the Kent County Courthouse. A United States flag with a State of Maryland and county flags below shifted in the light morning breeze. Eliot, dressed in a suit and white shirt, stood on the steps. Alison stood beside him, clasping her light coat around her dress to ward off the morning chill, nervously eyeing the crowd. Ben Horowitz, his head barely reaching Eliot's shoulders, reached for a microphone on a temporary podium and signaled Eliot to begin.

"We have a brief statement to make concerning the loss of my campaign manager, Kerry Lightner." The candidate cleared his throat. "Ten days ago, while we were celebrating the opening of our bed and breakfast in Port Anne, Kerry was discovered dead in the pool house. The Kent County Sheriff's Office is diligently seeking a suspect for her murder."

He looked up across the crowd and into the cameras. "Rumors of who is responsible are rampant. One of them affects myself, my family, and my campaign for state senator. We have met with the police and confirmed Kerry attempted to extort us before her death. Kerry claimed Isaac Hollowell was her grandfather, my grandfather's partner in Eastern Shore Marine Piloting. She also claimed my grandfather, Spencer Davies, was responsible for Isaac Hollowell's death. In actuality, Hollowell disappeared while night fishing alone off Osprey Point in 1967."

Eliot took a deep breath, his voice unwavering. "My grandfather, along with the Coast Guard and local police, searched three days for Mr. Hollowell. His boat was found, washed ashore. The Coast Guard determined that his engine failed and declared his cause of death was accidental drowning. His body was never recovered."

"Kerry Lightner's claim against my grandfather has not been validated nor do we expect it to be. In the meantime, the Sheriff's Office will continue to

111

investigate her murder, and we will assist in any way we can."

He put an arm around his wife. "Concerning my campaign. I continue to have a deep commitment to the State of Maryland and the welfare of its citizens. However," he swallowed, "I have decided to suspend my campaign temporarily until we draw closer to finding the person responsible for this heinous crime. Finding her killer is our priority. Thank you to all our supporters. We promise to keep you updated."

The press muscled forward, microphones waving in the air.

"Mr. Davies! Mr. Davies! Given Ms. Lightner was allegedly extorting you, isn't it logical to consider you or your wife suspects?"

Ben stepped forward. "It is not logical," he said. "We have no further statement to make at this time. The Davies family came here today to clarify this case as they understand it and express their condolences to Ms. Lightner's family."

A second reporter shouted out. "Who will be the candidate replacing Davies?"

"That has not been decided. Announcements from party headquarters will be released shortly. Thank you."

Helen swallowed. Tears came to her eyes. What a complete reversal from the optimism of eight days ago. 'Buck up, Helen,' Nora nudged. 'We've been in tighter spots than this. You'll figure this out.'

Her eyes traveled over the throng. She spotted Maggie Dyer, a voice recorder in her hand, and Ronnie and his assistant Pam a few steps to the right of the Davies. He was stone-faced, and she looked livid.

Diane squeezed her way over to Helen and touched her arm. "I feel so badly for them," she said. Helen pressed her lips together and nodded.

"Hi, do you have a couple minutes? I have a question for you," Helen asked.

"Of course." Together, they walked toward the parking lot.

"What's on your mind?" asked Diane.

Helen opened her tote. "I've been going through Kerry's files and came across this photo of you, Kerry, and Craig in D.C. Do you remember being there?"

Diane squinted at the phone. "Hmmm. Vaguely. It's one of the times we were all together. It was a regional conference regarding water conservation. Did I really wear my hair like that?" She chuckled. "Why? Is it important?"

"I'm trying to put together a timeline. Did you ever think Craig and Kerry were having an affair? They look awfully cozy. Could he have anything to do with her death?"

Diane's eyes opened wide. "I worked with them both when it involved Kent County. If they did, they certainly kept it from me. Why would he want to kill her?"

"Romance went sour?" asked Helen.

Diane shook her head. "If they were seeing each other, they kept it from me."

"If you think of anything that ties them together, will you let me know?"

"Of course. Anything to help." Diane's cell rang, and she glanced at the name. "Sorry, I need to take this. I'll give it some thought. It's too early for us to get discouraged."

Helen smiled. "Thanks. Let's meet for dinner soon."

The crowd started to break up. A truck tapped on his horn as he squeezed past her. A woman with a camera bag on her shoulder skirted around her. A high schooler in a hoodie jostled her. "Sorry," he murmured.

What does she do now? She pushed her cuff off her left wrist. Eleven o'clock. She texted Tammi.

On my way. Hungry?

I'm good. Picking up Kayla from school at noon. Doctor's appt. Back about 2.

Take your time.

* * *

The Wooden Mast in Port Anne had at least six people spilling outside its door as Helen eased by. "Guess late breakfast is out of the question," Helen muttered aloud. Two blocks down, Jean's Coffee Pot advertised fresh biscotti on her sandwich sign.

A bell chimed as Helen stepped through the door.

"Hello, stranger," Jean greeted. "What have you been up to?"

Helen pulled off her sunglasses. "My usual favorites are calling to me."

"Sounds like big news at the courthouse today. You there?" Jean asked.

"I thought I'd try to show Eliot and Alison some moral support." She pointed at the last blueberry muffin. "Heard anything I should know?"

Jean handed her a latte and set her elbows on the counter. Her coffee pot charms tinkled against the glass. "There's plenty of talk, even if people like them. Eliot's grandfather had a street named after him, then his partner disappeared. Now, his grandson and his wife are suspected of murder. Hard to believe." She tipped her head at an open table in a corner and signaled for her helper to take over the register. "I could use a little break. Want to sit?" She poured hot water onto a Tazo tea bag.

"Anyone in particular sound glad Eliot's in trouble?"

"Hard to tell. There's always someone jealous of someone else's success." Jean nursed the hot tea. "Owen Reese told me you asked about Isaac."

"Seems like everyone knew about that grave except me. Are people surprised Eliot is suspending his campaign for now?"

"Not really. Ronnie Mann and his girlfriend are looking for sympathy from anyone willing to listen. They're blaming Kerry for all their woes." Jean finished her drink.

"He's not anxious to help Eliot which doesn't make any sense."

"Maybe he's still mad Eliot brought in Kerry. Don't forget, Pam's an instigator. She's not a forgiver."

Helen's cell rang. "I need to run. If you hear anything whatsoever, call me. By the way, if you hear any rumors about Craig Olsoff or his company, let me know those too."

Jean chuckled. "Anyone else on your list?"

Helen called back as she opened the door. "I'll check with my squad and let you know."

* * *

Safe Harbor was a ghost town. Did she actually say that? She laughed to herself. 'You've got spirits on the brain,' commented Nancy. With Tammi out, she waved hello to their receptionist, settled into her office, and opened her laptop. Britany's appraisal was almost finished. She zoomed in on her cost versus value calculations, studying the comparisons from one sold property to another for the past three to six months. Grace Harbor market activity was strong, and she hoped the report would ward off any complaints from Britany's husband. Mortgage rates were creeping up, and she worried Britany might not qualify for a mortgage if they didn't agree on a value quickly. After one more proofing, she sent out the report.

Standing at her window, she watched Water Street's activity as she dialed Britany. Her call went to voicemail. "Hi. It's Helen Morrisey. Your appraisal should be in your email. Let me know if you have any concerns. If you want me to call your attorney, let me know."

Her phone rang. "Helen Morrisey," she answered.

"Helen?" A deep voice sounded familiar. "This is Craig Olsoff. We met at Eliot's headquarters Thursday."

Helen started. "Of course. I remember. How can I help you?"

"I came into town to meet with Ronnie and Eliot. I'm sure you're aware he's putting his campaign on hold."

"Yes. I was at the courthouse this morning."

"I thought you might like to have dinner with me tonight. I'm leaving in the morning for Baltimore."

Helen examined the plaster white ceiling and prayed to her Detection Club for help. 'How do I get out of this?'

'You don't,' Agatha hissed. 'Take advantage of the invitation.'

Nora chimed in. 'She's right. Try to find out what happened between him and Kerry.'

'And press him on Alex Jordan's water tests.' Helen let out a deep breath. "I'd love to, but I have an appointment at seven. Would you like to meet for a drink? Maybe the Riverside Inn?"

"Sounds great. Five thirty?"

"Perfect. See you there."

Tammi tapped on her doorway. "I'm back. Why do you look like you're being tortured?"

Helen rolled her eyes. "I will be. I just accepted an invitation to meet Craig Olsoff for a drink. He wanted me to meet for dinner, but I couldn't imagine enduring it."

"Is he really that awful?" Tammi's dangling blue crabs grazed her brown cheeks.

"Oh, trust me, he's awful. He thinks slick is an attribute and a too-tight suit a style. Nora Charles would use the 30s word 'smarmy.'" Helen gave a little shiver. "I wonder if he's married." She inputted his name in a Google search with the word 'family.'" She heaved a sigh. "Yup. He lives north of Washington, D.C., south of Baltimore. He's fifty-eight years old, his wife's name is Maryanne, and he has one daughter." She opened her desk drawer and pulled out two Twizzlers. "I need fortitude."

"Do I need to text you in the middle of your cocktail? You're a little old for using 'the babysitter is calling me home' excuse to cut your date short." She motioned quote marks with long sparkly nails.

"Don't you dare put this in the date category. By the way, my meeting with Alex Jordan went well yesterday. He's frustrated because his water tests aren't complete. I'll ask Craig if he can help."

"You're not exactly dressed to enchant him," her assistant observed.

Helen looked down at her slacks and comfortable wedges. "You're right. I think I'll run home, feed my kitties, and change. Might as well make the best of this." Her cell rang. "It's Lizzie."

She picked up. "Hi. Where are you?… I'm leaving the office…I have to meet Craig Olsoff for a drink at five-thirty…Okay. See you about four."

"Lizzie just finished her airing on ShopTV and is staying with me tonight. She's visiting Alison in the morning."

Chapter Fourteen

"Hello? Mom?"

"I'm out here on the deck."

Lizzie pulled open the living room sliders. "Kind of cold out here, don't you think?" She studied her mother, bundled under a thick navy throw. "Aren't you rushing the spring season?" She leaned over and kissed her mother's cheek.

"I needed some fresh air. Trying to bring down my temperature in anticipation of meeting with Olsoff."

"I saw him at the grand opening. He seemed nice enough."

"Jane Marple doesn't like him."

"Jane isn't exactly the best person to determine who's dateable. She never married."

Helen stood up. "She has good instincts when it comes to people's character. Let's go inside, and you can help me decide what to wear to this little meet-up."

Watson and Trixie loyally trooped behind them into her bedroom. Lizzie pawed through her closet, and Trixie helped.

"Obviously, you'll need to put on your Nora style. Or Agatha. How about this?" Her daughter waved a short, knit dress in front of her.

"Hon, this is Port Anne on a Wednesday night. I need something casual."

"You need to improve your attitude," Lizzie declared. "I think I need a glass of wine to help decide this. I'm glad I'm staying home." Lizzie was back with a glass of Cabernet. "How about black jeans, a short sweater, and dangly earrings? I'll make up your eyes."

"Let's do it. I need to be in the car in fifteen minutes."

* * *

It may have been a Monday, but the Riverside Inn was busy. Helen spotted Craig at the far end of the bar and took a deep breath. He gave her a delighted wave.

"Hi." He was dressed in a suit, his collar open and no tie. "I have a table for us."

"Great," Helen followed him to a two-top and hung her purse on the arm of her chair. She ordered a cosmopolitan in a Nick and Nora glass. He added a gin and tonic, then turned, his eyes grazing over her cream V-neck sweater. Gold dangling bars hung from her ears against her short dark hair. She wore gold and silver bangles on her wrist.

His eyes glowed with pleasure. "How was your day?" He swirled the ice in his glass. "Is the market busy?"

"Frustrating. There's such a shortage in inventory, agents are climbing through hedges to deliver flowers to sellers. Anything to encourage them to sell. With rates creeping up, buyers are nervous they'll be shut out of their price range. Sellers are afraid they can't find their next house. It's a vicious cycle." Helen took a sip of her drink, looking resigned. "I've lived through wicked markets before."

"I guess I'm lucky." He said. "In the water testing business, our contracts lock down clients for a couple years regardless of the economy. Real estate strikes me as a roller coaster."

She tilted her head. "It's definitely not for the faint of heart."

He glanced up at their waiter and lifted his empty rock glass.

"I have a question for you." Helen decided to apply a little feminine flattery. She gave him a coy glance enhanced by her daughter's makeup magic. "As CEO, would you have any influence on scheduling?"

"I'm not sure what you mean."

"I have a builder with a construction project on the water at Ferry Point. He's hit a snag because OMT hasn't completed their studies for the county."

Craig stroked his jaw, deliberating. "I don't usually get involved in our day-to-day operation, but I can certainly check for you." He pulled out his cell phone. "What's the name of the project?"

"Baywood at Ferry Point. Jordan Builders. It's a big site. Alex Jordan and I have been working on this for years. He's worried about the weather and his construction schedule. He's got a lot of big equipment sitting idle right now."

Craig tapped a note into his phone. "I'm emailing my personal assistant, and I'll let you know the status. Do I get a date for dinner?"

Helen ignored the question. "Thank you. That's such a big help. I can see there's an advantage to being top dog." She leaned in, folding her hands under her chin, and planted a big smile across her face. "Why don't you tell me a little more about how you got to know Kerry? From what I've read, you two go back ten, twelve years at least."

The CEO hesitated. "Kerry worked for me years ago. When she left and started working with big campaigns, she'd let me know. In my position, I get contacted by government people from Maine to California. People like Kerry try to encourage us to support their candidates."

"I can understand. Your work is important." Helen held her glass to her lips and wondered if she was pouring it on a bit thick. "How does the bidding process work? You do very well when it comes to winning government contracts."

Craig preened. "Our chemists are well trained, and we keep our costs down. I heard you've been going through Kerry's records. Any particular reason?"

"I'm trying to help Eliot. His world is collapsing around him."

"According to the press, he had plenty of reasons to shut her up. How do you know Eliot isn't guilty?"

"I don't. I can only operate on instinct. What about her personal life? Someone she snubbed in business? A colleague, old boyfriends, her ex-husband?"

Craig looked startled.

"Isn't there anyone?"

He shrugged. "Can I get you another drink?"

"Sure. That would be great. I'll run to the restroom." She gave him a little Nora wink. "Be right back."

Helen's drink was waiting for her. She took a sip and set the glass aside. "How long have you known Diane Gleason?"

Craig reached for his glass. "Diane's a good county commissioner. I've worked with a lot of them. Do you know she's naming a new Save the Bay project after Kerry as a memorial?"

"I'm not surprised. She's very thoughtful." Helen wrinkled her brow. "I wonder how Ronnie will react to that news."

"He'll need to get past his resentment if he wants to work for Diane. He needs friends. Speaking about alliances, what's your connection with the lead detective? Joe McAlister? How's he feel about you nosing around?"

She stiffened in her seat. "We cross paths from time to time."

His lips began to curl. "I've heard you've done more than just cross paths." He glanced down at the gold chain around her neck. "I'm surprised he's your type. I'd think you'd be more interested in movers and shakers than cops."

Helen flushed. "I'm not sure what you mean. Do you not like cops?"

"They have their purpose. Just not my kind of people if you want to have a little fun." He said. "You'd be better off spending more time on real estate deals and less on crime. It tends to annoy some of the locals."

"By locals, do you mean Ronnie or James Corcoran?"

He shrugged. "I've little to do with any of them. Candidates come and go, and local commissioners like Diane have very little influence."

"And influence is what interests you, no doubt." Helen couldn't hold back her taunt. "Seems you have a direct line to the comings and goings of Eliot's headquarters."

He touched her fingertips across the table. "I'm suggesting that chasing loose ends could cost you future business. That's a shame for someone so competent. My guess is McAlister would prefer you backed off too."

Helen glanced down at her watch. "Whoops. I need to run." She eased herself off her chair. "It's a shame quitting goes against my nature. What's the expression? When the going gets tough, the tough get going? Craig, thanks *so* much for the drink. I really enjoyed it. Thanks again for checking on the Jordan application."

The large man stood up. "I'm sorry you can't stay for dinner."

"Next time. By the way, you should try their crab bisque. It's excellent."

She turned, and, tossing her wrap onto her shoulders, she wove out of the restaurant without a look back.

'Snakes and bastards,' uttered Agatha in her ear.

'Got that right. He's a snake.'

* * *

The streets were empty as she drove through Port Anne. A few miles down, she neared the sign for Blue Point Road. On a whim, she made a sharp turn and drove toward the water and Captain's Watch. At the top of the turn to the Davies' drive, she jammed on her brakes, and the Mini fishtailed to a stop in the dark woods. She swore under her breath. Someone had graffitied the carved blue and gold bed and breakfast sign with blood-red paint strokes. She locked her doors and listened to the deadly quiet. Through the trees, lights glimmered on the water. She stared at the damage for a few minutes, then reached for her phone.

"Joe? Can you call me?" She opened her phone's camera app, lowered her driver's side window, and clicked off three pictures of the obliterated sign. Her phone rang.

"Hi. What's up?"

She gulped. "I was on my way home from meeting Craig Olsoff for a drink and decided to pull down the lane at Captain's Watch."

"You sound upset. Olsoff's a...never mind. Did he pull something?"

"Never mind him. Someone graffitied the Davies B&B sign."

"Likely teenagers, looking for fun."

"Joe, they wrote 'killer' across the sign in huge red letters." Her voice wobbled. "We all worked so hard to save this house. The Davies are good people. It's so cruel."

121

"I know." His voice lowered. "Do you want me to come out and meet you? You shouldn't be there alone."

"I'm fine. I'll be home in a few minutes and Lizzie is staying with me tonight."

"Once again, I've missed my excuse for an overnight. You know, a little police protection." His low laugh was balm on her nerves.

"Once again," she said.

"Text me when you're home. If I don't hear from you in ten minutes, I'm in the car."

"Thanks. Good night."

Chapter Fifteen

Lizzie stumbled down the stairs in the dark, wearing a long pink sleepshirt, her short hair squished and her feet bare. Helen was sitting with sheets of paper scattered across her kitchen island, with Watson and Trixie munching on a snack at her feet.

"Mom, it's four o'clock in the morning. What are you doing? Talking to yourself?"

Helen rubbed her eyes. "You caught me. Go back to bed. You know I'm a terrible sleeper. I can't get the image of the Davies sign out of my mind, and my sleuths keep badgering me to come up with a solution to this murder." She crumpled up a piece of paper and tossed it across the counter in disgust.

Lizzie filled a tea kettle and switched on a burner. "I can't imagine Jane or Nora badgering you. Any new ideas?"

"I've decided one thing. This list of suspects is too short, and we're not getting anywhere. There have to be other people involved in Kerry's life we're not considering."

Her daughter added hot water to her mother's mug. "Sure. But how many of them despised her enough to kill her?" Lizzie opened the refrigerator. "You have nothing in here but four eggs, wilted lettuce, and…" She opened a container of half and half, sniffed, and looked at the label. "What's the expiration on this, anyway?" Her mother ignored her. Lizzie pulled out a jar of strawberry jam. "I'm having a peanut butter and jelly sandwich on toast. I can always count on gourmet in this house. Want some?"

Her mother waved her pen in the air. "Her murder wasn't planned. She triggered someone into attacking her. Maybe they only meant to threaten her."

"Who did she know at the party?"

"Craig, Ronnie, Pam, Diane, James Actually, tons of people," Helen said, staring at her pad.

"Eliot, Alison and Sarah, and their travel agent Jill Sullivan?"

"Of course. Who else?" Helen asked.

"Any shopkeepers?"

"Plenty, but the killer certainly wouldn't be Calli or Owen."

"What about catering staff?" Lizzie shut the refrigerator door and dunked her tea bag in silence.

"Kerry might have dealt with James Cameron. As town historian, he's got his fingers in all the local business." Her mother jotted down his name. "He helped the Davies get their historic designation. Did they owe him for some reason?"

"James doesn't fit personality-wise. He's so milquetoast.

"He exhausts me with his ridiculously big words."

Lizzie giggled. "He is obnoxious. But, you know what Jane would say. People can surprise you when they're under pressure." She rubbed her eyes. "James and Kerry seem like odd partners. Kerry strikes me as caring about two things. One, the campaign. Two, blackmailing Eliot."

"Now you sound like me. I wonder if there's someone on the incumbent's staff who resented Kerry and Eliot. His campaign was doing well. It was building a lot of momentum."

"Maybe someone wanted to eliminate their competition?"

"Joe's partner, Rick, interviewed them all. He didn't see any connection."

"Maybe Rick missed something."

"He's pretty sharp." Helen jotted 'Incumbent staff?' "How about what's her name? The one who works for Howard Travel?"

"Jill Sullivan?"

"She's annoying." She added her to the list with a dramatic swish. "Do you know she delivered travel folders the day after Kerry died? She's emailed me twice about making plans." Her voice rose an octave.

"Mom, you sound really petty. She's doing her job. That doesn't mean she's a murderer."

"I'm keeping her on the list," Helen pouted. "I've told her my mind's not on trips right now."

"If *ever*," Lizzie moaned. "I get the timing is lousy, but why don't you want to consider a vacation? Is it Joe? If you don't think he's right for you, you should cut him loose."

"Joe is great."

"So, what's the problem? If you're not sailing *Persuasion*, you're working. That's not a life."

Helen avoided her stare. "Taking a trip is a big decision. I'm not ready to go traveling with someone besides your dad."

"You and Dad never traveled much. Don't you think you should find the time? Joe's not suggesting a world cruise. He wants to get out of town for a week or so, with *you*. I should be so lucky."

"Maybe that's the problem. I feel guilty your dad and I didn't."

"Mom," her daughter's voice softened. "You need to let someone else into your life. It's not healthy. I'm sure Joe crosses paths with plenty of women who would jump at his invitation."

"That's not a reason to go on a trip with him."

"Of course, it's not. But if you don't want to go with Joe, then consider someone else. Where's Pete Askin been lately?"

"He's been out of the country on business for his law firm. Pete's wonderful, and we go back years. He's just a little too three-piece suit for me."

Her daughter raised her eyebrows. "I like him. He's good-looking. He's smart. Besides, he's loaded. You could cruise the world."

Helen shrugged.

"Mom, pick one. Have some fun."

"This from a daughter whose boyfriend hasn't been here in months." Helen gathered her papers into a neat stack. "Let's get a little sleep. We both have long days ahead of us." She kissed her daughter on the cheek, and they turned off the lights.

* * *

Lizzie was dressed for airings and wearing a full face of makeup by eight am. They followed each other to the front door.

"Darn. I don't have my keys." Helen poked around in her purse. "Can't remember what I did with them." She pulled out her wallet and makeup bag. A slip of paper fell at their feet, and Lizzie handed it to her.

"Need this?"

"Probably a grocery store coupon. I toss them into my purse, forget them until three days after they expire." She hesitated. "What *is* this?" Helen opened the folded slip and gasped. "Oh, my God, look!" Lizzie snatched the note from her mother and read out loud. "Times up. Mind your own business or you'll get hurt!!" The two exclamation points were bigger than the letters. The word "hurt" was underlined.

"Mom. You've got to call Joe. Right now."

"You go to work. I'll call him."

* * *

Joe caught up with her in the Chessie Café. "When did you last use this purse?"

Helen had handed Joe the note.

"Think back." Joe fingered it. She'd dropped it inside a sandwich bag for protection. Other than the big black letters, the sheet was completely plain. One side was ragged as if torn in two.

"I'm trying to retrace my steps. I take this bag everywhere. On Tuesday, my first stop was Eliot's headquarters. I tossed it onto an empty desk while I dug through Kerry's files. It wouldn't have been hard for Ronnie or Pam to pass by and jam this inside. I never zip my bag shut, and I was focused on my search. They were super annoyed I was there. Agatha kept telling me to ignore them."

Joe scribbled in his spiral-bound pad, ignoring her Detection Club reference. "What time did you leave there?"

"About noon, maybe a little later. I went into the office and worked the rest of the afternoon. I left about six and went directly home."

"Where were you yesterday?"

"At ten am, I was standing with the crowd at the steps of the courthouse. I wanted to hear Eliot's announcement in person."

"Where'd you park?" he asked.

Helen glanced across the busy cafe. "Behind the administration building off Bridge Street. A lot of people did."

"Stop anywhere between the courthouse and the car?"

"Nope. I walked directly to the courthouse and then returned to my car. On the way through Port Anne, I stopped at Jean's. That place is like this. There's always people milling around. Jean took a break, and we sat at one of her little tables. Then I went into the office until about four. Lizzie was coming home from ShopTV, and I decided to change my clothes for my big date with Craig Olsoff." Helen rolled her eyes. "I met him at The Riverside at five-thirty."

"How'd that come about?"

"He called me at the office and suggested dinner. I wouldn't have gone if Nora and Agatha hadn't egged me on. They called the invite research. I agreed to drinks. Told him I had a work commitment later."

"When you walked into the restaurant, were you carrying your purse?"

Her mind raced, retracing the meeting. "Yes, I carried it into the restaurant. I wore black jeans, leather boots, and my white, off-the-shoulder sweater. The one you like."

Joe grunted. "You had to wear *that* one to meet Craig? That should have softened him up."

She laughed. "Lizzie and Nora told me to wear it."

He raised his eyebrows. "I'd call that entrapment."

"I was on duty," she protested. "I wanted to find out more about how his company bid for government contracts. I swear Craig is like sitting across from a reptile. I kept picturing his long, narrow tongue shooting out at me across the table." She made a little shiver.

Joe chuckled. "Did you learn anything?"

"Not a lot." She groaned. "He made it all sound pretty run-of-the-mill. Oh! Look at this." She pulled out the photo of Craig with Kerry on Lake

Michigan. "They were dressed for a night out."

Joe lifted the photo toward the morning sunlight streaming through the café's picture window. "They look pretty friendly, but that still doesn't tell us much about their relationship. Could be two business people out for dinner after a meeting."

Helen wrinkled her nose. "I don't agree. There was something happening between them. There's chemistry. He's married, by the way."

"Let's stay focused. Could he have dropped this note into your purse?"

"Pretty hard to do. I looped it over my chair at the table." She hesitated. "I did leave to use the restroom. Couldn't have been a couple minutes."

"Take your purse with you?"

She paused. "No. Forgot."

"Were you gone long enough for him to stick this inside?"

She nodded.

"That's one explanation," Joe said.

"After I left Craig, I came home, put on my PJs, and had a little dinner with Lizzie. Girl's night."

"Except for the detour to Captain's Watch," he interjected.

"That's true," she admitted.

"Are you sure no one else has been following you the past couple days?"

"Nope. I think I'd notice."

They watched customers coming in and out. Two young mothers chatted next to them, their toddlers happily chewing on pieces of buttered bagel. One man nearby discussed an Orioles baseball game on his earbuds.

Helen eyed three teenagers in sweatshirts and baggy jeans, placing their orders.

"Joe?" She tilted her head toward them. "When I left Eliot's speech at the courthouse and started walking to my car, a kid in a hoodie bumped into me. Could he drop a note into my purse?"

Joe's dark brown eyes lit up. "Did he say anything?"

She shook her head. "He said 'sorry' and kept on going. Happens all the time at those types of events."

"Bingo. Could you identify him?"

"I saw him for a split second. He looked like every other kid in the county. Do you think he's tied up in Kerry's death somehow?"

"I doubt it. Someone could have slipped him a twenty, pointed you out, and asked him to drop the message into your purse. What kid would turn that down? It was easy money."

"Someone wants the police to stay focused on Eliot and Alison. I've made them nervous."

Joe tucked the plastic bag into his breast pocket. "Let's go over that dreaded *Pro Con* list you have."

She brightened. "Lizzie and I worked on my list in the middle of the night."

"You two need to learn how to shut this stuff down."

"This from the man who answers his phone twenty-four seven."

"Lucky for you. I've never dated someone who makes a habit of being in the wrong place at the wrong time so often."

"It's the Agatha in me. Well, Nancy too."

He pressed his lips together. "Let's start with Ronnie and his assistant Pam."

"Okay." She dived in. "We know Ronnie's *Pro*. He detested Kerry because she took his job away. He was angry with Eliot for hiring her after promising him the top job. He was embarrassed. I can't say I blame him. He grew up here. That's two *Pros*. The *Con,* no one describes him as especially ambitious. It's hard to picture him hating her that much."

"It wasn't planned, remember?"

"You're right." Helen tapped her cup. "A man disappears. His partner, Spencer, was a leader in Port Anne. Sixty years later, a woman blackmails his grandson, who wants to protect his family's reputation. That's where I get stuck. It's not enough of a reason for Eliot to pay her."

"I agree. There's something more."

"Moving on. Craig. He's got money, but I doubt if he ever has enough. He and Kerry are the perfect match. We just don't know what they were working on. Our suspect list is too short." She picked up her pen. "Should I add Owen Reese from the tackle shop? He was at the party."

Joe shrugged.

"He knows a lot about how to use fishing shears. He grew up on this bay and handles them every day in his shop."

"As does half this town," Joe objected. "Owen's been in business for years. People around here say he's solid as a rock."

"Am I sounding desperate for ideas?" Helen bit her lower lip. "What do you know about Kerry's ex-husband?"

"He was in Arizona Sunday night."

She held up her index finger. "Last one on my list, Isaac's ghost."

"You've lost your mind," Joe declared. "Who's the stubborn one in your club?"

"They're all stubborn in their own way, like me." Helen chuckled. "Think about it. Why has this man's disappearance become local talk again? Who defaced the Captain's Watch sign?"

Joe's cell rang. "McAlister."

Helen recognized Rick's voice.

"Yeah. Got it. I'll be there in twenty minutes."

He stood up and rustled in his pocket for his keys. "I've got to go. Another case. I've got two more names for your list. Alison Davies and her mother, Sarah Howard."

Helen sat back and crossed her arms across her chest.

Joe said, "*Pro,* Alison may have asked her mother for her help to get rid of Kerry."

"But why in the world would they call me for help?"

"Acting the victim is a great defense. Ask your Jane Marple. She'd agree with me. They knew you liked to play amateur sleuth, and they hooked you into providing them a cover."

"You're annoying," she pouted.

He shrugged. "They confronted Kerry in the pool house, and their argument escalated. We need to find something incriminating. Other than Eliot's payments to Kerry, nothing's traceable."

"Have you noticed that large body of water next to the property? No better place to ditch evidence."

Joe's cell rang again. "With a case like this, I'm thinking of moving to landlocked Nebraska. See you later." He narrowed his eyes, his brows drawn. "Be careful. You've ruffled someone's feathers. They might decide to ditch you too."

She stuck out her chin. "I'm a very good swimmer."

"Not *that* good."

Chapter Sixteen

"I was about to call you! You will not believe who just called." Tammi's dark eyes sparkled, and her earrings danced. Today, they were lime-green fish.

Helen tossed her bag and laptop onto her desk. "Hmmm. Let me think. Who would be my dream client? Tom Selleck? Keanu Reeves? Matthew McConaughey? You know I only go for the gentlemanly types."

Her assistant plopped down in a chair. "Sorry to disappoint. They apparently haven't heard about you yet."

"The key word is *yet*." She wagged a finger. "Who was it?"

"To be fair, it's more about why. Look at this." She opened her iPad and scrolled across her screen. "Do you remember the Deale Island Lighthouse that went up for sale? We were talking about it a few weeks ago."

"Sure. Built around 1902, the Coast Guard operates the lamp. I'd love to see it in person." Helen perused the screen. "Take me out of my misery. What does this have to do with the Morrisey team being discovered by gorgeous men?"

"Remember Gavin Khan? You sold him the old house on Dove Lane."

"Of course. We had dinner together a couple months ago. He's a cardiologist at Johns Hopkins Medical Center. He's brilliant. So's his partner, William."

"He called us today. He wants to make an offer on the lighthouse, and, according to him, he's competing against someone from New York City."

"Really!" Helen reeled back. "Never sold a lighthouse before. Wouldn't *that* be a first for us. Could even be good publicity."

"Wouldn't it? You haven't heard the real kicker. Gavin says the only way to deliver the agreement to the owner is to take a private seaplane to the lighthouse."

"Wait. What? Why in the world would I need to do that?" Helen pulled open her desk drawer. "Just a minute. I need some sugar." She pawed around inside. "I'm out." Her face looked stricken. "This is going to be a long day. Tell me, why can't we submit his offer by DocuSign?"

"He said the owner is this odd hermit who communicates through his ham radio system. No cell service."

"Ham radio? I didn't know they existed anymore. Haven't they gone out with the flip phone? There has to be another way. Besides, you know I hate heights. An edge of a balcony gives me the shakes."

"He sounded pretty adamant. The lighthouse is in the center of the bay."

"Good grief." Her mind raced. "I'll charter a powerboat. There's no way I'm getting in a tiny seaplane with one engine and two pontoons for a landing. I'll call him right now and work this out." She shooed Tammi out of her office.

* * *

Her call went to voice mail. "Gavin? It's Helen Morrisey. Tammi said you want to buy a lighthouse. Your house on the point too big for you?" she teased. "Call me when you can."

She hung up as a text came through from her builder.

Hi. It's Alex. OMT showing up tomorrow to finish water supply testing. Thanks for your help!

Nice. When will you get their results?

They say within the week. Let's hope.

Her phone rang. "Gavin, what in the world are you up to? A lighthouse, seriously?"

The doctor chuckled at her reaction. "Always fascinated me, and now's my chance to own one."

"What will you do with this lighthouse? I assume you know it's on the

National Register of Historic Places. I'm sure there's restrictions for use."

"Not worried. I'll restore it. May even stay there occasionally."

"Good thing you're a cardiologist and physically fit. Talk about all vertical living."

"And lots of privacy." He laughed. "I'll have to install a special transmitter to pick up cell signals so the hospital can reach me. Once it's safe for the public, I'll turn it into a kind of floating museum. I'm working with the Coast Guard. They'll let me install a small, movable dock that can be raised and lowered with a power winch. The wave action and winter ice make the location too unprotected to install a permanent dock."

"Sounds like a huge task. Good luck finding contractors willing to work on a floating house. I have a hard enough time finding someone to show up to cut my grass."

"I'm not worried." He sounded undeterred.

"If I ever need a heart surgeon, I'll call you. 'I'm not worried' is exactly what I'd want you to say as we go into surgery. Fill me in on the logistics and timing. Are you really communicating by ham radio?"

"Actually, William is. Used them for years as a hobby."

"I was going to ask you how he felt about this."

"He's used to my insane ideas."

She laughed. "This may top the list. Tammi said you want your offer delivered by seaplane. I'm a sailor. I'm not in the Air Force. Can't I take a boat?"

"Helen, we're dealing with a hermit in his eighties who captained boats for a living. I need the right person to hand deliver this offer and get it signed. Once it's in my attorney's hands, it's his problem."

"Perhaps your attorney should handle this."

"I need gumption. Someone who can deal with a recluse. That's why I'm calling you."

She chewed on her lower lip.

"I have a pilot who'll meet you at the county private airport. She'll fly you twenty-five minutes south and land on the water. The lighthouse sits on a tiny island. She'll help you get onto the walkway and wait in the plane to return you home."

"She may have an hour or two wait."

"That's not a problem. She's an ex-Navy pilot, does rescues for hospitals. She backs up the Coast Guard on searches."

Helen took a deep breath. "Just don't tell me she plans to lower me down in a basket. Or gets impatient and abandons me. I don't want to be the Coast Guard's next missing person."

Gavin made his dry, quiet laugh. "She belongs to the 'leave no man behind' school."

At ten minutes after two, she opened her office door and glared at Tammi. "Well?"

"Looks like I'm delivering a contract by seaplane. Gavin's talking to his pilot right now."

Tammi jumped up and clapped her hands together. "I knew it! I knew you'd do it!"

Helen groaned. "Gavin said I need to bring someone with me. The plane requires a minimum of three people. Something about weight distribution, which doesn't make me feel any better. Want to come?"

"Come? With you?" She sat down with a thud. "Fly in a tiny plane and land in the middle of the bay on two pontoons? No way. I'd have to be insane to agree to that."

"So, you're all talk. George would never turn down Nancy."

"Oh, yes, she would. Besides, someone has to stay behind and keep this ship afloat."

"Let's not talk sinking ships either. I do not want to do this alone. I'll lend you a life jacket and a parachute."

"Very funny. Invite Lizzie or Shawn. Ask Joe. I'll bet he'd love to go."

Helen wandered down the hallway, peeking into cubicles for volunteers. She came back and leaned over Tammi's desk. "You might be right. I'll call them all."

"What's the next step?"

"His attorney and I will work on the offer now. Gavin's hoping I can fly down tomorrow morning if the weather's clear." She dove back into her office, energized.

At about three o'clock, she came out, her bag under her arm. "See you around four-thirty. I'm running over to the courthouse. Want to catch up with Diane about some photos I found. By the way, good news. Alex Jordan's water samplings for Baywood will be done tomorrow."

Tammi gave her a thumbs up.

Helen weaved through the narrow streets and across the narrow two-lane bridge leading out of Port Anne. A town maintenance crew was planting red, white, and blue flowers in careful rows around the blue *Welcome to Port Anne, Maryland – Top of the Chesapeake!* sign. Memorial Day was only weeks away. A line of cars and boats on trailers passed her on their way through town. She'd texted Diane to see if she could fit her in and headed east toward the county seat.

"Hello, I'm Helen Morrisey. Commissioner Diane Gleason is expecting me," she said at the front desk. A security guard punched in a phone extension. "Helen Morrisey is here. Shall I send her in?" She handed her a pass and pointed to the elevator.

Diane greeted her as she stepped out. She wore a light wool dress with a blue, geometric patterned silk scarf and low heels. Soft shadow accented her grey eyes, and her silver-streaked gray hair brushed her shoulders. Her nails were freshly manicured in light beige.

"Hi, I hope you don't mind. I only have about twenty minutes. I've got a board meeting."

"Not at all. I had a few questions I thought might be easier to ask in person." Helen stepped back and studied her friend up and down. "You cut your hair! You look amazing."

Diane laughed, patting the bob. "Thanks! I finally took the plunge. Thought it was time to update my look."

"I love it."

"Come, take a seat." She closed her door behind them.

"Got to be ages since I've been in your office," Helen said. In a grey-walled room, Diane's plain metal desk, with scratched legs, sat near a single window and overlooked the rear parking lot. She had a high-backed chair with plush, black leather. Helen guessed her friend had purchased it herself. One wall was covered with press, awards, and educational certificates. A handful of family pictures sat on the commissioner's crowded bookshelf next to three oversized grey metal lateral files.

"Hasn't changed much." Diane rolled her eyes. "Government issue decorating." She glanced at her watch.

"I'll make this quick." Helen crossed her legs, placing her palms on her knees. "You know I'm trying to help Eliot with the murder investigation. Sarah and I have been talking. You know everyone in the county and beyond. I'm hoping you've had a little time to think about that night."

Diane rubbed her temples.

"Did you notice anyone coming in and out of the pool house before Alison screamed?" asked Helen.

"You forget, I left the party about six-thirty for a Far Hill planning meeting. I only heard about Kerry through a text early the following morning. I couldn't believe it. I called Sarah right away, but my call went to voicemail. I was so shocked, and my phone was blowing up."

She leaned her elbows on her desk and folded her hands. "Are you sure the Sheriff's Office wants you involved? Isn't it uncomfortable for Joe?"

Helen shrugged. "You know me, I'm not likely to be put off. It's a strength and a curse, according to Shawn and Lizzie."

Her friend tilted her head and studied Helen. "You don't want to hear this, but I think you need to tread carefully. They're right. This case has rattled a lot of people. Like it or not, a lot of them are backing away from the Davies. No one knows where this investigation will go, and they don't want to be on the wrong side of this. Joe's had years in Baltimore State Police homicide. Makes me think he'll figure this out." She paused. "You might need to prepare yourself for news you won't like."

"Joe told me the same thing." Helen frowned.

"I don't get day-to-day updates from the Sheriff's Office. It's not my bailiwick. Once in a while, I might have a conversation with the Baltimore D.A.'s office when we cross paths. He did, by the way, mention to me that your amateur detecting is intrusive. He doesn't appreciate you running around like Jessica Fletcher."

Helen waved her away. "The D.A. can't stand the idea that I might help solve his cases. He's also annoyed I keep refusing his dinner invitations every time he's in town."

"You'd never make in politics. Once in a while, it wouldn't hurt you to accept."

Helen wrinkled her nose. "What do you think we can do?"

"I don't know. Kerry's death was horrible." Her friend gazed out her window. "It's no secret I was disappointed to not be chosen for the senate run. But I supported Eliot's candidacy because I understood his appeal. With all this news milling around, I'm worried. It's become pretty obvious he and Kerry were not getting along, especially since we know she was extorting money from him. Why he didn't go to the police when she first approached him, I do not know." Diane sighed. "It's a shame. He should have shown better judgment."

"I agree. I don't think he's telling us everything about her threat."

"Did he lose all control during an argument? Who knows. I feel terrible for Alison and Sarah. My heart would be breaking if I were in their position," Diane said. "Maybe this investigation will stall out, and no one will be charged. It might be the best we can hope."

"That's a terrible cloud for the Davies to live under if he's innocent." Helen tapped her index finger against her lips. "Was there anyone at the party you were surprised to see?"

Diane slowly shook her head. "No one stands out. You need to understand. Most everyone involved in state politics crossed paths with Kerry. She made a lot of friends over the years." She paused. "She also made a few enemies. She was a great fundraiser, but she didn't know when to stop pressing people. It became uncomfortable for some of us. She also had a reputation for being hard on her staff."

"I've heard. Especially from Ronnie Mann. As a commissioner, what do you know about how contracts are awarded during bidding? I've noticed Craig Olsoff's company has won at least three, if not four, huge contracts for water testing in Kent County over the past couple years."

"I have little to do with awarding them contracts. I can't discuss the bids either, but OMT is very reputable. We checked them out long before we hired them."

"You think their bidding success is normal?"

"Given the size of their operations and their track record, Kent County is just the tip of the iceberg. Look at the scope of their business. I'd expect them to win a few."

"It seems more than a few."

"I'm not sure why that surprises you. There aren't many companies specializing in commercial water tests."

"Perhaps I'm being hard on them. I have a client, Jordan Builders, waiting for his results. It's costing him a lot of lost work hours for his crew while he waits. We don't understand the hold-up."

"I haven't any idea how OMT handles its process."

Helen placed her left hand on her chin and grunted. "I understand. It's not fair to expect you to be able to influence Craig."

"You'd have as much luck as I'd have. I've only known him for a few years now. Since we met at that D.C. conference."

"Hear me out," Helen added. "First, OMT wins the job for initial tests. Later, the local government infuses the bay with tons of funding toward cleanup efforts. Later, OMT tests again, and their tests prove big improvements. It strikes me as so unlikely."

"Good grief," Diane declared. "Isn't that the point? If we invest a ton of money into water cleanup, wouldn't it be logical that we see improvements?"

"Absolutely, but doesn't it seem odd that virtually *all* their results show improvement?"

Diane groaned. "It's not all. Now you're exaggerating."

"Seems like every press release I came across talks about great results. Maybe I'm jumping to conclusions."

"Have you ever seen a press release from a politician that tells bad news?" Diane reminded.

Helen laughed. "You're right." She paused. "By the way, how was your Five Star meeting? I love that event."

"Long. Those meetings are one big blur."

"You've got more patience than I do. Any prediction as to who will take Eliot's place in the upcoming election?"

Diane rose from her chair. "As a matter of fact," she beamed sheepishly, "I'll be announced as the new candidate tomorrow morning."

Helen jumped to her feet. "Oh, my goodness! Congratulations." She gave Diane a hug. "I'm so happy for you! This could be such a big step! You earned it. We'll need to pick a night to celebrate, or will you be too important for old friends?"

Diane grinned. "It's not a problem if you focus on work and stop ticking off every law agency in the state."

Helen kissed her on the cheek. "Stop worrying. You're the one whose always trying to be in more than one place at the same time."

Diane grabbed her wrists and shook them. "Don't try to change the subject. Someone isn't happy you're poking around. It's dangerous. Put your Detection Club buddies back on your bookshelf and leave police business to the police. I don't want my phone blowing up with bad news about you. It would tear me apart. Please, leave this to Joe."

Chapter Seventeen

Helen's phone rang as she strapped on her seat belt. She recognized the raspy voice. "Maggie, what's up?"

"I picked up a little interesting news. Diane Gleason is taking Eliot's spot as candidate for state senator."

"She just told me. She said the official announcement will be made tomorrow morning. I'm sad for Eliot, but excited for her. They should have supported her the first time."

The reporter grunted. "Got another interesting tidbit for you."

"Oh?" Helen pulled away from the curb and turned toward Safe Harbor.

"I don't usually pay attention to small talk, but given her political ambitions, thought it might be useful."

"Don't keep me in suspense."

"Two different people around the courthouse told me she and her husband divorced about a year ago. Apparently, it got ugly. He squeezed her for a big settlement, and her attorney bills alone were at least forty thousand dollars."

"That's a reason to give marriage counseling one more try. I didn't get to know her husband. He was never around, and I felt badly for her. She cried on my shoulder more than a few nights during their divorce. Hear anything more about Kerry's connections? Husband, boyfriend, siblings?"

"You got me there," Maggie said.

* * *

It was after five, and Safe Harbor was quiet. Tammi was shutting down her desktop as Helen walked in.

"I've got to get Kayla." Tammi handed her a thick envelope. "I just printed out the final agreement from Gavin's attorney. I put it in a waterproof envelope."

"Thanks for the vote of confidence. Now I'm *really* worried about this plane hitting the water. I meet his pilot at ten-thirty. I doubt you'll see me tomorrow. By the time we've landed back in Port Anne, I'll be looking for the closest bar to help me forget the whole trip."

"Maybe you need that drink before you go to build up your courage."

"Not a bad idea. I'm meeting Joe at Prime and Claw in a half hour."

"Is he going with you?" Tammi pulled her giant purse up onto her shoulder.

"He thought the whole idea was insane."

"He turned you down?" Her voice rose in surprise.

"I convinced him it would be a little break for both of us."

"Not exactly a day on the beach with a Mojito in his hands and you in a bikini."

"He'll have a long wait for that unless we're talking Rehoboth Beach, Delaware, two hours away. And minus the bikini."

"I think he's envisioning something a little more exotic."

Helen made a face.

Tammi eyed Helen's light jacket and heels. "I hope you're not going dressed like Jessica giving a book talk. Something more casual? Could be cold too."

"I'll be in Nancy Drew mode, dressed warm and comfortable. Gavin said the plane is heated, but who knows what it's like on the island. Temperature tomorrow will only be about sixty-two degrees."

"Be careful. Your record with climbing lighthouses isn't exactly stellar."

"Don't remind me. I'll text you tomorrow. That's if I get any cell service." She gave Tammi a quick salute. "Wish me luck."

* * *

Early the next morning, Helen pulled off Hollings Point and up a long, narrow paved drive along an open field near Osprey Point peninsula, a few miles from Port Anne. A one-story frame building was set to one side of a single runway. About twenty-two miles of level land, the little airport had two large hangars beyond it to house private planes.

She walked to the edge of the parking area. Above her, white clouds scuttled across a blue sky with a pale sun dodging in and out between them. Wind socks lifted and dropped in the light, crisp breeze. I guess if I have to fly in a four-passenger plane, this is the day to do it, she thought. She heard another car approach. A black Ford Explorer pulled in next to hers.

Joe climbed out. His faded jeans and short brown leather jacket fit the scene. Good to see him out of his standard 'nothing but the facts' attire.

"You sure know how to arrange an unusual day together," he said. He pulled her close and gave her a quick kiss, studying her anxious face. "You ready? Maybe this will get you interested in taking an island puddle jumper next winter with me."

"Or convince me to never go." She made a little nervous flick of her hair. "You'd need to get me focused on margaritas."

"Now? Or later?"

"Now would be handy. I really don't want to get on this plane. Thanks for coming with me."

"It took a little maneuvering to clear my schedule, but I didn't want to hear later you fell out of a seaplane into the bay." He eyed her olive backpack. "Got what you need?"

"Yup. I've got Gavin's agreement." She rooted around. "Sandwiches, water, an extra pair of socks and sneakers, a hat and gloves, and my phone. No cell service, but I need to take pictures. You?"

He handed her leather gloves and a knit cap, and she stuffed them inside.

They spotted a woman about five foot seven, in her late thirties, strolling across from the hangar. Her thick black hair, pulled up in a ponytail, stuck out the hole of her navy baseball cap. A Coast Guard insignia was embroidered in gold across the front. Her pants were straight and tucked into brown low-cut leather boots.

"Here comes our *Top Gun*," Joe remarked.

Helen took a deep breath. "Let's hope she's that good."

"Hello, you must be Helen Morrisey. I'm Morgan Quintero." She reached out a strong hand. "Is this your passenger?"

"Joe McAlister. Good to meet you."

"You too." Her dark eyes assessed her passengers as she buttoned up a khaki jacket lined in fleece. "The cabin has heat, but once we arrive at the lighthouse, we'll feel the wind coming across the bay. Ever flown in a small plane before?"

Helen shook her head. "Heights are not my thing. I don't even like open staircases. If I'm not on land, I'm on a sailboat."

"I belonged to the Corps, got plenty of rides," Joe added. "I was also with Baltimore State Police, did searches by helicopter."

Morgan flashed bright white teeth at Joe. "You'll like this. It's like swimming. It comes back to you real quick."

"Could we not discuss swimming? I'd like to think it's not on our agenda today," Helen said. "Sailors like to cruise on top of the water."

Morgan nodded. "Let's get going. I've completed my pre-flight check. The wind is light, so we should have a flat ride. Technically, we're flying a Cessna float plane because it can land on both water and land. A seaplane can only land on water. This particular model lands on pontoons, not on its hull." She signaled for them to follow her across the tarmac.

The blue and white plane appeared relatively new and ready for takeoff, its single engine humming. She climbed into the cockpit. Joe followed, helping Helen strap herself in next to Morgan. He took a seat behind. Their pilot handed them each a headset. "We'll need these to communicate over the engine noise." She adjusted hers over her ears.

"Hollings Airport, this is Bay Flight 21." Slowly, she rotated the seaplane ninety degrees and faced the airstrip. A voice came across Morgan's VHF marine radio."

"Roger." She glanced over at Helen.

"Do pilots really say 'roger'? It thought that was only in movies." Helen tried to put on her game face.

"Absolutely. It means 'received, will comply.' Technically, for a plane this size and a trip short and low, I don't have to radio in to a private airport. Do

I need to say, 'welcome to Bay Flight 21' to you? Are you ready?"

Helen swallowed. The little plane picked up speed down the runway.

"Here we go." In seconds, its nose lifted up, and they swooped above the tree line. "You can exhale now," Morgan grinned, shouting over the wind noise as she headed toward the mouth of the bay. "If you're a sailor, you'll get a kick out of seeing the water from here. Do you want earplugs?"

Helen shook her head and pressed her hand against the glass. "Now I know how new sailors feel when we're skimming across the top of the water. Out of control."

"Don't worry. We're in control," she said.

Helen peered at Joe. "I certainly hope so."

In seconds Osprey Point Lighthouse and the state park appeared directly below them.

"Do you mind swinging over to the Port Anne River side of the peninsula? I'd like to spot my house along the cliffs."

"No problem." The pilot swung the nose of the plane to the west and cruised along the sandy yellow cliffs. They watched as Port Anne appeared at the top of the river.

"Joe," Helen said, clicking off pictures. "There's the proving grounds and Grace Harbor west of Buoy Two. There's my house!" The three peaks of the grey and white contemporary poked out among the trees. Her stairway leading from the house zigzagged down the hillside to the dock.

The little plane swooped along the tree line then turned again, heading south. "We have about twenty minutes before you spot your client's lighthouse. We'll pass over Middle River and Baltimore Inner Harbor soon."

Helen sat forward, her shoulder muscles releasing an inch or two, and took in the views. An enormous star shape started to appear in the distance.

"There's Fort McHenry on Locust Point. What a location. Looks right down the bay. Protected the harbor from the British during the War of 1812." She looked at Morgan. "I guess you know that. Have you ever toured the fort?"

She nodded. "Birthplace of our national anthem."

Helen pointed. "You see those cargo ships coming north? What do you know about the pilots steering them through the channels?"

Morgan shouted over the engine. "Those jobs are often handed down through their families, generation after generation. Half the goods shipped to consumers would never arrive without marine pilots. Look there!" She pointed. "I'll try to sweep by this ship coming north. Can you see the harbor pilot's boat? It's tied to the port side of the cargo ship." They watched a man deftly jump from his pilot boat onto narrow metal stairs affixed to the side of the ship and start what had to be a thirty-foot vertical climb to its top deck.

Helen snapped a picture. "Fascinating. They're steering ships from around the world. Looks like that one's from Japan."

Morgan adjusted her rear mirror. "Coast Guard and the Natural Resources Police depend on them too. If the pilot sees any goods they suspect are being transported illegally, they're obligated to notify us and harbor police."

"I've worked some of those calls," Joe said.

"Goes back to pirates who used to sail up and down the bay. If we find out a pilot's complicit, he'll lose his license."

"And jail," Joe added. "What's your plan to land at the lighthouse?"

"We're approaching now. Can you see it?" She began to pull back on the throttle and point the nose down and toward the right.

Helen's stomach took a flip-flop. She'd managed to avoid thinking of landing until she saw the battered lighthouse, four stories high, straight ahead. Worn and discolored white stucco covered the exterior. A rusty red metal railing encircled the upper third, forming a narrow balcony. The glass at the top was murky. Gavin's out of his mind. No, I'm out of my mind being here.

"Let's circle around a couple times so I get a better feel for the wind conditions and how we'll tie up."

After the third trip around, the plane pulled away.

"It's tricky. I'll have to land about a hundred yards out in the bay. We'll cruise up to that little patch of land and those old pilings on the south side. I'll put the lighthouse between us and the wind." Their pilot glanced at Helen. "I'm glad you're familiar with docking a boat. This is much the same, except this engine can't go in reverse. We won't have a lot of room for error."

"Joe, you need to be ready to push open Helen's door. Neither of you have much time to climb out onto land." Morgan pointed to their feet. "The dock lines are on the floor near the door."

Joe signaled okay. He turned and searched behind their seats, then handed a Coast Guard-issued life jacket to Helen. They strapped them on.

"Helen, be ready to hand the lines to Joe and climb out after him. You got it?"

"Roger that."

"Here we go, everyone. Hold on. You'll feel a hard jerk as we hit the water. I'll be cutting the engine and using water rudders to increase my drag." Morgan swept out and encircled the lighthouse again. She backed down the engine, it whined, and the plane slowed with the water below seeming to slip beneath their feet. The plane touched down on the water on its two pontoons. She cut the propeller, and it slowly spun to a stop. They could feel the plane struggle to make headway against the strong current and wind action. Yard by yard, they edged up toward the pilings.

Morgan laughed. "You're catching on quick. Remember, it's like docking your sailboat, except the plane is a lot lighter. Our biggest challenge is this strong current since we're in the center of the bay." She eased the plane forward. "Joe, you head for the piling toward the nose," she shouted. "Helen, you tie up the rear when I give you the signal." They nodded.

The Cessna grazed the pilings. "Ready? One, two, three, go!"

Joe shoved open the passenger side door and leaped onto the ground. Helen tossed him two lines and jumped out after him. The grips on their boots slid on the soft, squishy ground as they pulled on the heavy lines. Helen's feet skated across the mud. She grabbed a wooden post, struggling to get her line around it while keeping her balance. Joe's line strained as he pulled his end around the forward piling and tied it down. Helen levered her line from the plane's tail around the rear one. The current fought their efforts to bring the plane to a halt, jerking in protest. Joe gave one more huge heave, and together they secured the tail.

All three of them gave a relieved hoot. Morgan climbed out and checked on the straining lines. They grabbed two more and tied off at the nose and the wing a second time.

"Wow!" Joe said. "I wouldn't want to do this every day."

"It's why Gavin needs to build a drop-down dock," Helen shouted above the wind. She leaned in and grabbed her backpack from under her seat. "How much time do we have?"

Morgan glanced at the wave action. "About an hour max. The wind will be picking up but backing off this island is a lot easier than the approach. Good luck," she called out as she climbed back into the cockpit.

Helen raised her hand to shadow her eyes, taking in the relatively smooth water open for miles down the bay. She looked at Joe.

"I guess you're on," he said.

"Here goes," she answered and reached up to pull a dirty grey rope hanging off an old brass bell. It clanged next to the lighthouse's small door, the red paint weather-worn to a greyish-pink cast. Albert Einstein opened the door.

Chapter Eighteen

The wrinkled old man with bushy white brows and a heavy black wool sweater led them into a round room with iron stairs winding up along the side walls. "I wondered if you would actually show up," he grunted.

The two of them turned to take in the first floor. Natural light seeped in through four narrow, tall windows. Feeble light from three gas lanterns lining the walls helped Helen and Joe's eyes adjust to the dimness.

Joe spoke first. "This is a lot bigger than I pictured."

Two lumpy brown chairs jutted out from one wall and divided the room in half. A cast iron, Victorian-styled wood stove with a stove pipe winding out a side wall supplied heat. Two cooking grates held a dull copper teakettle and a cast iron frying pan. To their right, a wooden cupboard leaned against the curving wall, its doors open and displaying a stack of white plates, bowls, and mugs. A metal sink on four legs stood beside it. This is a step back in time, Helen thought to herself.

She and Joe unclipped their life jackets and hung them up with their coats on iron hooks set into the wall near the door. The room was surprisingly warm.

* * *

"Captain Lawry, I'm Helen Morrisey. It's a pleasure to meet you. This is Detective Joe McAlister, who agreed to come along and act as our witness." The two men shook hands. "I'm here to represent Dr. Gavin Khan of Port

Anne, Maryland. I believe you've been communicating about his offer?" She lifted her backpack off her arm and pointed at the small square oak table near the stove. "May I?"

The old man dropped his eyes. "Of course."

"Our sea pilot tells us we only have about an hour to discuss Dr. Khan's offer before we have to leave. The wind will be picking up."

"Please, sit down."

The three pulled out small oak chairs, the varnish worn down over the years, and Helen spread out her paperwork. "I'm sure you realize this is a very unusual transaction," she started. His wise blue eyes met hers. "I have to ask, how did you come here?"

With gnarled hands, Henry Lawry stroked his sparse mustache. "I grew up on the bay and was a pilot since I was a lad. When my wife passed, I decided I wanted to live here, and the Coast Guard agreed to sell this lighthouse if I continued to monitor its lighting operations. Which I did." He took in the circular room. "It's time to return to shore. It's become harder and harder to get provisions. And I'm not well."

"Do you have family?"

His eyes lit up. "I have a daughter. I'll be with her and my grandson."

"Good. I'm glad to hear. I assume you're ready to review the details of our offer?"

"I am. I've stalled long enough. I considered another offer, but my sailor's instinct tells me your buyer is the more honorable person. I'm impressed you're here in person."

"I'll tell you this. I've worked with Dr. Khan twice in the past few years. You can trust him. He'll stick to your agreement. He hopes to convert this building into a kind of educational site. Does that appeal to you?"

He pulled on his mustache. "People, especially young people, need to appreciate the history of these buildings. I'm interested in a buyer who'll open her to the public."

Helen touched her watch. "Let's review. Stop me if I cover anything too quickly. I'm hoping you'll take us through the lighthouse before we leave."

"I'd like that. I don't get many visitors." He chuckled.

"I'm sure you don't."

Quickly, Helen laid her agreement before him. One by one, she reviewed its points, and the old sailor signed off with a few changes.

"Congratulations." Helen offered her hand. "Your daughter will receive your copies tomorrow."

He grunted with satisfaction. "I have a friend arriving here next week to help me pack my things and bring me back to the Eastern Shore."

"We'll be ready to settle within the next few weeks. The Coast Guard will need to sign off on the island land use rights." Helen hesitated. "You mentioned you were a channel pilot. Any chance you crossed paths with Eastern Shore Piloting Services? They were in business from the early 1950s until the 1980s and based in Port Anne. I'm working for Eliot Davies, the grandson of Spencer Davies, one of their original owners."

He studied her, then shifted to look at the detective. Slowly, he motioned them to a window. Flashes of light off the water streaked across the glass. Only the glazed white brick wall of the lighthouse separated them from the tumultuous bay water. "All the piloting companies knew each other when I was a young sailor. It was a close community because there weren't many qualified for the work. Later, marine conglomerates started buying them out, and the government tightened licensing restrictions."

"Spencer Davies' partner, Isaac Hollowell, disappeared while fishing in 1967. They never found his body. Ever hear any rumors?"

The waves slapped up against the window, their crests a bit higher than when they arrived.

"There's still a few of us pilots alive from the old days," Henry said. "We're like old veterans from past wars and we chatter by way of radio. Eastern Piloting knew the channels better than anyone." He hesitated. "There were rumors Isaac and Spencer were taking bribes on the side. When Isaac died, the rumors of bribes died with him. A few of us wondered if Spencer wanted him gone." Henry raised a heavy white eyebrow.

"What kind of bribes?" Joe asked.

The old man gestured. "Follow me upstairs. I take these stairs as seldom as I can nowadays. It's a young man's place."

* * *

The three trudged up the narrow circular staircase. Different from her Osprey Point Lighthouse, these stairs wound along the exterior wall rather than up the center. Their footsteps reverberated on the iron treads. Joe glanced at Helen as she took a shaky breath. She gave him an uneasy nod and gripped the iron handrail. Twelve steps up, the stairs stopped, and they entered another circular room of white-washed brick walls and narrow slanted windows.

A neatly made bed against the wall sat opposite the stairway. A rudimentary closet with a rough wooden toggle for closure and a long wooden mirror with cloudy glass leaned against another wall. Helen took pictures of the room and edged toward the window, taking in the endless view.

"You see that dome of land out there?" Henry pointed with a shaky hand.

"Yes, not far," Helen said.

"In 1965, the feds passed the Clean Water Act. It outlawed dumping of waste from factories, including on the Chesapeake. They designated that area as a federal landfill. Some companies weren't happy about hauling their waste over there and paying government fees. Story was Davies and Hollowell piloted boats for companies that continued dumping their toxic waste. Slowed down the bay's recovery."

"Never got caught?" Joe asked.

"Most pilots I knew were afraid to go up against them. Should have." He shook his head. "Years later, government closed the landfill, cleaned it, and created a park."

Helen chewed on her lower lip. "Do you remember anything about Isaac's family?"

"He was married. Don't remember much more."

"Isn't Spencer's grandson running for state senator?"

Helen gave him a quick appraising look. "Yes, until now. He and his wife restored the family's house and opened a bed and breakfast. Last week they found his campaign manager stabbed in their pool house, and Eliot's under investigation as a primary suspect. He bowed out of the campaign. I'm surprised you know anything about him."

Henry stroked his chin. "I get supplies, newspapers, and mail once a week. Since he's Spencer's grandson, I couldn't help but follow the story. Read about the murder."

"Is there anything else you can tell us? The pressure to indict him is growing," Joe asked.

He shrugged. "Stories of illegal dumping stopped when Isaac disappeared." Joe and Helen exchanged glances.

They took the next set of stairs to reach the third level serving as an office. They climbed again to the fourth floor and the tower room. From here, the sun emblazoned the room in the afternoon light, reflecting off the beacon sitting in the very center. The lamp's internal works captured solar energy, flashing every few seconds. Outside, a ring of iron formed a balcony around the room.

"Wow. What an incredible view." Joe reached out to touch one of the floor-to-ceiling pieces of window glass.

The sensation of total exposure to the wilds of the bay made Helen shiver. She planted herself in the center of the room, snapping photos from every direction. "Tell us about the lamp."

Henry frowned. "The lighthouse had an original Fresnel lens built in Paris in 1888. Vandals stole it about forty years ago. That was a historic loss. I believe your Osprey Point has one of the few left. The Coast Guard replaced this one with a solar optic beacon."

"Will you miss being here?" Helen asked.

He cracked a wistful smile. "I will, but it's time to pass the lighthouse along. Hopefully, to someone who can afford to preserve the structure."

"The view is mesmerizing." Helen turned to the captain and made a sad face. "I'm afraid we're out of time." She touched his arm. "Thank you. I've sold a lot of real estate and all kinds. This is truly the most memorable. If you haven't caught on, I'm petrified of heights." She made a little nervous laugh. "Is going down any easier?"

Henry chuckled. "Just don't look through the treads."

At the bottom of the stairway, she turned and hugged the old man. "Thank you for the agreement and for telling us about Davies and Hollowell. Next time, we'll see you on the mainland." Joe shook his hand. With that, they grabbed their life jackets and snugged their caps down over their ears. Helen hooked her backpack onto her right arm.

"Let's go!" She shouted.

* * *

The roar of the wind took their breath away. They spotted Morgan through the cockpit glass. She looked relieved to see them. Helen tugged the door open and handed up the backpack. She and Joe untied the lines, keeping them looped around the pilings. From the cockpit, Helen and Morgan gripped the tail line while Joe released the floatplane's nose. He let the second line slide through his hands as he leaped inside and slammed the door shut behind him. The sound of the wind dulled.

"I thought you'd never come out!" Morgan shouted as the wave action began to push them off the little island.

"Let's not do this again!" Helen shouted as the plane rocked from side to side like a child's Weeble.

They cheered in relief as the plane's propeller picked up speed, and they turned northward toward home. It coasted across the water and then took flight. The western sun glistened across the tips of the waves as the rays ebbed their way down to meet the water.

Helen sat back and sighed. "I don't know about you, but I need a drink," she declared. 'I'll second that. Martini, please, three olives,' Nora chimed in.

"Good meeting?" Morgan squinted, adjusting her headset.

"We got what we came for. A signed agreement." Helen beamed. She looked at Joe. "Perhaps a lot more than we expected. What do you think about Davies and Hollowell?"

"I think Henry was right. We'll never know if Spencer killed Isaac deliberately. Kerry told Eliot his grandfather's company was guilty of illegal dumping, and she wanted to be paid off. She wouldn't back down. He didn't have the money, and his entire campaign was based on his clean water pledge. He reacted."

"Eliot didn't want to tell us the truth." Helen gritted her teeth. "Like father, like son. Or should I say like grandson?" She gazed out the window at gathering storm clouds. "What's next?"

"I sit down with Eliot and Ben again."

* * *

Gavin Khan's house was tucked deep in the woods on a peninsula. Built in the 1930s, two summer camp-like homes were connected by a walkway. Gavin and William united the two structures into one large house. Wide glassed-in porches stretched across the front to take in the water view. Helen teased them about their bathroom and walk-in closets. They were big enough to rent as a VRBO on their own.

Gavin opened his door at her first knock. "Helen! So glad you're here! Come in, come in." A slight man with a close-cropped reddish beard and brown eyes, Gavin's smooth-skinned hands, with their long thin fingers, reflected his profession. He peered into the dark. "Joe with you?"

"He had to get back to his office. Sends his regrets."

"It was good of him to take the trip with you."

"We really couldn't have made it without him. Besides, he loved it."

"Let me take your coat and get you a drink."

"I can't stay long. It's been quite a day. Still trying to get warm." Helen handed him a long wrap. She glanced over his shoulder. "I didn't mean to interrupt a party." She waved a legal-sized, sealed envelope. "Here's your signed agreement. I believe you owe me a very good glass of red."

His eyes lit up like a Christmas tree. Grabbing her elbow, he led her onto the porch and a small group of guests. "Hey, everyone! Meet my miracle-working Realtor who risked life and limb today to return a signed contract to buy Deale Island Lighthouse! Mission impossible, but she did it! A toast!"

His burly, kind-faced partner William, stepped forward to give Helen a bear hug. "I still can't believe he talked you into boarding a float plane to get this contract signed. I was half-hoping you would refuse, and he'd give up on the idea."

Spotting Helen from the living room, Diane Gleason escaped from a conversation and joined her. "Am I glad to see you in one piece! When Gavin told me what you were attempting, I almost had a stroke. Told him he was insane to send you.."

"I'm still shocked he talked me into going."

"What's the lighthouse like?"

"A complete wreck, but fascinating," Helen said. They listened to Gavin's excited chatter about his plans. "Come follow me." Helen meandered to the sideboard and scooped up a plate of warm food.

"Hungry?" William topped off her wine glass.

"Starving."

A tall woman in a flowy dress stepped in. "Congratulations. Sounds like quite a little adventure."

"Not one I'll soon forget," Helen said in between bites.

"I'm Leslie Darrow. Did I understand you're a friend of the detective investigating the murder at Captain's Watch? I was at the grand opening."

"Really? I don't remember meeting you. Joe McAlister is in charge."

"He introduced himself while we were getting drinks. Handsome. Are you dating?"

Helen shifted her head to study the woman. "Ah, yes, as a matter of fact, we are."

"I heard you've gotten involved in a few of his murder cases. Is it true Eliot Davies might be indicted for murder?"

Helen deliberately took her time sipping her wine. Her antennae went up. Agatha might have sniped back, but Jessica told her to hold her tongue. 'Time to ask the questions,' commented Jessica to her. Helen gave the woman a bland look. "The police are checking all sorts of motives. Did you know Kerry Lightner?"

The woman shifted her shoulders importantly. "My husband and I met her during political fundraisers. In fact, I believe William had also. That's how Diane and I became friends." Her eyes traveled to the commissioner with a gleam. "I've used Howard Travel for years. Sarah must be beside herself with worry. She mortgaged her travel agency to help them finance all those renovations."

Helen made a Nora shrug, trying to hide her reaction to the snarky tone and the new information. What was this woman after?

"Know anyone who disliked her enough to kill her?" She clamped her mouth shut and waited. "Or wants to make Eliot look guilty?"

The woman examined Helen again, then glanced around the room. "Kerry won't be missed by many people."

"Can you be more specific?" Helen asked.

"I doubt it's appropriate. Give my best to Sarah." Leslie stepped away.

"I will."

"Ignore her," Diane said under her breath. "She likes to stir the pot."

"Got that right."

A bit later, Helen made her goodbyes to her hosts. She touched William's arm. "William, can I ask you a question?" He followed her to the front door and helped her with her wrap.

"That woman talking to Gavin. She seemed to be very interested in the Davies case."

His open, friendly face shuttered. "She's a bit of a local pain in the ass. I've worked with her husband."

"Hmmm. She's got a bit of a nasty streak about her, doesn't she?"

Chapter Nineteen

Grey water cresting into waves broke against her dock below with a wind that had howled all night. A crack of lightning flashed across the bay. Barely daybreak, she was already up and wearing out her living room carpet. It was raining so hard Helen could hardly see the bay from her deck.

The trip to Deale Island Lighthouse and Henry Lawry's comments about Spencer and Isaac's business kept bouncing around inside her skull. What really happened between the two partners? If Isaac's death was accidental, why didn't Spencer call the police? Did Spencer end their partnership by ending Isaac's life? The rumors from every direction were mounting up and impossible for her to ignore. They made Kerry's threats more legitimate. It made Eliot's retaliation more likely.

She poured herself a second cup of coffee, added half-and-half, and paced again in front of her windows, watching the churning water. Matched her brain, she thought. Trixie pawed and sniffed at the corners of the cardboard carton Helen had dropped onto her dining room table two days ago.

"What are you getting into?" She'd rooted through the junk from Ronnie late last night. This time she reached in and removed each item. Kleenex, pens, half-used note pads, breath mints. 'Take your time,' advised Jane. 'Don't discount the mundane. The everyday can be informative.'

One by one, she continued to empty the box. Nothing else besides a scattering of old business cards. Networking events? She flipped through the cards. A local florist, Jill Sullivan from Howard Travel, Commissioner Gleason, Port Anne Yacht Club, McFadden's Marina, historian James

Corcoran, and an incumbent's staffer.

Wearily, Helen rubbed her eyes. She unfolded a wrinkled receipt and read, "Owen's Bait Shop, windbreaker, total due thirty-eight dollars." Another receipt was for gas. A third, lunch at The Blue Crab. She set them down on the table in front of her and hesitated. She stared at the bait shop slip and slowly smoothed out its wrinkles, then rose and headed into her kitchen, coming out with a pair of rubber gloves and a handful of plastic baggies. Gingerly, she dropped the receipt into a bag and sealed the top.

Helen reached for her phone and dialed Joe's number.

Joe picked up. "You're up early. Get your contract to Gavin last night?"

"I did. He's thrilled. Thanks again for being my co-pilot. You were a Godsend." Her voice climbed. "Joe, Ronnie gave me a box of junk drawer stuff from Kerry's office. I didn't see anything worthwhile the first time I looked in it. I decided to sort through it again this morning, don't ask me why."

"Anything interesting?"

"Very. There's a receipt here from Owen's. Kerry shopped in his store, even though he denied it. Maybe you can get him to admit they met. She was in that shop."

"Damn. Nice find."

"Could I go along with you? I'd like to see his reaction." She waited.

"You can. If you promise to keep quiet."

She grinned to herself. Nice. "I'll be Jane. I'll leave Agatha and Jessica at home."

He grunted. "My gut tells me you've got something else on your mind."

"I found something else."

"Oh? Were you keeping it from me?"

She issued a guilty chuckle. "I was tempted. Good thing you agreed to let me come along to interview Owen."

"Your club is not a good influence. Spill it."

"There's a bunch of business cards in the box. One of them is McFadden's Marina."

"So...? Stop leaving me in suspense."

"Why would she stop into McFadden's?"

"Maybe she was asking about her grandfather's business years ago."

Helen turned the business card back and forth between her fingers. "What if she owned a boat? We haven't found any more old notes or journals to support her claim against Spencer. We haven't found any of the cash Eliot paid her. We found nothing at Captain's Watch. Could she have stashed them on a boat? This could be a breakthrough."

Joe went quiet for a moment. "I'll meet you at the bait shop at ten. From there, we'll find this boat. Don't mention any of this to anyone, not even your sleuths."

"Don't worry. They won't say a word."

* * *

The rain pelted against her windshield all the way through Osprey Point State Park. Two deer stopped on the shoulder of the road and watched her pass. Helen could barely see in front of her as she crawled over the cliffs into town. Her wipers were working in overdrive, thumping across the glass. She parked in front of the bait shop and shut off the car behind Joe. Together, they opened the door to the bait shop. She stamped her rubber boots onto a meager mat. Joe, in a long tan raincoat, ran his hands through his soaking wet hair.

"Raining cats and dogs," she muttered under her breath. She reached up and tugged off the hood of her yellow foul-weather gear to expose her wet head. "What does that mean, anyway?"

The shop was empty. No sign of its owner.

"Good morning. Is Owen in?" asked Joe.

A young man, dressed in a brown sweatshirt and worn jeans dropped well below his hips, stood behind the cash register. His dull eyes traveled from one to the other with a disinterested glance. He continued to scratch away at a lottery ticket on the counter with a pen knife. "Nope."

"That's a shame," Joe said calmly. "We were hoping to catch him."

Owen's helper picked a second ticket from his pocket, giving them a view of the top of his mop of brown hair and nothing else.

"Any idea when you expect him?"

He gave an indifferent shake of his shoulder.

"Excuse me." Joe's temper was starting to rise. "Do you work here?"

Helen heard the edge in his voice.

The mop slowly lifted to show his face. "Yup. Assistant manager."

"I don't know your name." The detective's eyes drilled him.

"I'm Dustin, Dustin Wills." He snapped the knife shut and leaned on the counter behind him, refusing full eye contact with the taller man in the dark suit. "Something I can do for you?"

"I'm Joe McAlister. Kent County Sheriff's Office." Joe flashed his badge. "This is Helen Morrisey. I didn't realize Owen had an assistant manager."

"I'm seasonal."

"Sounds like code for occasional," Joe snapped.

Helen looked around the crowded shop. "I talked with Owen a few days ago about Kerry Lightner, the woman killed at Captain's Watch Bed and Breakfast. Did you know her?" Joe flashed her a warning shot.

This time Dustin's chin dropped, his brow became damp. "Nope. Never heard of her."

"Really?" Joe said. "She was stabbed in their pool house during a party. Surprised you haven't followed the news."

"Sorry. Never heard of her. Never met her."

"Any idea if Kerry owned a boat around here?"

Dustin gave an insolent stare. "How would I know? Like I said, never met her."

Joe slid his business card across the counter. "Tell your boss to call me when he returns. Make it sooner than later."

* * *

"Insolent creep," Joe muttered as he opened her car door. "Follow me to McFadden's."

They wound along the river off Lance Point Road, turned in at the marina's gate and wove in between dozens of dry-docked boats up on jacks. A handful of boat owners were prepping their boats for spring launch in spite of the rain and chill.

Inside McFadden's office, a woman in her early twenties with long light hair and a navy collared shirt was hanging up her phone. She rose to her feet. "Good morning. Can I help you?"

"I'm Detective McCallister from Kent County Sheriff's Office. I need to know if a Kerry Lightner has her boat here." He flashed his badge.

She started at the sight of the badge. "Um. Let me look through our client list." With a click, click on her keyboard, she scrolled along. "We have a Lebner on A Dock." She squinted at the screen. "Here." Turning the screen toward the detective, she pointed. "Lightner, Kerry. She rented a slip in late February for a 2017 Beneteau forty-foot sailboat. It's in the water on G Dock."

"I wonder why she didn't dry dock it for the winter," Helen spoke up.

"The note on her file said she wanted to access the inside. If an owner brings their boat into our yard late winter, it's cheaper to keep it in the water."

Joe turned to Helen.

She nodded. "That's true."

"Thank you for your cooperation." Joe turned to Helen. "Let's take a look inside. I assume there's a padlock. I'll get a bolt-cutter from my trunk."

"And flashlights."

The rain had slowed to a light drizzle. They traipsed across the gravel. Up and down and in between lanes, boats of every size and shape all seemed to be waiting for warmer weather. G Dock was empty except for two.

"Be careful. The docks are slippery," Helen warned. "Here's the Beneteau. It's named Get Away. That was overly optimistic of her." Together they tugged on one of the lines tied to the finger pier and pulled the sailboat closer. She looped her legs over a white lifeline encircling the boat's stern and jumped on. Joe climbed on behind her.

The padlock was a typical Master lock, not much of a deterrent for someone determined to break into the boat's cabin. They lifted up the three teak slats forming its hatch cover.

"Wait." Joe reached into his coat and pulled out rubber gloves. "Put these on. I'll have forensics here tomorrow to find out if she had any visitors." They stepped down the short narrow ladder into the boat's galley.

"Brr." Helen shivered. "Nothing like an empty boat on a cold, wet day." Helen stamped her feet as she looked around. The salon seating was white leather, the teak handrails running along the port holes glistened, and the U-shaped galley was stocked with mini appliances. The navigation table had all the electronic bells and whistles for ocean cruising. She opened the refrigerator and peered in. "Looks like this was her home away from home."

"I'm guessing she planned to make this her escape route after she got her money from Eliot."

"Could have. She was single with a high-powered job. Eliot's payments were her icing on the cake."

"Let's start searching for paperwork."

"Take off all the seat cushions. There's storage lockers under them. You take the starboard side, and I'll take the port." She flicked on her flashlight.

One by one, they popped off the plush seats, kneeled down on the cabin floor, and searched around water pumps, batteries, and waste lines. Joe shoved a case of water to the side and probed under wiring. Helen pulled out spare sail bags and life jackets. A narrow closet of clothes was next. She dug through every pocket.

"Nothing," she said in disgust. "How about inside the food lockers?" She started opening plastic containers, coffee cans, and Yeti cups. Joe pulled magazines and paperbacks off a bookshelf, shaking each one.

"We're running out of options." He pulled off his jacket and tossed it aside. "We'll be losing our daylight soon."

Helen reached across the chart box to the electrical panel and flipped on battery power. "It won't turn on all the lights, but we'll get a few. Try the aft berth. There's storage under the mattress. I'll check the forward."

"Take a break. Let's think about this." Joe shoved the mattress back into place and sat down on the salon cushions. He propped his feet up on the opposite seats.

"Yikes. I just got a glimpse of myself in the head's mirror. I'm proof of the expression 'what the cat dragged in.' Worn makeup, stringy, straight hair, smelly damp sweater. I could scare small children."

"I'm going to owe you a fancy dinner," he said.

"Not tonight, you don't. Nora wouldn't dare be seen in public like this. Come to think of it; she wouldn't step out of her own bedroom looking like this." She tugged on her bangs in disgust. "I really thought this boat was going to give us some answers."

"I know. We're done here for tonight. I'm hoping forensics might pick up some fingerprints other than Kerry's."

"You realize you'll find the last owner's prints along with any boat mechanic who serviced it."

Joe shrugged. "Let's go to my place. Rocky's been alone most of the day. I can pick up a pizza in Port Anne."

"Hot pizza sounds good. Is there any wine in my future?"

"I can arrange it." He made a weary smile.

"Except, I'm so cold. I'm dying for a hot shower and dry clothes. I have a feeling your wardrobe isn't a fit."

"You forget I've got three older sisters wandering in and out of my house whenever they want. My guest room drawers are filled with their spare sweatpants. I can find you a pair of warm socks."

"That'll do. Let's get out of here." Helen's eyes traveled around the perimeter of the cabin. "Sure is a beautiful boat. It reminds me I need to get a port hole resealed on *Persuasion*. I've got a stubborn little leak that drips down onto my heating and A/C duct in a hard rain. Annoying as...." She paused, then rose to her feet.

"Joe, open the chart box and find a utility knife and a screwdriver." She reached for her flashlight and ran the light up and along the round flexible ducts tucked behind the teak trim. "Hmmm. Looks untouched. Normal."

She followed the ducts around the cabin. "What about the heat and a/c returns? This boat has two or three. Hold my light." Kneeling on the forward berth, she unscrewed a teak, louvered cover about six by eight inches. She squeezed a hand inside. "Nothing." She shifted to the aft berth and crawled across the mattress to the second return on its far side. Two screws held the cover. It popped off, and she stuck her right hand into the small open square, scrapping her skin along the fiberglass.

"Oh, my Lord, what do we have here?" Triumphant, she twisted around and faced Joe, holding a small brown leather pouch on a braided strap. Engraved into the leather were two initials, IH. Her eyes gleamed. She reached down again and pulled out a newer, waterproof nylon pouch. She unzipped the top. Stacks of hundred-dollar bills were stuffed inside. "Jackpot!"

Chapter Twenty

"Careful." Joe whipped out a plastic baggie from his pocket. Helen crawled out from the aft cabin and dropped the two pouches inside.

"Let's close down this boat. We can look at this later," Joe said.

"Agreed. I'll follow you home."

Ten minutes later, they passed a wooden sign set into a grey stone column and marking a private gravel lane among the horsing facilities of Far Hill. A large Victorian farmhouse came into view. Joe's lane split off beyond the lane and led up to a two-story restored carriage house. Three twenty-foot-long sliding wooden doors had accommodated horse carriages and equipment coming in and out. Rocky heard their approach and went wild.

Joe swung open the main door, and the old Golden bounded out into the yard, swishing his big, plumed tail, happy to relieve himself and wander across the nearby fields.

"Come." Joe led Helen up the iron stairway to his guest room and pointed to the bathroom. "Plenty of towels. Help yourself to whatever you want in those dressers. Meet you downstairs."

Fresh and warm from her shower, Helen pulled on sweats, a hoodie with Baltimore Police Department imprinted on the front, and heavy cotton socks. In the closet, she found a pair of worn Minnetonka moccasins. 'Like old home week,' she told her chums. The bathroom was stocked with hairbrushes and moisturizers. She dug through her purse for a few bits of makeup.

A fire blazed in the oversized stone grate as she padded into the living room. Joe stood up, reached for a bottle of pinot, and poured. They both sank into his couch.

"Cheers." They raised their glasses, sighing in relief.

"What a day," she breathed. "And it's not over yet."

He chuckled. "Promises, promises."

The smell of steaming margarita pizza wafted up from the wooden cutting board in front of them. She handed him a piece and took a big bite of hers. "I'm referring to our discovery."

He stretched his legs toward the fire. "Let's savor the moment first. Besides, you smell good."

"Better than pizza?" she asked.

"Better than pizza. And I love pizza," he responded.

With the wine bottle nearing empty and Rocky enjoying scraps of crust, Joe eyed Helen. "Not knowing what's in that pouch is killing you, isn't it, Nancy?"

Helen's face flushed.

"Since you found it, you get the honors." He handed her gloves, and she pulled open the baggie.

"Obviously, the initials IH tell us the leather one belonged to Isaac Hollowell. How do you think Kerry got it?"

"I think we can assume someone in her family handed it down to her."

With careful fingers, Helen opened the bag and pulled out a thin ledger about the size of her hand. Made of hard cardboard and water stained, the inside cover read 'Isaac Hollowell, Eastern Shore Marine Services' in faded blue ink. Beginning on the first page were numeric notations, each with a date, time, and a check next to them. A fourth column listed names of businesses.

Helen was puzzled. "These pages go on and on. What do you think they are?"

Joe rubbed his temples. "My bet, Henry would recognize some of these companies. Most of them aren't around any longer."

She frowned. "The dates are spread out over about four years."

"He kept this journal to track his payoffs for illegal dumping," Joe said. "He was smart enough to pace how often to take bribes and avoid the law."

She ran her index finger along the page. "The last date listed was July 9, 1967."

"Only six days before he disappeared."

"You think it's likely Spencer did kill him."

"I also think it's likely Eliot killed Kerry. He was determined to keep this out of the news."

"He'd want this toxic dumping kept quiet. Doesn't mean he killed Kerry." Helen pulled her knees up to her chest and wrapped her arms around them.

Joe reached for her hands. "No one will contest your loyalty. Or your stubborn streak. I'll have him come into the station." He stood up and moved toward the kitchen, his back to Helen, and picked up his cell. "Rick, can you order forensics to examine a boat at McFadden's first thing tomorrow morning?" ... "Yes, we might have a break in the Lightner case."

He turned around, tossed his cell onto the couch, and pulled Helen to her feet. "Time to change the subject, don't you think?"

* * *

"Good morning," Helen answered as she pulled out of her driveway the next morning. Tammi sounded relieved to hear from her.

"Sorry I went dark on you yesterday. I think I owe you for picking up the slack."

"That's okay. When you texted, you were with Joe. I figured the day got out of hand. What were you up to? It was a miserable day to be out."

"For sure. I spent the entire day in wet clothes. Long story short, we discovered that Kerry had a boat at McFadden's. We tore the hull apart, trying to find more information. Unfortunately, what we found only made Eliot look more guilty. Hear anything from your end?"

"You had a visitor. Jill Sullivan from Howard Travel stopped by. She said she had more info on vacations, but I really don't think that's why she was looking for you."

"Really?"

"She said she needs to talk to you. When I told her you were out for the day, she seemed kind of upset. Anxious. Do you want to call her?"

"I'm ten minutes away from town. I'll stop in."

"Coming in after?"

"Yup."

"Don't forget you have a home inspection at one o'clock on Shady Lane."

"Yes, Sarge. Your husband's military service is rubbing off on you. Any word from Britany? I'd think her attorney would have gotten a reaction from her husband on our appraisal by now."

"Haven't heard from her."

"I'll call her today. See you later."

* * *

Howard Travel's windows on the corner of Water and Wallace were plastered with colorful posters advertising an array of exotic warm places. Helen studied a photo of a huge catamaran with a happy couple sunning on its deck, a British Islands coastline in the background. She'd met strange men in dirt basements, but she wasn't brave enough to accept Joe's invitation to stay last night. 'Why aren't I taking one of these trips?' she asked her sleuths. 'You're passing up a good man,' Agatha whined. 'What do you know about good men? You fall in and out of love with the wrong ones every other day,' Helen retorted.

Jill spotted her as soon as she stepped into the tiny building. She blanched, then offered a tentative smile. Sarah set down her phone and joined them, her face dejected.

Helen gave her a little squeeze. "I haven't talked to Alison or Eliot since Monday. How are they doing?"

Sarah fingered her bracelets with a nervous hand. "They're hanging on."

"They'll get through this," Helen commiserated. "Make sure they know how many people believe they're innocent."

Sarah nodded. Jill gave her boss a cautious look. "I guess Tammi passed on my message." She glanced at their receptionist handling phone calls. "Want to get a cup of coffee next door?"

Helen was surprised. She didn't consider vacations a confidential conversation.

"Um, sure."

Jill picked up her purse and eyed her boss. "Since you're here, do you want to join us? I might as well discuss this with both of you." Together, they crossed the street to the cafe.

"How's business? Busy?" Helen started.

"Slow. Our corporate clients are skittish about using us while Eliot is under suspicion for murder. I'm hoping they'll return after the killer is found. Diane's campaign is starting to work with us now that she's gained the party's endorsement," said Sarah as she chose a small table in the far corner. "The situation irks Eliot and Alison, but we need the business."

Jill fidgeted with her napkin, her cockiness deflated. She avoided their eyes.

"Why do I get the sense this conversation isn't about my travel plans?" Helen folded her hands in front of her in true Jessica business-like style.

"I need to tell you about a conversation I had with Kerry a couple days before she died. It's been worrying me ever since."

"What conversation?" asked her boss, sitting back.

"Kerry called me. She suggested we have lunch together. I assumed she wanted to plan more of Eliot's campaign trips. I was wrong. She accused me of pocketing some of the campaign's payments instead of sending them out to the hotels and bus lines. I was shocked. I told her I didn't' know what she was talking about. When I pulled up their account, I realized that I never forwarded their deposits."

"What did you do?" Helen asked.

"I told her it was an accounting mistake on my part and showed her the funds were still with Howard Travel. Kerry said she didn't believe me. I'd deliberately planned to squirrel away the money. She threatened to pull their account."

Startled, Sarah narrowed her eyes. "But we're still representing them. What happened?"

"I told her I would straighten out the arrangements and forward their deposits immediately." Jill swallowed. "She said I had to make it up to her or she'd tell you and Alison. She'd be sure I lost my job and never get hired by anyone else." Her voice quivered.

Helen glanced across at Sarah. "What did she suggest?" she asked Jill.

"She said I needed to arrange a month-long luxury trip to Europe for her after the election. I'd have to either pay for it myself or work out an expense-paid deal through my contacts. In exchange, she would keep my mistake between the two of us." Her agent sniffled. "I told her I needed a couple days to figure out how to arrange the trip. That Sunday, she was killed."

"Why did you wait to tell anyone?" asked Helen.

"I was intimidated. Eliot's campaign travel was a big account for us. Ronnie and Pam told me how vindictive she was when she didn't get her way."

Sarah's eyes blazed. "You should have known Eliot would back you."

"She hammered me about how important she was to Eliot."

"That woman had no conscience," Sarah retorted, rubbing her temples.

Jill's face was scrunched into a near cry. "Do I still have a job? I like it here."

"I'll need to discuss this with Alison. We'll talk later." Sarah made a rueful little smile. The two friends waited in silence as Jill left the café.

"Well?" Sarah asked.

Helen set down her coffee mug. "It's a shame she didn't tell you when it happened. Eliot would have fired Kerry. She might have left town and never been killed."

"I'm thinking the same thing."

"In Jill's defense, Kerry was an expert at manipulating people. Her ego was off the charts."

Sarah's voice quivered. "What a horrible woman."

"Kerry recognized Eliot as a fresh young candidate who would be going places politically. Joe told me the money from her divorce settlement was running out. She liked living well and was looking for new income streams."

Sarah's voice dropped to barely a whisper. "Even if he avoids a murder charge, with all this negative press, he may have lost his chance to run for office."

Remembering Isaac's journal, Helen didn't respond. She knew Eliot's odds weren't improving.

"I don't think we should let Jill go. We need her at the agency more than ever."

"I agree. Kerry had an agenda. Give Jill credit for telling you." Helen hesitated. "I'm not good at admitting when I'm wrong, and I'm usually a good reader of people. When it comes to Jill, I blew it. I've been annoyed with her persistence in trying to sell me a vacation. To be fair, that's my personal problem, not hers." Helen stared down at her hands. "This trip with Joe is weighing on me. I'm much better at helping other people make decisions. I'm stuck in second gear when it comes to our relationship and may decide after it's too late."

"How long have you known him?"

"Almost two years."

"The older we get, the faster time flies. You know my opinion. If I'd met him before you, I wouldn't feel guilty about pursuing him."

"My kids would use the expression, "Called it!" The two friends laughed. "Can I ask about a rumor I heard two nights ago?"

"Oh?" Worry lines returned to Sarah's face.

"Did you mortgage the travel agency to lend Alison and Eliot money for repairs?"

Sarah nodded slowly. "I probably shouldn't have." She gave a little shrug. "Anything for your daughter, right?"

Helen smiled. "We'll always be mama bears. That never goes away. Keep your chin up." She picked up her bag. "Let's head off. Poor Tammi hasn't seen me in days."

* * *

It was almost noon when she entered Safe Harbor. An agent passed her in the lobby with clients. Another was in a settlement room down the hall. Kids were on the floor in another room while their mother chatted with her agent.

"Hi there." Helen leaned across Tammi's desk. "Busy day, huh?"

Little red airplanes swung from side to side as Tammi lifted her head. "Three-ring circus. Are you coming or going?"

"I'm going to make a few calls and catch up on emails. Where did you get those?" Helen exclaimed, pointing at her earrings.

"Aren't they hysterical? I picked them up at Calli's today. Thought I'd commemorate your trip."

"You are a one and only."

Tammi grinned. "You have an inspection at one, remember?"

"Yes, Major General." Helen saluted. "Anything I should know?"

"Britany emailed you this morning and copied me. She needs to talk to you."

"I'll call her now." Helen opened her office door and tossed down her tote.

"I almost forgot. Calli told me she remembered a big car coming out a dirt lane just before the Davies driveway. She thought you should know."

Helen paused. "Huh. That's interesting. It was probably a guest who took the wrong private drive. I've done it twice." She reached for her phone.

"Britany. How are you?" She jotted down a note on a scratch pad. "I'll be glad to call your husband. Sounds like you've made some progress. Call you afterwards."

She pulled up her appraisal while she dialed and wondered if the conversation would be contentious.

"Todd? This is Helen Morrisey from Safe Harbor Realty. Your wife, Britany, said you wanted to discuss the appraisal I provided. How can I help you?"

He cleared his throat. "I discussed it with my attorney. I also contacted two other appraisers for their feedback."

"Oh? Do you mind telling me who they were?"

"George Matters at Intelligence Real Estate in Bel Air and Margaret Nevin at Jamestown Realty in Far Hill."

"I know them both. We've crossed paths over the years. What did they have to say?" She jotted down their names.

"George said he would have used 87 Devon Court. Margaret thought 6 Triton Street would have been comparable."

"I'm online right now. Let me pull them up." Her fingers clicked over her keyboard. "I remember them. Devon has a lot more square-footage and a three-car garage. It's not comparable. I've been inside Triton. Its condition is excellent, but the house is three towns away. A mortgage company would never accept it. Frankly, I didn't think either would increase your value. They may even work against you."

Todd was quiet.

"Did your attorney have an opinion?" The line went silent again. She waited.

"He said we could hire a second appraiser," Todd said, "if I want to dispute your numbers. Frankly, George and Margaret backed up your price. They both described you as experienced and ethical. One of the best."

Helen made a silent little fist pump to herself. "That was very nice of them. I did forewarn Britany my report would reflect the market and not who happened to hire me."

Again, silence. Helen had learned years ago to bide her time, which was not a trait that came easily. The first to speak often loses the debate, she reminded herself.

He let out a breath. "I don't want this decision to hurt my kids. I know it would help if they could stay in the house. Tell Britany I'll notify my attorney to agree to your number so we can move on."

"Thank you. I'm sure Britany will appreciate it. Is there anything else you want to ask me?"

"No." His voice sounded lighter.

She started to hang up, then stopped. "Could I ask you a question having nothing to do with this appraisal?"

"What about?"

"Britany told me you're a marine pilot. She gave me some articles off your desk at home about smuggling through the channels?"

174

"Smuggling? I wasn't expecting that to be the topic." He let out a little snort. "She may have told you we used to follow all the updates on Captain's Watch because Spencer Davies was a pilot. In those days, smuggling was easier."

"What about dumping by companies along the water?"

"Between the Coast Guard and Natural Resources Police, they keep a pretty tight clamp on marine activities and companies on the bay. We don't hear much about toxic substances going into the water. Water testing like Olsoff Marine helps agencies control cheaters."

"Todd, thank you. I'm glad we talked."

"Me too. I'll call my attorney now."

Helen sat at her desk, listening to the chatter outside in the hallways. Toxic dumping and water tests. Interesting. She turned back to the Bowers file and breathed a sign of satisfaction. As badly as she felt about their divorce, she was relieved Britany wasn't in for a long nasty process. Dialing her with the news, she hoped Todd didn't change his mind.

Chapter Twenty-One

Her cell rang the following morning after her inspection as she drove back to Port Anne. Joe.

"I thought you'd like to know that Rick and I had a conversation with Owen and his helper, Dustin. When we pressed them about who sold Kerry a sweatshirt, they both denied it. When Owen pulled out the store's work schedule that matched the time on her receipt, it proved Dustin worked that afternoon."

"That's a gotcha. He couldn't have been happy."

"Owen got upset. Asked what he was hiding. Of course, Dustin clammed up. Said he didn't even remember who she was."

"Do you believe him?"

"He's lying through his teeth. We'd already run background checks on both of them. Owen is clean as a whistle. Dustin, he's a different story. He's actually up on fraud charges. Owen would be far better off without him."

"Fraud? How?" Her voice climbed.

"Did you read about the two fisherman who competed in a regional bass competition last fall and were caught cheating?"

She couldn't help but snicker. "How does someone cheat during a fishing competition? Sounds fishy?"

Joe moaned. "Dustin and a buddy sliced open the bass they caught, filled the guts with sand, and then turned them in for weighing. They won a $25,000 prize for biggest catch."

"You have to give him credit for creativity."

"Someone questioned their win, and the judges reexamined the fish. The story made national headlines. A lot of people were furious."

"I'll bet. It's embarrassing for the county, for sure. Sounds like Owen needs to kick him to the curb."

"I think after our interview, he knows Dustin's a problem."

"I'm adding Dustin to my *Pro Con* list. What do you think he's hiding?" she asked.

"Not sure. I told him to come into the Sheriff's Office tonight for a little private talk."

* * *

"Tammi? Hi. I'm heading for home. Hope you don't mind. I didn't get much sleep last night." She listened to Tammi's finger running across her keyboard.

"Totally fine. I'm leaving soon. I'll be in tomorrow morning but out in the afternoon." She hesitated. "Um, could I ask for a big favor?"

"Of course. What do you need?"

"Kayla has an event tomorrow at three. She's in a little play Diane and her arts council started a few months ago."

"I remember. It's a great program. We need more of them."

"All the kids are bringing their families to watch. Her dad is obviously not here, and my mother is home with a bad cold. Kayla will be short of adoring fans. Do you think you could come? It'll be about two hours between the program, and some treats parents serve afterwards."

"I'd love to," she said. "Maybe Lizzie is nearby and can join us too. I'll check."

Tammi breathed a sigh of relief. "That would be wonderful. She's been feeling a little sorry for herself."

"Text me the location and time. Tell Kayla I'll be there."

* * *

Close to six o'clock on a Thursday, Port Anne was looking pretty quiet.

Fingering a short stack of envelopes on her passenger seat, Helen decided to park and walk up the street to the post office. Jean's Coffee Pot was dark, finished for the day. The lights were on at Calli's. Viv was rearranging books and pottery in the windows and waved. Dustin, in a tan knit hat, was turning the front door lock of the bait shop as she passed. Their eyes met. He glared, curling his lips at Helen. She ignored him and kept on walking. In front of the post office, she dropped her letters into the big, blue mailbox.

Back on the sidewalk, Helen considered the iron-gated entrance to St. Cecilia's Cemetery across the street. A five-foot-high stucco and stone wall encircled the property, making much of its interior not visible from the street. 'Come on, Nancy. This is your kind of scene. Let's find Spencer Davies's family plot. And Isaac's memorial,' Helen said. She returned to her car, slipped off her heels, and pulled on her boots. Tossing her purse into her car, she locked the doors and strode across the street. The sun was dropping, and she hiked up her hooded jacket around her ears to ward off the chill.

Neat little brick and concrete walkways wove up and down, forming a patchwork quilt of grave plots. The sweet little estuary off the river to the bay traveled along the top of the cemetery toward the north side of town. Other than a few teenagers sitting on a memorial bench at the water's edge, the graveyard was deserted. She tucked her jacket closer in the weakening sunlight.

Methodically, she followed a path, pausing at a plain marker for a young Civil War soldier and leading to the little church's arched, deep red door. A scripted black plaque read *St Cecilia's Church, Founded 1706*, in gold. Arched, paned windows with curved, glossy black wooden shutters flanked the entrance. A circular, pale blue stained-glass window was near the peak of the white steeple. She stood on her tiptoes, cupping her eyes to the window glass, and peeked into the chapel. Inside, rows of ancient wooden pews faced the front altar. Neat stacks of leather hymnals placed at the end of each pew were ready for Sunday services.

She turned around and gazed over the rows of uneven and tilting gravestones among the tufts of early spring grass, so worn many of their names and years were illegible. To the far south side, a four-by-four crunched on the narrow gravel drive, and a young woman clambered out with a toddler's high-pitched chatter following behind her. Helen watched as they carried a spray of flowers to a newer-looking gravestone near the stone drive. Her long light brown hair draped over her shoulder, she pushed the mass back in place, gently set down the flowers, then turned. A few minutes later, she and her child were gone.

Helen searched for larger plots. An eight-foot obelisk to the east of the church stood in the center of a large grassy square formed by round iron bars about eighteen inches high. Inscribed at the top of the obelisk was *Spencer Davies, Born April 12, 1911. Died November 8, 1974. Beloved captain, husband, father, generous benefactor.* Below was an inscription for Eliot's grandmother. She died seventeen years later. Two more stones marked Eliot's parents.

Her boots continued to scrunch among the graves. She finally spotted another plot surrounded by a thick iron chain in the opposite corner. *Isaac Hollowell* was carved into the granite in large block letters. *Born January 9, 1912 – Missing July 15, 1967. May he be free of earth's boundaries.*

"How interesting," she muttered to herself. "His plot is as far away from the Davies family as physically possible." She glanced over her shoulder and made a little involuntary shudder. Stepping over the chain, she moved closer to an open rectangular grave edged in worn red brick. The opening was covered with five long, narrow rectangular slabs of white-gray stone. They bridged the distance from one side to the other with about ten inches between them, just as Calli had described.

Dropping to her knees and then her stomach, she inched her way to one end. She pulled out her cell and switched on the flashlight. 'Can't see a thing,' complained Nancy in her ear. Helen rested her chin on the dirt and brick, trying to adjust her eyes in the gathering gloom. Her flashlight traveled around the interior perimeter.

Inside, a long narrow container, shaped much like a canoe, hung from four narrow chains on four chunky eyelets. The container appeared to be filled with a metal-like shroud. Beyond it, she could see a couple flashlights and bits of debris scattered four or five feet in the dirt below. The smell of damp earth and rotting leaves filled her nostrils.

'I see I'm not the first person who came to investigate our wayward sailor,' she said to her sleuths. Holding her breath, she listened to the soft, almost imperceptible creak of the shroud rocking. She could feel the hair on her neck raised against her skin.

Inching her way back from the edge, she began to rise to her knees.

"Why are you here? Want to join him?"

Helen jerked her head in the direction of the low voice.

A hand grabbed a hank of her short hair and jerked her neck. He pressed a sharp piece of metal against her Adam's Apple. He drove his knee into her back, shoving her to the ground, and Helen gasped as her chin scraped along the brick.

"Get off me!" She writhed under the person's grasp.

"Leave Isaac alone, or you'll disappear too." He grunted.

She opened her mouth and managed to bite down on a finger. She tasted blood. With a quick thrust, her assaulter tossed her aside, turned and sprinted across the cemetery and beyond a break in its brick walls.

Helen sat up, touching the scrape, then leaped to her feet. Too late, he was out of sight. Darn! She wiped grit and grass from her mouth and looked around. My cell phone is gone! She retraced her steps to Isaac's grave, spotting it on the cusp of the grave. Thank God. She hit Joe's cell number and dialed.

"Joe?" Her voice trembled.

"What's wrong?"

"I'm in St. Cecilia's Cemetery on Water Street. Someone just attacked me."

"Are you hurt?"

"No, just roughed up."

"Stay there. I'm sending a nearby patrol car. I'll be there soon."

"My car is parked in front of Calli's. I'll meet them. Thanks."

By the time she approached her Mini, two uniformed deputies were pulling up behind her, their lights flashing.

"Are you alright?"

She drew a deep breath. "Yes, I'm fine. Just frightened."

"Can you describe your attacker?" the older one asked.

"Strong, deep voice. That's all. It happened too fast."

They turned as Joe's Explorer screeched up behind them. He jumped out, flashing his badge at the uniforms. Pulling her into his arms, he studied her face with worried dark eyes and touched the graze on her chin. "Are you sure you're okay?" She nodded. "Any idea who it was?"

"If I took a guess, I'd say Dustin Wills. But I could never attest to it. I only saw his back."

"What makes you think it was Dustin?"

"I passed his shop as I was walking to the post office. He was locking up and sneering at me through the glass door. He could have followed me into the cemetery. Whoever he was, he was agile enough to bolt across the cemetery afterwards."

Joe turned to the deputies. "Can you circle around town? Try to pick Dustin up. Find out where he's been the past hour. I don't think there's much else we can do but make him aware he's on our radar."

He opened her car door. "Why don't I follow you home? I'll fill you in on my day." Helen's face brightened. Joe laughed. "You are *so* predictable."

Trixie and Watson greeted them at the door. Helen filled their dinner bowls while Joe pulled out a bottle of red from her cabinet and poured her a glass. He dug around her fridge and came out with a Yuengling and a block of cheddar. "Tell Shawn I owe him a beer."

"Back in a minute. I need a shower." Ten minutes later, she came out in washed-out jeans and a cotton sweater, her hair damp.

Joe sprawled on the couch, his shirtsleeves turned up to his elbows and his tie gone. His Glock and its case sat on the mantel. "Take a look at that sunset." The sun was an orange ball dropping into the water.

"Spring is here, thank goodness. Hungry?"

He chuckled. "What do you think?"

"I have ravioli in the freezer and homemade tomato sauce. Just have to boil water."

"You made homemade tomato sauce?" His eyes lit up in shock.

She laughed. "Get serious. You're in luck. Lizzie made a batch and dropped some off to me last week. It's delicious." She headed into the kitchen and started rustling pots on the stove. Joe leaned on the island countertop.

"I'm not used to watching you cook. It's usually me. Kind of nice."

"I'm not sure if boiling water qualifies, but thanks." She handed him a sleeve of romaine lettuce and a cutting board. "Why don't you put together a salad?"

Happily, he sliced up black olives and red onion.

Helen stirred ravioli into boiling water. "So, are you going to tell me about your day or keep me waiting?"

He gave her a sheepish grin. "We took a statement from Dustin. He admits Kerry hired him to haunt the Davies house."

"Wow. That's progress. How did he do it?"

"Kerry paid him to flash lights along the docks and the pool house at night. She convinced him that reviving the old rumors of Isaac haunting the house would unglue the Davies."

Helen served him a hot bowl of pasta topped with parmesan. "You think Dustin helped pressure Eliot to pay up."

"I do. He also defaced that sign. Bought a can of spray paint in town. He planned to continue scaring them after she died but lost his nerve."

"Still doesn't mean Eliot was driven to kill her."

"We've got his argument with Kerry and his fingerprints on the pool house rear door."

"What are you working on tomorrow?" asked Helen. "I told Tammi I'd show up at her daughter's play, and I'm hoping Lizzie can come. With Kayla's dad still deployed, the little kid doesn't have much of an audience without us."

"When I was a kid, I was spoiled. With three older sisters, my brother and I always had a personal fan base." He spooned more sauce into his bowl. "Tell Lizzie she saved me from starvation tonight."

"I will," she grinned. "I assume you heard Diane is taking over Eliot's candidacy."

"I did. She'll be good for the state. I always thought it was a tough choice between her and Eliot."

"I'm sad for Eliot, but he's young. If he can put this all behind him, he'll get another shot." Helen's cell kept pinging with new texts. She glanced down. "Lizzie is coming to Kayla's show." She scrolled again, then winced. "Did you tell Shawn about my attack?"

"I did. He needed to know."

"Now he's coming for an overnight tomorrow. You really didn't need to do that. He's so busy, and it's at least an hour's drive from Baltimore."

Joe sighed. "He's a grown man and your son. He can make up his own mind what's important to him."

"You know he doesn't approve of my getting involved in local cases."

"That's because he thinks you've got an obsession for saving people. And putting yourself in danger."

She made a little pout.

"Speaking of fixing lives, when are we going to get out of town together? I need a break, and so do you." He reached for her hand.

She pulled back and picked up their plates. "Maybe we can decide after this Kerry thing is over."

Joe went silent, studying her. He stood up and set his beer on the counter. "Do you know how many cases I've got on my plate right now? Helen, this isn't just about Eliot Davies and Kerry Lightner. You have to know I'm crazy about you. I really can't believe it either." He looked away and back. "You're a woman who rearranges furniture once a week, talks out loud to yourself in public, and keeps nothing in your refrigerator other than white wine and old cheese. I'm even crazy about your group of sleuth buddies. I didn't even know who they were until I met you. Can you guess how hard it was to clear my schedule, get on that plane and be unreachable for a full day?"

"I know I couldn't have made the trip without you," she replied, her words barely audible.

"I've been on bay rescue missions. They don't always end well. I went on that plane because I didn't want you to be my next rescue. You are more obsessed than I am when you're involved in a murder case, and this is *my* job. You can't help yourself." He stopped, his lips clamped.

Suddenly, Helen was keenly aware of Joe's physical bulk, his hurt dark eyes, his short brown, grey peppered hair. She swallowed hard. He started to kiss her, then dropped his hands.

"I need to go. Rocky's waiting." He strode over to the fireplace and reached for his Glock and its black leather holder. He picked up his jacket. The front door closed behind him.

Helen stood at the sink and watched the running water. Drying her hands, she walked to her dining room window and stared down at her drive. Joe was sitting in his car with the engine running. Slowly, he turned, looked behind him down the driveway and pulled out. He gunned the engine and climbed up Mauldin's Hill and out of Osprey Isle.

She tossed a dishcloth onto the island, picked up her wine glass, and walked out to the deck. The sun had set, leaving a thin orange-red streak floating across the distant waterline. Her resident owl made a few comments from his favorite oak tree. Trixie and Watson sat at her feet, their eyes regarding her thoughtfully, their tails still. She wiped her cheeks with the palm of a scraped hand.

Chapter Twenty-Two

Tammi. **Two stops. Be in about eleven.**

She weaved around the back streets of Hollings, the county seat, and pulled up in front of an old frame house housing the Kent County Historical Society. She hoped she'd catch James Corcoran.

"Helen, what brings you in here?" He lifted his head above stacks of old books when she opened the door.

"Hi. I brought you a few homemade muffins from Jean's. Thought you'd enjoy them."

"Thank you. That's very thoughtful." He gestured at a broad, spindled wooden chair in front of his desk. "I rarely get to visit her shop."

"You're literally buried. What project are you working on?"

"You might be interested. Given what happened at Captain's Watch and the rumors, I got inspired to gather materials for a Kent County history of ghost stories." He offered a slightly embarrassed look. "I guess I have you to thank."

"James, what a fantastic idea."

"Well, I'm not sure about that, but the locals will like it." He bit into his muffin. "Delicious. Jean does know how to bake. Tell me why you're here."

"I guess I've got perfect timing. " Helen drew in a breath. "I was struggling to find reasons why Isaac's spirit was active again. Which leads me to you. No one knows more about old buildings and unsolved mysteries from years ago. Can you help me?"

He paused and studied her anxious face. "I know Kerry claimed Eliot's grandfather had a hand in Isaac's death. What else do you know?"

"Bits and pieces. When I sold the Davies their house, I really didn't pay much attention to ghosts. Thought they were nonsense. After they closed on the house, they started to notice lights out on the water along their docks. Given all the local boaters, I thought it was business as usual. I see them all the time down at my point," she explained. "The Davies started seeing lights around the pool house. I suggested they install a few solar security lights. After all, the house sat empty for years, and everyone knew kids broke in. The neighbors used to call the police and complain about parties at midnight."

"A week after Kerry was killed, I stopped in to check on the house. Someone defaced their carved sign at the end of their lane with the word 'killer.' Last night, the police traced the vandalism to a local troublemaker. Turns out Kerry hired him to help frighten the Davies."

"Helen, you know I worked with Eliot and Alison on their special funding. I like them. Unfortunately, being blackmailed makes him look bad, even to me," he said..

Helen hesitated. "You've been on the town council for years. Can you tell me anything about Craig Olsoff and his company? I asked Diane why she thought they kept winning the big contracts. She said it was a group decision by the council, and OMT was a logical choice. It seems like they have a lock on these contracts. Did you have any sway in them happening?"

"Sway? That's an odd word." His eyes narrowed, and the warmth in his voice dropped. "I have strong opinions when these contracts are reviewed. That's my responsibility as a board member. But my allegiance to OMT is strictly fact-based. They get the job completed professionally and on time." He started to stand up.

Helen offered her hand. "Please don't take offense. I hoped you knew more about them than what's published in local news. Neither of us wants the wrong person to go to jail."

He walked her to the door, then hesitated, pressing an index finger to his lips. "One thought. Eliot was going to contribute some of his grandfather's library to the society. You might take a close look at his collection. Perhaps you'll come across some family history."

Helen's eyes widened. "We've searched in the attics, not their library. Leave it to you to know where to do more research. I appreciate your suggestion." She squeezed his arm. "Thank you."

* * *

Back on the street in the bright sunshine, she glanced at her watch. She wanted to stop at Safe Harbor, then meet Lizzie at Port Anne Yacht Club. She dialed Britany.

"Hi. Checking on you. Did your husband sign off on my appraisal?" She could hear Britany's kids shouting in the background.

"Sorry. It's a little noisy here. I've got Gavin's soccer team for a pizza party. Hang on a second." A door banged. "Phew. Much better. Yes, I got Todd's paperwork late yesterday. I'm so relieved we can stay."

"I am too. Make sure you lock in your mortgage rate ASAP. Let me know when their appraiser is coming. I want to meet him with my numbers."

"I'll call them right now. Helen, can't thank you enough for getting Todd to agree."

"The appraisal was the easy part. Give him credit for not arguing with you. Not all of these situations get resolved this easily. By the way, thanks for leaving those articles about pilots and the MDE." She heard a crash. "

Britany gasped. "I'd better go before there's no house to mortgage."

Helen's next call was to Alex Jordan. "Hi. I'm checking in on your water test results."

He shouted over the line. "We're good to go. Water quality is fine."

"Fantastic." She tossed three folders onto her own desk, picked up two more, and grabbed her tote. She leaned on Tammi's desk.

"Unless you need me, I'm supposed to meet Lizzie for a quick bite. You're welcome to join us."

Tammi's aqua and gold stars swung. They matched her bracelets. "Thanks. I'm running home to get Kayla dressed for her show." She tilted her head, studying Helen. "What's with your chin? Did you scrape yourself?"

"Can you see a mark? I better touch up my makeup."

Tammi's voice dropped. "You didn't answer my question."

Helen pulled out a compact. "You might say I had a little altercation in St. Cecilia's Cemetery."

"Excuse me?" Her assistant rose from her seat. "The graveyard? What were you doing there?"

"I was checking out Isaac's memorial, and someone didn't like it."

"Do you know who?"

"I have my suspicions. Don't worry. It was nothing. I'll see you at three."

* * *

Only a handful of boats were in the water as she walked past the docks and into the Port Anne Yacht Club's Burgee Lounge to find Lizzie. Their lunch crowd was in the Commodore's Dining Room enjoying the view.

"Sorry I'm late." Helen sank into her chair. A server in a neat navy polo shirt with PAYC emblem printed across the breast pocket handed her a menu. "No need. I'll have a Caesar Salad and iced tea. Thank you."

"I'll do the same." Her daughter's blue eyes widened. "What did you do to your face?"

"Not you, too," her mother protested. "I scraped my chin on a brick."

"A brick? What were you doing with a brick?"

"It's a long story. I had a little dust-up with Dustin Wills, Owen's helper. At least, I think it was him."

"Does Joe know about this?"

"I called him afterwards."

"Wait until Shawn hears about this. He'll be fuming."

Helen sighed. "He knows. Joe talked to him. I got an earful from Shawn early this morning."

Lizzie shook her head. "I spoke with Alison this morning. Eliot is very depressed. They've had a total of five guests since Kerry died. Remember the movie *Ghost Busters*? They're all curiosity seekers, members of a paranormal club. Eliot thinks they should start advertising for ghost tours since anyone else is too afraid to stay with them."

"Maybe we need to invest in an EMF meter," Helen chuckled.

"A what?"

"I've been reading up on spirits. The meter measures electromagnetic changes in a house. We could try to communicate with Isaac's spirit to solve this case."

"Very funny," Lizzie said.

"How was your show this morning?"

Lizzie scrunched her nose. "ShopTV is having a stroke. One of our most popular skin creams treating acne got taken off the market. We found out the manufacturer was scamming their test results. We're not responsible, but it makes us look bad. Guilt by association."

"That's terrible." Helen stopped chewing and stared across the room toward the water.

"You look like you saw a ghost," said Lizzie.

"Don't mind me. I had a quick thought, but I've already lost it." She checked the time. "It's almost two-thirty. I'll meet you at Kayla's play."

Helen and Lizzie stepped inside Grace Harbor's Opera House lobby. They wound around and up a wide staircase to the second floor and into its two-hundred-seat auditorium. Helen recognized Britany and her entourage three rows down and gave her a wave. They settle into grey plush seats next to Tammi.

"Hi! They're about to start the performance." Tammi squeezed Lizzie's knee. "Thank you so much for coming."

"I wouldn't miss it," Lizzie whispered. "Reminds me of my days with Shawn. We performed in one play after another."

Tammi spotted a tall, young man in a suit striding down the center aisle. She jumped up and gave him a hug. "Shawn, I can't believe you came all this way."

He straightened his tie and offered a sly grin as he sank down next to his mother. "I didn't have any court appearances scheduled so I slipped out of town. I'd much rather watch Kayla than another boring attorney talking case law."

"She will be thrilled." Tammi's dark eyes teared.

With a trill, a piano announced the beginning of the program, and the director welcomed their guests.

"Thank you for being here today. Before we start, I would like to introduce one of our strongest supporters, County Commissioner and state senate candidate Diane Gleason. "Diane, can you say a few words?"

Diane, dressed neatly in a navy and white pantsuit with a colorful silk scarf at her neck, joined the director on stage.

"Welcome, everyone! As a member of the Grace Harbor Cultural Center Board, I am honored to be here in this beautiful, historic building that has served the public since 1870. A task force of wise citizens restored the century-old, three-story brick building into a haven for artists and performers." She paused. "Let's welcome the entire cast of today's performance from Port Anne's first grade. Then they will begin." Everyone rose up and clapped. On the stage, Kayla jumped up and down as she recognized her fan club.

As the house lights dimmed, Diane slipped in next to Helen. "Bring back memories?" she asked.

"You bet," Helen said. "We thought we were destined for Broadway."

An hour later, after taking final bows, the children swooped down the aisles. Lizzie handed Kayla a gift bag of treats, and Shawn gave her a small spray of pink carnations. Slowly, they worked their way up the rows toward the exit. After goodbyes, the Morrisey family headed to the parking lot. Helen filled them in on James' advice. "We have to search the library. It may be our last chance to solve Isaac's disappearance."

"I'll help search," Lizzie offered. "I don't have any airings until tomorrow night."

"That would be great. Meet me at six."

Shawn opened his cell. "I have to return calls. Thought I'd work from your house." He leaned closer and squinted at Helen's scrape. "We need to talk about what happened in the graveyard."

Lizzie gave her mother a woeful eye. Helen ignored them both.

* * *

Captain's Watch was deserted. Alison, thin and pale, opened the door.

"How's Eliot?"

"He's struggling. We're working on house projects and combing through old files. He'll be right down. Can I offer you something to drink? Vodka tonics? Wine?"

"The vodka tonic sounds great," Helen said, setting her tote on the floor at the door.

Eliot trundled down the staircase in jeans and a short-sleeved polo shirt. "Hi, ladies. I hear you have news."

He led them into Spencer Davies' library. It was dark, almost cavernous, and felt damp. Alison handed Lizzie and Helen their glasses, and they settled into the fat, brown leather chairs beside the fireplace. Eliot struck a match to a log. The scent of local pine and oak mixed with the varnished wood of the paneled walls and high coffered ceiling. Eliot looked thinner, and the lines around his eyes seemed deeper.

"I know you didn't come here for a drink. Fill us in."

Lizzie eyed her mother.

Chapter Twenty-Three

Helen set down her glass. "The Sheriff's Office traced a recent purchase of red spray paint at the Dollar Store in town back to Dustin Wills. He admitted that Kerry went into the bait shop and offered him cash to stalk your house. She'd read about how he cheated to win a fishing tournament cash prize and decided he'd go along with her con to make a few bucks. He began sneaking around for a month or so, setting little fires, flashing lights down at the dock and inside the pool house. Anything to stir up rumors that Captain's Watch was haunted and get people talking again about Isaac's disappearance. She knew the gossip would help you feel pressured to pay her off."

"What's McAlister doing about him?" Eliot asked.

"There's not a lot to do at this point. At least, anything that helps you. His pranks add up to nuisance charges. It's not a lot of progress, but it's breadcrumbs. Each piece gets us closer to why all this is happening to you."

"My mother's not telling you everything," Lizzie interrupted. "She was in St. Cecilia's graveyard, checking out Isaac's memorial late yesterday. Someone jumped her. We think it was Dustin."

"What!" Alison sat up. "Did he hurt you?"

"I'm fine. Just a little roughed up. I couldn't get a look at him, so it's only an assumption. I admit, he scared the bejesus out of me. I thought he was going to toss me into Isaac's open grave."

Eliot looked stunned. "Helen, you have to be careful." Sarah reached for Helen's hand.

"Blame my Detection Club. They keep needling me to keep going."

"Anything more about Kerry?" he asked.

"Quite a bit. She owned a boat. It's sitting in McFadden's Marina. It was kitted out for a long trip. Looks like she was planning to sail to the Caribbean with your cash after your campaign was over. Probably putting it into an offshore account. She also booked a one-way flight back to Chicago." Helen hunched forward. "We found most of the hundred thousand you paid her. We also found a log book belonging to Isaac with records of payoffs. There's lists and lists of dollar amounts. Kerry must have come across his log with family belongings passed down to her. She was smart enough to recognize its value and came to you."

Eliot swallowed. "Now what?"

"I'm hoping you want to know why Isaac disappeared."

"I do, but it could hurt my case."

Helen rubbed her eyes. "It's a chance you may have to take. But you already know that, don't you?"

Everyone was silent. Her eyes roved around the room, stopping at the large portrait of Spencer Davies and Eliot's grandmother to the side.

"Eliot, Kerry didn't have proof your grandfather killed Isaac. We're still not sure what happened. She did have proof that Spencer and Isaac accepted bribes for helping polluters in the sixties. They acted as channel pilots for crooked companies who continued to dump their waste into the bay and avoid new government fines. That's really why you paid Kerry. You wanted to protect your campaign. People might not vote for a candidate running on a clean water pledge if his inheritance came from a polluter. You lied to us." Everyone went silent.

Helen took another breath. "With the argument James overheard earlier Sunday and your thumbprint found on the rear door of the pool house that night, the police are about to charge you."

He hung his head. "I didn't kill Kerry, but I was afraid to tell McAlister why she was really blackmailing me. I was ashamed of my grandfather, and I knew it would give him a stronger motive."

"You were petrified when she wouldn't back off. You knew you could never come up with the entire four hundred thousand. There's no doubt, it gives the police a very strong motive." Helen said.

Tears started to dribble down Alison's cheeks. "What do we do? How do we find Kerry's killer?"

"Isaac's death and the hauntings Kerry and Dustin stirred up are diverting our attention from the real killer's motive. I suspect her killer is thrilled to see them muddy the investigation. It keeps all eyes on you." Helen sighed, got up and poured herself some tonic.

"Let's go down the list of possible suspects. Ask yourself, what's the motive? Why would they kill her? Why would they not? First, there's you, obviously." She sighed. "Then there's Alison. *Pro,* comes to her husband's defense. *Con,* not in her, ever." Eliot held her hand.

"Next, Ronnie Mann. *Pro,* detested Kerry for taking his job. *Con,* a question mark. Next, his girlfriend, Pam Breen. *Pro,* furious with Kerry for taking Ronnie's job. She resented your decision. She's known for a bad temper."

Eliot raised his eyes. "That's true. I actually threatened to fire her after she tore into a volunteer. Pam practically attacked her."

"Why'd you keep her?" asked Lizzie.

"Ronnie promised he'd keep her in line. He convinced me it was a one-off. Between Kerry's bullying and Pam's attitude, I had my hands full with staff problems, and we'd just launched the campaign." His lips formed a straight line.

"What about Dustin Wills?" Alison asked.

"Could he? Sure. He's a local hoodlum and drifter. Ghosting for Kerry and expecting to be paid. Maybe he came to collect, and they argued. Jane Marple and Jessica Fletcher would tell us simple is often the right answer. It's why police consider immediate family first. My *Con* is, he doesn't strike me as smart enough, and he wasn't at the party."

"We think," Lizzie interjected. "He could surprise us."

"Craig Olsoff is next," Helen said. "*Pro,* had an affair with Kerry. Wanted to keep it from the wealthy wife."

Eliot shook his head. "I never knew."

Helen walked the carpet. "Another *Pro* for Craig, I think Kerry helped

Olsoff win contracts. Did Kerry get a piece of that action? Most likely. She doesn't do anything just for love. Craig's *Cons*, did he still care about her? Did he want her to keep steering bids to him?"

Eliot rubbed his hands together. "I never saw anything that looked like Craig had an illegal advantage. I liked Craig. He encouraged his company to contribute to local campaigns, and not just mine. He and Kerry seemed friendly, but I wrote it off as traveling in the same circles."

Helen frowned. "I can't figure out if I suspect him because of his contributions or getting contracts. Maybe it's because he's such a womanizer. It's hard to separate the three. When I asked him about winning bids on contracts, he got very huffy. He also denied any personal relationship with Kerry." She examined her list. "Next is Diane Gleason."

"Mom, seriously? Diane?"

Helen waved her away. "*Pro*, she has influence over awarding contracts even though she denies it. She also could use the money. And she wanted to run for state senator and lost it to Eliot. That's big. *Con*, I've known her for years. No one has worked harder for this county than Diane."

Lizzie raised a finger. "What about James Corcoran?"

Helen nodded. "James is very involved in who gets state and county support. He's important but manages to keep his private actions private. He also hated your plans to convert the house into a B&B. I was surprised when he helped you with the qualifications."

"What's his *Pro*?"

"Protecting his reputation. If he steered funds only toward friends or pet projects, he'd have to keep them concealed."

"*Con*?"

"No proof as of yet. His personality doesn't seem to fit the profile. Always seemed kind of bland, and he's obsessed with using highfalutin words." They groaned together, breaking the tension in the room.

"Mom," Lizzie reminded her. "We wanted to search this room tonight."

"Why?" asked Alison.

"I stopped into the historical society, and James suggested your grandparents may have stored journals and notes among their old books." Helen hesitated. "What we find may not help exonerate you. It may even hurt you."

Eliot glanced up at his grandparents' portraits. "I ran scared when Kerry threatened me. Let's finish the search."

He and Alison began on opposite ends of the room. Lizzie, Sarah, and Helen worked from the center toward them, rolling an old-fashioned library ladder across a metal track. One by one, they fingered though books, flipping pages and poking under cover flaps.

Alison started sneezing. "I think most of these haven't been read in fifty years."

"Given the topics, no wonder," Lizzie agreed. "Here's *The History of Anchoring* and *"Duck Decoys of the Eastern Shore."*

"Now I know how to get to sleep. I'll borrow some books from your house," Helen commented.

Eliot tossed another log on the fire. The doorbell rang, reverberating through the big house like a gong. Everyone jumped. "Who is that? It's after eight."

A muffled but familiar voice floated in from the hall.

"We've got another helper," Eliot exclaimed, clapping Shawn on the back.

Alison gave him a big hug. Shawn tossed his jacket onto a chair. "When my mother and Lizzie didn't answer my texts, I decided to come see what you're doing." He chuckled. "Besides, there's absolutely nothing worthwhile to eat at my mother's house other than a Lean Cuisine. I was desperate."

"I should have warned you," Lizzie said.

"I'll order two large pizzas from Tella's and get them delivered." Alison picked up her cell and started dialing. "I want to keep you all energized."

"I knew there was hope. Where do you want me to start?" Shawn rolled up his sleeves and grabbed three books off a top shelf, handing them down to his sister.

The curved mantel clock struck ten-thirty. Crusts littered a side table. Helen dropped onto the old tapestry sofa and set her feet on a coffee table. "How many are left?"

Alison stood back, crossing her arms. "Two more rows across the top."

Shawn heaved the ladder to the center and climbed. He handed them to

CHAPTER TWENTY-THREE

Eliot. He searched, then handed them back.

With a little cry, Eliot stopped. "These are diaries. They're my grand-mother's!"

Three covers made of cardboard were decorated in '60s patterns with tiny gold-colored latches, one with a key. He opened the first. Alison shot a hopeful look at Lizzie.

"First date is January 1, 1964. The last date is in December, 1965." He paged through the diary, running his fingers down each leaf. Alison fingered a lock on the second, jiggling the miniature key. She shook her head in frustration, her ponytail loose on her neck.

Shawn reached out. "Let me try. My dad had jimmying old locks down to a science."

Gently, he shifted the key about. It didn't budge. "Alison, get me a letter opener or a big paperclip." Shawn rotated the tip of the paperclip around the lock's opening. The lock sprang open.

"You do the honors," he said, handing the diary over to Alison.

Alison lifted her eyes to her husband and started. "It's dated February 1966, seventeen months before Isaac disappeared. Your grandmother says, 'Spencer had a big argument with Isaac. I could hear their voices from the water. He won't tell me why.'"

She paused. "'September 1966, Spencer not sleeping. December 1966, wanted to invite Isaac and his family to our house for dinner. It was his birthday. Spencer refused. March 1967, Spencer working from the pool house. Haven't seen Isaac in days, not speaking to each other. Sad.'"

Alison glanced at her husband.

"Go on," he said, gritting his teeth.

She continued to flip. "There's nothing here but grocery lists and notes about the children. Notes on meetings Spencer had in Port Anne."

The friends looked at each other. The only sound in the big Victorian was the old grandfather's clock chiming eleven.

She continued. "July 13, 1967."

"Two days before Isaac disappeared." Eliot rubbed his eyes. Everyone held their breaths.

Alison read, "'Terrible row. I could hear Spencer and Isaac in the pool house. I went up to the widow's watch. Why were they fighting? Spencer said he wanted out. Lots of shouting. My stomach hurts from worry.'"

"'July 15, 1967. Isaac went night fishing. Spencer called the Coast Guard for Osprey Point Lighthouse and Port Anne River about seven o'clock. Isaac missing. Never returned. Spencer worried. Left to meet Coast Guard. Returned about midnight. No news. I told him Isaac is very experienced. They'll find him.'"

"'It's been three days. Spencer has been searching from his trolling boat with our neighbors. No sign of Isaac." Alison's voice quivered. She swallowed. "July 18, 1967. Isaac's empty boat washed against the jetty rocks at the point. Nothing more we can do. He must be gone.'"

Alison gripped the diary. "When did Spencer die?"

"November 1974. Why?" Eliot said.

"Your grandmother says he never seemed the same after Isaac drowned."

* * *

The next morning Shawn and Lizzie sat outside on Helen's deck, watching the mist lift off the water.

"You two are up early," Helen declared, a mug in her hand. "It's a little chilly."

"Feels good to get some fresh air. I need to get to court by eleven."

She took a seat across from him.

Lizzie cleared her throat, her face pale. "Since you're both here, I should give you a little news."

"Oh?" Helen brightened.

"Jason and I split up. I'd like to move back here until I find my own place."

Shawn didn't look surprised.

Her mother set down her cup. "I thought you were about to tell me you set a wedding date." She glared at her son. "You knew."

"She told me on the phone yesterday morning."

Helen hesitated. "I haven't seen him in months. Why?"

"Either he's on a plane or in meetings twenty-four seven. I know my schedule is erratic, but he never finds time for us. It's not what I want. Can you understand? I know you liked him."

"After three years, I thought of him as family. But family makes an effort to spend time together. He never did," Helen said. "You need someone who wants to build a life with you. Do things together even when they're not fun. For your dad and I, rehabbing our old house in town was so much work and yet those days created some of our best memories." She gazed across the water, then eyed her daughter. "I've one warning. Don't break up because you're afraid to commit. That goes for you too, Shawn." She reached for her daughter.

Lizzie pressed her lips together and offered a brave face.

"When are you moving?" Helen asked.

"I'm picking up my clothes later today. Shawn will help me move my furniture once I know where I'm living."

Helen gave her daughter a big hug, rubbing her shoulders, kissing her cheeks. She studied her son, "What about you?"

"Don't start on me." Shawn pleaded, holding up his hands. "I have to get to work. Did you talk to Joe yesterday?"

"What about?" Helen tried to sound indifferent.

"Dustin and his attack on you, of course."

"Let's just say we're not talking much." Her mother avoided their eyes.

"Why?"

"He's upset. I told him I won't consider a vacation with him until this case is resolved."

Lizzie put her hands on her hips. Her voice climbed. "You just told me I need to know when to commit."

"You're young. I may never be ready."

"I'm leaving Lizzie to handle this discussion." Shawn got up and gave his mother a quick kiss. He gave his sister a hug on his way out the door.

"What time do you need to leave?" Helen asked Lizzie.

"About nine. We've got time." Lizzie's cell rang. She bit her lower lip. "I better take this." She stepped inside. Helen could hear a male voice on the other end.

"Hi. Jason, we can't talk about this one more time. You're always on the road, and I'm always alone. I can't keep waiting for you to decide when we're your priority. I'm sorry too." She hung up, turned, and stuck her face in between the sliders.

"I'm sorry you're going through this," said Helen.

"It's for the best. I'll be showered and ready in about thirty minutes." Lizzie had tears in her eyes.

The sun on the distant shore was climbing. Helen sat down on a chaise. Tucking her knees up to her chest, she listened to the morning squawks of eagles as they searched the water for breakfast. 'Your daughter knows what she needs,' Nora whispered in her ear. 'Yes. I'm proud of her.'

'Don't worry. She'll find her match. And Joe?'

Helen gazed across the water and didn't answer. She walked inside and picked up her phone. No missed calls.

Chapter Twenty-Four

"Lizzie!" Helen called up the stairs. "I need to leave in five minutes."

"I'm right behind you."

"Any chance you feel like stopping at Eliot's old headquarters with me? He wants me to pick up the last of Kerry's files."

Lizzie came to the top of the stairs with a hairbrush in her hand. "Sure. I'd like to see it. Isn't it Diane's now?"

"That's why I need to claim those files."

* * *

The banner, *Diane Gleason for State Senator,* felt a little odd. What a mess, she thought. Two friends, wanting the same thing. Helen tugged the front door open, and Lizzie stepped in behind her. Pam was at the front desk.

"Helen." She clearly looked annoyed. "Can I help you?"

Helen stuck out her hand, along with an exaggerated smile. "Good morning, Pam."

Pam kept her hands in her pockets.

Helen pretended not to notice. "Eliot wanted me to stop by and pick up the last of Kerry's boxes. This is my daughter, Lizzie."

Lizzie's eyes widened as she offered her hand. "Pam? I didn't realize you worked here."

"You know each other?" Helen asked.

"Pam and I graduated the same year from Port Anne High School. I don't think we've bumped into each other since. Have we?"

"Maybe the five-year reunion. How's your brother?"

"He's fine. He's a D.A. now for Baltimore County," goaded Lizzie. "How long have you worked for Diane?"

Pam gave a little flip of her hair. "Ronnie's my fiancé. He was Eliot's campaign manager. Now, he's running Diane's campaign. We've been together two years."

"Congratulations. My mom told me a person named Pam was helping Ronnie. I didn't make the connection. I'm sure you enjoy the challenge."

The two young women dropped into an uneasy pause.

"Well," Helen said. "Let's grab those boxes, and we'll be on our way. I'm assuming Diane isn't in yet?"

"Ah, no. She'll be in later."

"Remind her we're happy to help with the campaign."

"I will." Her blank eyes told them she wouldn't. "Good to see you, Lizzie." Pam picked up her phone and turned her back.

* * *

"*That's* the Pam you have on your *Pro Con* list?"

"I didn't realize you knew her." Helen opened the trunk of her car, and Lizzie shoved three boxes inside.

"I had no idea she was the Pam I knew."

"What's her story?"

Her daughter rolled her eyes. "She's a nightmare. Ask Shawn. When he was running for class president his senior year, she was dating the other candidate. She was over-the-top competitive. Vindictive. She sent nastygrams to our volunteers. When the principal announced Shawn won, she got up, cursed him out in front of everyone and stomped out of the auditorium. The principal gave her a day's detention."

"I forgot all about that."

"When we were together for our five-year reunion, she wouldn't speak to us. Talk about holding a grudge."

"Do you think she's capable of murder?"

Lizzie pushed her bright hair off her face and glanced up at Diane's headquarters. "Be careful," she said under her breath. "She's staring out the window at us. Probably sending us bad karma. Or wondering how she can key your car. Could she murder someone? I'd hate to think so, but she's definitely unhinged."

* * *

The tourist season had arrived. The sun was warm, and foot traffic up and down Water Street carried bags from the little shops, a healthy sign. Diners sat outside at Tacos Etc. and The Blue Claw under their blue and yellow umbrellas. Helen slowed to allow a Jeep in front of her time to jockey into an open parking spot. A familiar figure caught her eye.

Joe was chatting with a curvy woman with shoulder-length, reddish-brown hair in a powder-blue dress and heeled sandals. Helen couldn't help but stare. He picked up a beer. She lifted what appeared to be white wine to her lips. Clearly, she was enjoying their conversation. Joe gave their server their order and returned to the woman with an appreciative look.

Helen's jaw dropped open. 'Humph. What do you think about that, Agatha? Certainly didn't take long. Kind of underhanded, don't you think?' 'Maybe it's business,' Agatha responded. 'If that's business, his job just improved.' 'You did blow him off,' Nora admonished. 'It's all your fault,' Helen objected. 'If you didn't distract me with Kerry's murder, I might be more available.' She could sense them rolling their eyes.

Tammi greeted her at Safe Harbor with a stack of invoices. "You don't look very happy."

Helen opened her office door and tossed her belongings onto a chair in disgust. She dug around inside her desk drawers and pulled out a handful of bent Twizzlers. "Don't ask." She sat down with a huff, and Tammi retreated from the room. A few calls later, she reached for a snapshot of her sailboat. She dialed McFadden's Marina.

"Good morning, this is Helen Morrisey. My boat, *Persuasion*, is still on the hard and winterized. Can we get her scheduled for launch soon?"…"The next couple days would be great. I'll move her out of your slip as soon as it's in the water."

Her cell rang.

"Helen? It's Craig Olsoff."

"Oh. Craig," She started, choking on the piece of red licorice in her mouth. "How are you?"

"Just fine. I had a meeting in town this morning. I'm on my way to Lance Point Marina to check on my boat. It's a fifty-foot Carver. I want to give it a short run, find out what needs to be serviced for the summer. Any chance you want to join me?"

"Ah, gee," she stumbled. "I'm kind of jammed up."

"It's a beautiful day," he said warmly, ignoring her tone. "All work and no play makes Helen a dull girl. It's just a little cruise to the point and back."

'Go on.' Agatha urged. 'The sun's out.' Jessica prodded. 'Maybe you can ask about his romance with Kerry.'

Helen inwardly groaned. "What time should I be there?"

"About three?"

She bit her lip. "How should I find you?"

"Meet me at the end of the fuel docks." He sounded elated.

"See you at three."

Her cell rang again. Gavin Khan. "Hi. How's my favorite lighthouse owner?"

"Moving ahead. You should hear more from my attorney in a day or two."

"Great. Anything I can do for you?"

"I'm relaying a message from Henry Lawry by way of William's ham radio. He said to tell you to search the pool house for old records. Eastern Shore Piloting used it for their office."

She chewed on her lower lip. "Thanks. The Davies redid the building before the party, but there's still some original cabinets and a desk they use for a bar. We'll check."

That's very interesting, she thought. The diary from Eliot's grandmother mentioned Spencer and Eliot arguing in the pool house. Now Henry brings it up. Forensics examined the pool house the night Kerry died. Did they miss something?

'What do you think, Nancy?'

'It's an old building. Worth checking,' she replied.

* * *

Lance Point Marina was tucked along the river coastline south of Port Anne Yacht Club and across the river from the Baywood job on Ferry Point. A convenient stop for boaters to fill up their fuel tanks and pump out their waste before they aimed for the open bay. Like the cargo ships, even pleasure boats couldn't discharge into the water. Pump-out stations were every few miles up and down the bay.

Ten after three, she locked her car and jogged to the end of the docks. Craig's luxury Carver was easy to find. A high school student was filling his freshwater tanks.

"Sorry, I'm late. I ran home and changed." Helen handed him a bottle of white wine and her windbreaker.

"I thought maybe you decided not to come." Craig's voice lifted at the sight of her. He offered her a hand as she stepped onto the deck and leaned in to give her a little peck.

Helen grabbed a rail and dodged the kiss. She adjusted a navy baseball cap, tucked her hair behind her ears, and claimed a broad, white leather seat up on the boat's flybridge next to his steering station. She gazed down the river toward the point. "This was a good suggestion." She had to admit, even Craig couldn't spoil the chance for boating on a sunny spring day.

Craig shifted the boat's throttle forward, his dock hand released the lines, and two big diesel engines roared as they pulled away. "Get out on the water often? Or aren't you a boater?"

"I'm a sailor. McFadden's is launching my boat later this week. I enjoy powerboats, but for me, there's nothing better than turning off the engine and listening to the quiet." She looked around. "This boat is certainly beautiful. Own her long?" Mentally, she racked up the cost. He must have plunked down half a million easily.

His chest seemed to puff. "I bought it two years ago. I owned a thirty-two foot for a few years but wanted to travel down the Intracoastal Waterway and out to the Gulf. This can handle the ocean." He smirked. "I like to get to places fast."

He pointed to her bottle. "Want to open your wine? There's glasses in the galley. You can bring a beer for me."

She took two flights of steps down to reach the companionway deep in the hull and into to his spacious galley. White leather seating, three queen-size cabins, stainless and custom teak cabinets. Wow. Helen climbed back up, handing him a beer.

"I'm curious. Do you plan to contribute to Diane's campaign now that she's replaced Eliot?"

He tilted his head. "I'd like to support her. I'm encouraging my board to shift our contributions we earmarked for Eliot to her."

"I'm glad. How well do you know Diane?"

"Not much. We've met at regional conferences."

"Did Kerry introduce you?"

"She may have. I really don't remember. Why all the questions?"

She glanced away, taking a sip from her glass. "Someone mentioned you met while she was working a big campaign in Chicago years ago."

He shrugged. "In my job, I network all across the country. Hard to keep track."

"From the press clippings, you seemed to be pretty friendly. Can you think of anyone who wanted her dead?"

Craig ignored the hint. "I was told the cops thought it was an argument that got out of hand."

"Killing someone is quite an overreaction to an argument, don't you think? Must be someone with a real grudge."

"At this point, my bet is on Eliot. He admitted she was blackmailing him, and he sounded desperate to keep her claims a secret. It's a shame. He had a bright future." He attempted a sympathetic face.

"You really believe that?"

"Don't you?" Craig responded.

"I think the jury is still out. At least, I certainly hope so."

"News on the street, she had proof his grandfather killed his partner."

"Did Kerry tell you?"

"No, Ronnie and Pam."

She decided to change tracks. "My friendship might be skewing my outlook. When do you think you'll head south? I imagine your wife enjoys these trips."

His mouth made a little scrunch, and he reached for the throttle. "She grew up in Annapolis. We have a house there and one on the water in Savannah. She takes my daughter and her friends for much of the summer. I usually invite a few business connections along on my cruises," he said. "Good excuse for a write-off."

"Sounds like the good life. I've never seen South Carolina." She flashed him a little grin. "Your buddies like to party?"

"They'd better, or they don't get invited," he said, admiring her legs. "Want to take a little trip tonight? We could head to Baltimore's Inner Harbor for dinner. Be there in less than two hours." He raised his eyebrows. "Stay at the Four Seasons Hotel."

She gave him a sweet smile. "Until I figure out who killed Kerry, I'm sticking around here. I picked up the rest of Eliot and Kerry's files yesterday. I'm hoping to get through them by tomorrow."

His jaw tightened. "You've become quite the little amateur detective. I wish you'd take my advice. Someone might want to shut you down."

"Thanks for worrying. It's a chance I'll take. I have a thing about good people being accused of murder."

"If you're smart, you might want to rethink that. It's a dangerous habit."

"You may be right, but I'm not very smart."

His eyes met hers, and he reached for her knee. "Let me know when you're ready to let this all go. We could have some good times together."

Helen pulled away. "Why Craig, what would your wife say?" What a beast, she thought, repulsed. I wouldn't give you a second thought.

Craig's eyes narrowed, and with a sharp turn of the wheel, he headed back toward Port Anne and Lance Point Marina.

Chapter Twenty-Five

Alison called her the next morning.

"Hi, you sound upset." Helen turned up her Bluetooth and closed the little roadster's open roof. "I'm on my way into Safe Harbor."

"It's Pam. Ronnie found her lying on the bank of Little Elk Creek behind campaign headquarters. She's dead!"

"What? When did this happen?"

"No one knows. It's all over the news. Ronnie's at the office talking to the police."

"My God. How did she die?"

"We don't know yet. Can you talk to Joe? Ronnie's not picking up our calls."

"I'll call Joe right now." Helen dropped her cell onto her car seat and stared down the winding road from her house through the woods. She texted Joe, but the message didn't go through. Pressing on the pedal, she sped through the curves to reach a clearing two miles closer to town.

She dialed. His cell rang and went straight to voice mail. "Joe, Alison called me. What's happened with Pam? Call me." 'Either he's too busy, or he's still too angry to answer you,' commented Nora. 'Don't remind me,' Helen retorted.

* * *

Tammi was climbing out of her Prius at Safe Harbor as Helen swung in beside her. They walked up the office stone path together.

"Hear anything about Pam this morning?"

Tammi's eyes widened. "Should I have?"

"Alison just called me. She's dead."

"Good Lord! That's horrible. How?"

Helen's phone rang as they stepped onto the front porch. "It's Maggie Dyer." She picked up. "Maggie, what happened with Pam?" The reporter's response was terse. "Okay, thanks. Let me know what you find out."

"Well?"

"Diane's headquarters is blocked off. Joe's squad is questioning Ronnie. Maggie says all the local news is trying to get a statement. I swear this campaign, no matter the candidate, is doomed. The incumbent must be quietly ecstatic." She shoved her tote and laptop into Tammi's arms. "Take these. I'm going down the street."

She recognized Joe and Rick from a block away. Rick turned, pointing to a few bystanders craning their necks over a police barrier and motioning to keep back. A television van crept down the street until a uniformed deputy stepped onto the street and signaled him to turn around. The driver threw up his hands and shoved the vehicle into reverse.

She skirted along the curbs of the sidewalk and in between Calli's and a candle shop, deftly inching forward. She ducked her head and wedged her way toward Ronnie. He was sitting on the tailgate of an EMS vehicle with his hands on his head and a blanket wrapped around his shoulders. A black sedan pulled along a curve. Diane stepped out and hurried toward Joe and Rick. A deputy reached out to stop her until Joe recognized Diane and signaled her through. Joe took the candidate's arm and guided her to Ronnie. Glancing up, he saw Helen seated beside him.

"Helen, how did you get here?" He glowered.

"Alison called me. She wanted me to check on him." She offered a guileless look.

"Sit still and don't talk," he instructed. Diane sat down on the other side and reached over to pat Ronnie, shaking her head from side to side. She and Helen exchanged stricken glances.

Ronnie's eyes raised to meet theirs.

"When did you last see Pam," Joe started.

"About six last night," the young man said. "We've been setting up for Diane's campaign. Pam left here to go home and take a shower. She was meeting a couple of girlfriends at Uncorked on Rogues Point. I got a text about ten saying she was staying at a friend's house rather than driving home."

"How did you happen to find her?" Joe asked.

"This morning, I unlocked our back door on the creek side of the office. I made a couple trips into the building with some supplies. That's when I spotted a black jacket on the bank. I put down my last stack and walked over to the creek to take a look. I realized it was a body lying in the sand." He stumbled. "Pam. Face down, her hair wet. I couldn't believe what I was seeing."

"Did you touch her?" Joe was jotting down notes.

"Just enough to see her face. I put my hand on her back. I could tell she wasn't breathing. Her face was white, and her lips were blue." Ronnie took a deep breath, his shoulders quaking under the blanket. "How, how do you think she died?"

"Too early to tell. The coroner is on his way. Do you know the names of her friends she saw last night?"

"Rachel Hendricks. I'm not sure who else. She could tell you." Ronnie opened his phone and read off her phone number.

"Does she drink a lot when she's out with friends?"

Her fiancé gave a reluctant nod.

"Does she like to walk along the creek?"

"She'd go down there for a smoke break," Ronnie said.

The detective looked toward the wet grass along the stream's edge. "She may have slipped over the edge in the dark. Did you go directly home when you left here last night?"

"I stayed until about seven and then walked down to The Blue Crab to get a beer and a burger."

"Anyone there who can vouch for you?"

Ronnie ran his hands across his shaved head. "The bartender, Nate. I hung around, had another beer, and then left for home."

The detective studied his face. "Watch any television?"

"A Sixers game."

"Who were they playing?"

The young man hesitated. "Celtics?"

"What was the score?" Joe's face was deadpan.

Ronnie gave his question some thought. "Sixers won. I think 92-86. What happens next?"

"I need to talk to your boss. Detective Rick Lauer will escort you to the Sheriff's Office and take your official statement." Joe caught Rick's eye. "He'll decide when you can go home."

"Can I come to work? I'd rather keep busy." His voice broke.

"That's Detective Lauer's decision." Joe turned to Diane. "How did you hear about Pam?"

"I was getting ready to leave my house about eight-thirty this morning. One of your deputies called to tell me Ronnie found Pam in the creek behind headquarters. I jumped in the car and came right here."

"Diane, I have to ask you. Where were you last night?"

"I was with Ronnie and Pam and a few staffers until about five-thirty. I left for a dinner meeting," she said. "I got home about nine, nine-thirty. Undressed, then bed."

"Anyone with you?"

Diane gave him an amused look. "I live alone, Joe. Helen can tell you."

"Did you go straight to bed? Watch TV? Make a phone call?"

"Umm, no. I worked late. Time gets away from me."

"What were you working on?"

"A speech."

"Who is the speech for?"

She gritted her teeth. "This feels like an inquisition."

"Rather ask you here and now than down at the station." Joe's dark eyes didn't waver.

Diane's eyes roved over the curious bystanders and press gathered at the curb and nodded. "Of course. Thanks. It was for the Maryland State Library

Association."

"When did you stop working and go to bed?"

She hesitated. "About eleven thirty? Those speeches always take longer than you expect."

"Do you have any idea who could want to kill her? Anything to do with your campaign? She tick anyone off lately?"

Diane lowered her voice, leaning into Joe and Helen. "Pam was difficult. She tended to push around our staff. I reminded her last week they were volunteers, not hired help."

"Eliot gave her the same warning," Helen offered.

"Speak to Ronnie about her?" Joe asked.

"Yes. I told him he needed to either get her under control or let her go."

"I thought they were engaged," Helen said.

"They were, but he knew she was a liability. I told him he might have to make a choice between his career and her."

"How'd he take your advice?" asked Joe.

"He was upset, but he knew I was right."

"Lizzie told me Pam had a long history of carrying grudges," Helen added. "She liked to get even."

The detective scratched down a few more comments. "Diane, we'll need to ask you to work from home until my crime tech team goes over the office and surrounding area."

She gritted her teeth and turned to Helen. "I'll need your help to find a new location. I can't conduct campaign business from the county administration office. I'm beginning to think the Davies B&B may not be the only place that's haunted. The press will have a field day with this news. We'd be better off in a different building."

"I'll start a search today."

"Joe," Diane said. "Are you interviewing the incumbent's staff too?"

"Rick will. Two deaths connected to one campaign has upped the stakes."

"Can Helen and I claim a few of my files to take to my place? I've got meetings and deadlines."

"I can send you inside with a deputy. Give you ten minutes. I know your fingerprints will be all over the office." He looked at Helen. "Since you were there the past few days, we'll probably find yours."

"Lizzie was with me yesterday. You may find hers too."

Joe issued a long, resigned groan. "Count on the Morriseys to be where they don't belong."

"Here's my home address." Diane scratched it down on a business card. "Let me text Ronnie, so he knows where to find me when he's done. I want to help him with her funeral expenses."

Helen gave her friend a hug. "Don't worry. We'll get past this. Go pick out the files you need. I'll be right in to give you a hand."

A black coroner's van pulled up alongside the curb, and Helen spotted Ed, his medical bag in hand, climbing out. "Joe, can you call me later?" she asked.

"When I can." He turned and pointed the coroner toward a patch of creek bed between two buildings and the medics below. Yellow police tape was stretched around the perimeter. Joe followed him down the uneven bank to the water.

Helen saw Maggie Dyer's sandy hair among the reporters and a TV crew. Maggie flagged her over.

"Anything for me?" she asked.

"Nothing. The coroner is looking her over."

"Do you think she fell into the creek?"

"We'll find out soon. She'd been drinking. Rick Lauer took Ronnie into police headquarters to give a signed statement. Diane has to work from home until forensics finishes inside. I'm going to give her a hand loading her car."

"She's got to be upset."

"It's tough to keep a campaign on message when dead bodies keep getting in the way. It's what derailed Eliot."

Maggie gave her a little shrug, her reporter's face jaded. "Unless she can capitalize on getting sympathy votes. She's not dodging a grandfather with a tainted reputation."

Helen raised her brows at Maggie, turned, and trotted toward the building.

A deputy lifted the yellow tape across the front door. She dipped underneath and through the entrance.

Chapter Twenty-Six

It was only about five-thirty when she pulled into her driveway. Weary, Helen pulled out her keychain and reached for her front door. The door swung open with her pressure before she inserted the key into the lock.

That's odd. Did I forget to lock the house this morning? She turned the knob. "Lizzie? You home?" Silence. She stepped inside and dropped her bag on her foyer table. "Lizzie?" Watson and Trixie slowly crawled out of hiding. Watson issued a loud, long request for dinner. Helen kicked off her heels and wiggled her bare toes.

She stopped at her dining room table. Eliot's boxes from headquarters were dumped open, the files tumbled onto her carpet. She padded into the living room. All the books from her bookcase were tossed onto the floor, some with pages torn out. Two candleholders and all her picture frames were smashed on the floor. She started to pick them up. Pictures of the kids had been removed and torn in half. Her wedding picture with Andy was shredded. A shard of glass from a frame caught her right thumb and index finger. Ooh! She dropped the broken frames onto an empty shelf and sucked at her fingers. Standing in the middle of the room, she listened. The house was completely quiet. Not even the wind talked to her. This is when I could use a dog.

She pulled out her phone and tapped a shaky finger on Joe's direct dial. She spun around. What was the intruder looking for? In her bedroom, every drawer was pulled out. The clothes from her closet were on the floor and trampled. Her underwear was missing. Creepy.

In the bathroom, her cabinets were empty. 'If they were hoping for drugs, they picked the wrong house,' she said to her sleuths. 'Stay cool,' Jessica said. Joe hadn't answered. She texted him.

Call me! I've been robbed.

Ninety seconds later, her cell rang.

"Helen? Are you okay?"

"Yes." Her breath caught in her throat.

"Is anyone with you?"

"No. Lizzie's staying with me, but she's not home yet."

"You need to leave the house."

"Whoever they were, they're long gone."

"Was anything stolen?"

"It's weird. My underwear is gone. A lot of things smashed."

"I'm sending a car to check. I'm on my way. Sit outside on the deck and wait, okay?"

"Okay," she whispered.

In minutes, the sound of a police car wailed through the quiet of Osprey Point State Park.

"Mrs. Morrisey? It's Kent County Sheriff's Office," a voice called out.

"I'm here on the deck!"

A young, uniformed deputy and an older one climbed the deck stairs, guns drawn, eyes alert.

"Ma'am, stay here. We'll check the house. Have you been upstairs?"

"No. I waited for you."

The older one nodded, and they entered. She could hear them working room to room.

Another siren reverberated, and a car screeched to a halt in her drive.

"Helen?" Joe leaped onto the deck with Rocky at his heels and pulled her into his arms. She returned his grasp.

Her eyes welled. "I was fine until you arrived," she said shakily.

Joe lifted her chin and pushed her dark hair off her brow. "How do these things happen to you?" He kissed her forehead.

She gave a little laugh. "Lucky, I guess." Heavy feet trundled down the staircase.

Joe turned to the uniforms and walked them through the house again with Helen right behind. Every room on the first floor was turned upside down. Some of her pictures and paintings were trampled, lamps and tables cast onto their sides. The second floor was untouched.

"This wasn't a robbery," he said. "This was vindictive. A warning."

Helen trembled. "You're right. It's weird. My underwear and all my pajamas, gone. Even some shoes." She pointed to empty shoe slots. "Thank God I had my laptop with me."

"Jewelry?"

She kneeled down and pulled out a flat wooden case from under her bed. "It's not broken. They must not have seen it. Not that I have a lot that's valuable." She moved to her dresser. "Where's my mother's watch?" She dropped to her knees and pawed around the tossed clothes, bringing out a narrow black gift box with the name of a long-closed Philadelphia jewelry store imprinted in silver script. She opened the box and held up a delicate, narrow watch with tiny diamonds. "It's still here. Thank goodness."

"Looks old."

"My father gave it to my mother one Christmas. I was eleven. Before things got ugly. I always think of that Christmas. I was so happy he gave it to her." She sighed. "Not every marriage lasts."

"Mom!"

"It's Lizzy." She tucked her mother's watch into the box and pushed it into the top dresser drawer. "We're in here!"

Lizzie stepped into the bedroom. "I saw the police cars! What happened? Are you okay?" She reached for her mother.

"I'm perfectly fine. I'm grateful you weren't home before me."

Lizzie flashed a look at Joe over her mother's shoulder.

"I'll tell the deputies they can go."

The two women followed him, stepping between debris to the kitchen.

"What a mess." Lizzie opened the refrigerator and pulled out a bottle of Sauvignon Blanc. She reached for wine glasses. "Want one?"

"As Nora would say, make it a double."

Joe walked back inside, shedding his suit jacket. Helen handed him a Corona Light. He took a long swallow, his Glock and holster still on his hip, and his face glum.

Helen took her glass, shoved littered books and mementos off the couch and onto her coffee table, then collapsed. "Don't take off your shoes. There's glass everywhere."

Lizzie plopped down beside her. Her cell rang. "It's Shawn. Hi. I'm here with Mom and Joe. Someone trashed the house."... "We're fine. Want to talk to Joe? He's here."... "Okay, I'll tell her to call you in the morning."... "Thanks. Love you too."

Joe took a second slug of his beer.

"Shawn knows?" Helen asked.

"Of course, Shawn knows. I called him on the way through the park. I owe him that. We tell family when family's in danger."

"Humph," Helen folded her arms in protest.

"Well? Any idea who did this?" He scowled. "I'm sure you have an opinion."

Helen avoided his glare. "It's not like I asked for this to happen." She felt like a child being disciplined.

"Ah, huh."

Lizzie didn't say a word. Her eyes roved from one to the other.

"You've trampled on someone's toes. Who'd you talk to lately?"

"You mean other than you?"

"Don't get smart, Nancy Drew. What have you been doing since I was here two nights ago?"

She fidgeted in her seat.

Helen pulled her cell out of her pocket and scrolled through her calendar. "Thursday, I stopped at the historical society to talk to James Corcoran. I asked him how the county commissioners decided government contracts. He got a little testy." She scrunched her face. "He suggested we search in the Davies library for more information on Eliot's family."

Joe scowled. "Then what?"

"Lizzie and I went to Kayla's play for Tammi at the Opera House in Grace Harbor. Shawn met us. Diane was there and gave a nice welcome speech."

"You're stretching my patience. Obviously, Kayla's event was not a problem. Where else?"

"Lizzie and I worked with Eliot and Alison all last night. Shawn showed up about eight-thirty to help. We quit about eleven. I called to tell you we found a diary, but you never returned my call." She flashed him an indignant pout. "Shawn and Lizzie stayed overnight."

"Yesterday, which was Friday, Lizzie followed me into Port Anne. We stopped at Eliot's headquarters." She stumbled. "I mean, Diane's headquarters. Pam was there, glaring as usual."

Lizzie spoke up. "When I saw her, I realized I knew her from high school. She was always miserable. If she thought you crossed her, she never forgave you."

"She was annoyed we claimed the rest of Eliot and Kerry's personal files." Helen said.

"What did you do the rest of the day?"

"I went into the office. Made calls, some appointments. The usual work stuff. Walked in here, saw the mess, and called you."

He raised his eyebrows. "That's it? Nothing else? No personal calls? No stops? Look me in the eye. I'm a detective, remember? I sense a gap here somewhere."

"I called McFadden's Marina and scheduled a launch for *Persuasion* over the next couple days. I spoke with a lawyer friend. He offered to come down and help me bring *Persuasion* around to the house."

"Who called who?"

She stuck out her jaw. "Why is *that* relevant? I didn't ask you who you had lunch with yesterday, did I?" She glanced at Lizzie.

Her daughter rolled her eyes and stood up. "I need more wine." Helen jiggled her empty glass at her.

"Back to your afternoon. Talk to anyone about the Kerry Lightner case?"

"Craig Olsoff called me. He invited me along on a test drive for his Carver. I met him at McFadden's about three o'clock this afternoon, and we powered down to Osprey Point lighthouse."

Joe paced to her sliders, and back, his hands jammed in his pockets. "What did you talk about? Tick him off?"

"He was very pleasant. It's a beautiful boat." She smiled sweetly.

Lizzie couldn't contain herself another minute. "Mom, I know you. You asked him stuff. Admit it."

"Whose side are you on, daughter." Helen objected. "He's on our *Pro Con* list. I asked how well he knew Kerry and if he had any opinions on who killed her. Hinted that I'd seen pictures of him with her looking cozy. He said they only knew each other through conferences, which I still don't believe."

"Not surprising he'd be ticked off," Joe commented. "What else?"

"I told him I was digging through all Eliot and Kerry's records because I didn't believe Eliot killed her. I certainly didn't say anything that would drive Craig to this." She stood up and waved her arms around the room. "In fact, he wanted to take me for an overnight cruise."

"Mom, what did you say?"

Helen's green eyes flashed. "I said, no chance. I was out to find a killer, and he should invite his wife."

Joe chuckled. "In your usual abrasive Agatha Raisin way." He swigged the rest of his beer. "I need something stronger. A lot stronger."

Off the hot seat, Helen bounced up. "Lizzie, order a big pizza with everything. I'm taking a shower and then cleaning up this room."

They filled four big contractor-sized trash bags and stacked pictures and broken frames on top of her dining room table. Lizzie handed books to Joe, and he reloaded the living room bookcases. Helen swept up glass and vacuumed the first floor. Rocky, cordoned off on the deck, rejoined them. Watson and Agatha took their positions on the arm of a chair to listen in on their conversation.

"That's enough for tonight," she declared, flipping a Jane Marple mystery back and forth in her hands. "They destroyed my oldest copy of *Murder at the Vicarage*, the bastards." She looked up at Joe. "Any chance Dustin Wills did this? It seems like his kind of job."

"It does. Hired help." Joe glanced at his phone. "I've got to go into the station."

CHAPTER TWENTY-SIX

"Anything new on Pam?"

"Ed said she was drowned. Someone bludgeoned her with a river rock, then held her under the water. A lot of alcohol in her system. She was likely too drunk to know what was happening."

Lizzie closed her eyes. Helen covered her face. "If she texted Ronnie she was staying with a girlfriend, why was she found behind the office?"

"We're not sure she actually sent the text. We expedited a DNA request on her clothes and her phone. Her killer could have sent the text so Ronnie wouldn't come look for her." Stretching, Joe picked up his jacket, and Helen followed him out.

"I think I should leave Rocky here." He fondled the dog's gentle muzzle.

"Are you sure?"

"I'd feel better. I'll claim him in a day or two."

"I'll be in the office. I need to find a new headquarters for Diane. She's texted me twice."

He reached for the door.

"Before you go, I have an idea," she said.

"I'm too tired for your ideas." He breathed in with exaggerated patience. "What now?"

"I want to walk the woods around Captain's Watch." Helen reached down and patted his retriever, avoiding Joe's eyes. "In fact, maybe Rocky could help. Dogs sense things we miss."

Joe ran his hands through his hair as he mulled over her request. "Okay. We'll give it a try. You'll badger me until we do. I'll call you and set a time. In the meantime, go to work, straight to work. No wandering around town stirring people up. Where's Lizzie tomorrow?"

"She's staying with me for now. I'll explain later. She has a full day on air and won't be home until late."

"Good. I rather she not be here by herself."

"Do you mind if I bring Rocky into my office?"

He ran his hand over the dog's snout. His tail wagged. "No, he'll love the attention."

Helen turned to go up the stone walk. "Joe?"

He looked back, frustration all over his face.

"I'm sorry we argued. It's complicated."

"It's not complicated. You're complicated. We'll figure it out." He put his Explorer in reverse.

Chapter Twenty-Seven

"Who do we have here?" Chelsea Peet of Peet's Paws greeted Helen and Rocky. The little shop was bursting with dog and cat treats and toys. Dozens of collars and leashes of every color and type hung along one wall. Life jackets in every size hung near the entrance for all the boaters bringing their pets on board. Rocky's tail couldn't wag fast enough as he sniffed every shelf. He was like a kid in a candy store.

"He's not really mine. He's on loan from a police detective."

"Is he trained to help him?" Chelsea asked.

"He's trained to eat leftovers."

The red-headed shop owner kneeled down to stroke Rocky's face with two hands. A long cotton sweater scattered with embroidered cats and dogs reached her knees, covering her dark leggings. "I'm fascinated by how dogs can seek out drugs and people. Their commitment to their task is amazing."

"He's spending the day in my office. Any suggestions for treats? He'll deserve them after listening to me blather on the phone. I should get a water bowl too. If he's good, I may ask to borrow him on a regular basis."

The two women perused the room. Helen settled on a package of natural dog chews and a blue bowl inscribed 'work day is play day' along the rim. She spotted a section for cats, picked out two bowls with fish on the bottom, and set them on the counter. "I can't come home without presents for Watson and Trixie too."

* * *

Rocky was a big hit at Safe Harbor. It wasn't unusual for agents to bring their dogs if they weren't meeting clients. He paraded up and down the aisles and in and out of cubicles making new friends. Tammi filled his bowl with water, and they settled him in next to Helen's desk.

"You're looking kind of casual," Tammi observed.

Helen looked down at her jeans and sneakers. "I talked Joe into meeting me later today. We're going to check out the woods near Captain's Watch."

"What in the world do you think you'll find out there?"

"I really don't know. There's an abandoned road on the next property. It's not far from the pool house and leads to the water. He's humoring me by coming along."

It was close to one o'clock before Joe rang.

"I'm finishing up more interviews along Water Street. A neighbor noticed Pam pull up about ten p.m. and go into the building. They went to bed and didn't notice her leave, which we know never happened. At least our witness nails down her arrival. How's Rocky?"

"A darling. I'm thinking of keeping him."

"Oh? While you're considering it, I can stop by Safe Harbor and pick you up about three."

"Any chance you could bring a personal item from Pam for Rocky to sniff?"

"I'll find something. Don't be disappointed if he doesn't help. He's not trained for searches. He's trained for soft beds and chasing rabbits. See you later."

* * *

The wooden directional sign for Captain's Watch was straight ahead. Someone had cleaned off the graffiti.

"Slow down," Helen said. "Take this little dirt road right before the sign. I'm glad we have your Explorer. My Mini could never climb over these ruts."

Joe turned off and crawled along the route. Dips in the dirt threw them back and forth in their seats. Rocky sat behind them with his nose pressed through the open rear window.

224

"I walked this lane when Eliot and I were looking for land survey markers," Helen said. "James Corcoran came along with us. He was a big help. It brings you around to the town side of Eliot's property and circles fairly close to his docks and the pool house."

"You think Kerry's killer could have approached the pool house from this direction?"

"Maybe."

"It may seem too easy an answer to think Pam and Dustin may have been working together," Joe said.

"Dustin is a natural born liar, and Pam's spent her life finding reasons to feel cheated. They could have made the perfect, despicable combination. Jane Marple would say she finds the most likely people behaving exactly as she would have expected."

"Your Jane can be very annoying." Joe grimaced, the steering wheel jerking in his hands.

"That's because she's usually right." Helen let out a yipe as she gripped the handrail above her head. "You need to read *Murder Most Foul*. Jane told the inspector that while it may irritate him, sometimes women have superior minds, and detectives need to accept it."

Joe groaned. "How much longer?"

"Just around this bend. There's a tiny clearing."

They pulled up. Helen grabbed her baseball cap. Joe handed her a pair of heavy gloves. Pointing, she led the way. Rocky, delighted to be part of their adventure, bounded ahead.

"You're loving this, aren't you?" Joe said.

"Are you talking to Rocky or me?" she asked, ducking a briar branch. She flashed a grin. "You must admit, this is right up Nancy's alley. Or Trixie Belden's. Ever read *The Gatehouse Mystery*?"

"I can't say I have."

"I must have read that book ten times. You had a neglected childhood."

"Don't tell my mother."

"I've never met your mother or your sisters."

"Meeting them could be dangerous."

"Here's candy wrappers and two beer cans." She picked up a piece of fabric. "Could someone have torn their jacket on these sticker bushes?"

"More likely a kid rolling around in the woods with his girlfriend."

Helen pulled the tiny patch and the wrappers and tucked them into her pocket. "You're right." She stopped and picked up a shiny piece of gum wrapper. "You sure you don't want to run a DNA test?"

"If I start bringing in trash, forensics will want to kill me. Consider them mementos. Are we almost near the property line?"

She peered through the brush. "It's easier to see it today than when we were here months ago. Back then, the pool house was a dark gray, and the roof was brown."

Another hundred yards, and they reached the structure from the rear. Joe jiggled the back door. "Locked, of course. It was locked from the outside the night Kerry died. We never did find the key."

Helen pulled her left hand from her pocket and jiggled a set of keys in the air. "How about these?" She couldn't help but act triumphant. Alison gave me a set earlier this week." They unlocked the door and stepped inside.

The charming pool house wasn't quite so charming today. Dust from forensics covered the bluestone floor and every item hanging on the walls. A streak of blood stains marked where Kerry had fallen. The windows were locked tight, and the room smelled damp.

Helen made a sad face. "I loved this little building. I was so excited about restoring it." She poked along the edges of the room. "Do you see these original shelves and this drop-down desk? I never realized Spencer and Isaac used this for their office until Henry told us. I assumed Spencer used it for storing marine equipment years ago. It was Alison who made this into a changing room for the pool."

"It's less than a hundred feet from the water. Their workers probably arrived by boat years ago."

Rocky nosed his way around the perimeter. He snorted at the dust.

"Let's go," she urged. "I want to look around outside before the sun starts to drop. These woods are dark even in bright sunshine."

Joe hesitated as he started to lock up.

"Follow me." Helen treaded up a slight rise in the brush. "When we were here during the property inspection, there was a fair amount of trash scattered around. With the house vacant for years, the pool house was a favorite hang-out for teenagers." She tramped a few steps farther. "When Eliot and I came, we wanted to see inside the pool house, but we'd forgotten a key. This little hill gave us enough height to look through the pool house windows." She stopped. "Take a look."

Joe followed her. "Weren't the windows replaced?"

"Yes. Which means someone on this rise could see inside even more easily. They're new, and they're clean. It's a clear view inside."

"And yet, no one inside would ever spot them hiding in the woods."

Helen wrinkled her forehead. "Exactly." Shoulder to shoulder, they peered into the windows.

"Can I kiss you now?"

"Maybe later. I'm concentrating on a mystery."

"I'm hoping that won't be written on your tombstone."

"Very funny. Let's not discuss my tombstone just yet. I want to walk in a circle from where we're standing."

Together, they moved in concentric circles, Joe with his Maglite and Helen with her cell light. Reaching the broken branches of their path to the pool house, they stopped.

"I know what you're thinking."

Helen shoved her hair under her hat. "Let's walk this area one more time. If someone was here watching, they had a long wait. I'm a lifelong Girl Scout anti-litter freak, but plenty of people don't give any thought to 'leave nothing behind.'"

"Let's start from here and work toward the rise at the window." Joe headed for the waterside and Helen deeper toward the east and the woods.

The light was disappearing between the trees. "Joe! I found something!"

He strode through the brush.

"Three cigarette butts!" Her eyes were alight.

Joe stared down at her feet. "I'll be dammed." Reaching into his pockets, he pulled out two plastic gloves and kneeled. Ends of white cigarette papers poked out from under the leaves and trampled grass. He dropped them into a baggie. "Forensics would never have found these. We're at least twenty-five feet from the building. "They could be Dustin's. Kerry was paying him to creep around the property and cast spooky lights."

"My bet, these are Pam's and why she was killed." Helen's eyes glimmered in the dusk. "The killer found out she'd been watching."

Chapter Twenty-Eight

Helen's cell sounded two text notices as she stood in line at Jean's Coffee Pot the following morning. She handed Jean change with one hand while checking her phone with the other. She almost dropped the hot coffee when she saw Joe's message. A second message from Alison and Sarah was below.

"Oh, my God!"

"What's wrong?" Jean shoved a napkin across the counter.

"It's Joe." Helen held up her phone screen to Jean.

Eliot Davies arrested this morning for the murder of Kerry Lightner and Pam Breen. More evidence in. Couldn't get D.A.'s office to delay. Know this isn't good news.

She texted, **thanks for telling me.** She added a sad face.

"Sounds like he'll be charged for Kerry's murder next," Jean replied.

"So far I've been useless."

"You're too hard on yourself."

"Here's a text from Alison and Sarah."

Eliot arrested. Ben with him. Frantic.

"I better run."

* * *

"Tammi? I'm on my way into the office."

"Did you see the news? Eliot's been arrested."

"I just got a text from Joe. I want to try to catch Ben Horowitz at the

Sheriff's Office, and I've got Rocky with me. Can I drop him off with you?"

"Of course. He can run the sales meeting this morning."

"Probably better than anyone else."

* * *

Ben didn't pick up her call. She texted.

Can we meet?

Yes. Anywhere nearby we can eat?

Prime and Claw? Right on Water Street across from Calli's.

See you there at one.

* * *

Rocky got a big greeting as they entered Safe Harbor.

"Hi, Rocky!" Tammi stroked his head and snuck him a biscuit. His tail swished in thanks.

"I can't meet with Ben until one, which gives me time to check on Alison and Sarah."

Helen dropped her belongings on her desk, settled Rocky into the corner, and dialed her phone. "Alison? What can you tell me?"

"It's a disaster," Alison cried. "Ben's with him now. He's been charged and gets arraigned before a judge tomorrow. I won't be able to talk to him until later this afternoon. We don't know what to do."

"I wish I did. I took Joe out to the woods beyond your property yesterday afternoon. We think Pam was watching the pool house when Kerry was killed. Ben is meeting me for lunch in town. Do you want to come?"

"No, I trust you. We don't need more press following my mother and me around town."

"I know this is frightening. Try to stay calm. Call you later." Helen opened her desk drawer and pulled out a Twizzler. "Don't give me such a sad face," she said to Rocky. "I eat when I'm nervous, and you can't eat licorice." He set his face down between his paws and glowered at her.

230

She looked up at a tap on her doorway. A tiny woman with a smart grey haircut and round tortoise-framed glasses grinned. "Do you mind a visitor?"

"Olivia!" Helen swallowed, trying to regroup. "How nice to see you! Why are you here?" She gave the older woman a big hug.

"I was across the street at Silver and Gold to get a gift and thought I'd stop by and say hello."

"I'm so glad you caught me. I have an appointment at one down the street. Come in for a few minutes." She led the former principal to a seat.

"I brought some pictures of my new digs," Olivia said, pulling out her phone from an enormous tapestry-fabric handbag.

Olivia was the only woman approaching eighty Helen knew who would use the word 'digs.' "Your unit looks beautiful. Are you enjoying the community?"

"Love it. I'm so glad you encouraged me."

"It wasn't hard. You were ready for a change." Helen hesitated. "I have a question for you. Do you remember a student by the name of Pam Breen? She graduated with Lizzie and Shawn."

Olivia frowned. "She's the same Pam the police found in a creek yesterday, isn't she?"

"You heard the news."

"I knew immediately she was Pam from our high school. Terrible. Don't tell me you're involved with her."

"Not by choice. She was working with Ronnie Mann at Eliot Davies' headquarters. I assume you know Eliot had to bow out of his state senate race when his campaign manager was killed."

"I've been following the news. I never knew Eliot. His family didn't live in Port Anne when he was in high school. I know Alison. She's lovely. I've known her mother, Sarah, for years and years."

"I'm afraid he's been arrested this morning for killing Pam, and I think a charge for killing Kerry is coming. I'm making slow progress in coming up with someone else with a motive. What do you know about her?"

Olivia lowered her voice. "Pam was difficult. Her father was gone, and her mother did her best. We even assigned her one-on-one counseling. She seemed determined to get into trouble. I was relieved when she graduated. It was an uphill battle."

"No siblings? Anyone she traveled around with?"

"I'd run across her working in different shops in town. Then I heard she was dating Ronnie. I was glad. He has ambition."

"I think he does. He's working for Diane Gleason now. She's replaced Eliot in the race. Any possibility he could have killed her?"

She drew her eyebrows together. "I'd hate to think so, although Pam was good at fueling an argument, and Ronnie had a short fuse. He put himself through the University of Delaware, which wasn't easy. Did you know he has an older sister with M.S.? He's taken care of her for years." She glanced down at her wrist. "You'll miss your one o'clock."

"Thanks for reminding me." Helen stood up. "I'll walk out with you."

"I hope you'll be careful. How is your young man, the detective?"

Helen broke into a huge smile. "I'll tell him you called him a young man. Let's say we get along better when I'm not intruding in his cases. I'm also too slow in the romance department."

"You have a lot of years ahead of you." Olivia gave her the unwavering eye she'd use with recalcitrant students. "Don't make them lonely ones. I made that mistake." She gave Helen a kiss on the cheek and unlocked her Subaru.

"I'll keep your advice in mind." Helen turned. Olivia suddenly called out.

"Helen! Do you know Pam's related to Dustin Wills?"

"I'm sorry?" She felt slapped.

"Dustin is trouble."

* * *

Ben Horowitz was easy to pick out. Short, with thick dark hair, round wire-framed glasses, and the only man in Prime and Claw wearing a tie among all the t-shirts at the bar. He stood up to greet her.

"Good to see you."

"Hi, Ben. Thanks so much for meeting me. How's Eliot?" She signaled the bartender for a vodka tonic.

His eyes clouded. "Not good." He looked down the bar. "Let's find a quiet table."

They followed a host into the main room and requested a table in the far corner.

"I would have suggested meeting at your office, but I haven't eaten since last night. I got a call from Alison about five am and was in the car by five-thirty." He looked down at the menu. "I assume since this place is called Prime and Claw, I should order beef or crab cakes." Their server hustled off to the kitchen with their order.

"What do they have on Eliot?"

"A lot. Forensics found his DNA on Pam's jacket and his fingerprints on her phone."

"Oh, God."

"Nothing under her fingernails. She was hit from behind with a river rock and fell face forward. Her killer rolled her down into the stream and held her under the water until she drowned. She was definitely intoxicated and didn't put up a fight."

"Anything on her cell?"

"Pam's and Ronnie's, which, since they live together, doesn't surprise anyone. And Eliot's. No sign of any footprints. It's been dry, so the ground was hard."

"Couldn't she have picked up Eliot's DNA in his office?"

Ben munched on an onion ring. "She might have, although he hasn't been there in weeks. Other than her boyfriend, Ronnie, there wasn't any other DNA on her body. They also ran tests on those cigarette butts you found outside the pool house. They were hers."

"So she was there watching when Kerry was killed," Helen said.

"Which gave the cops more reason to suspect Eliot."

"I hurt him more than helped." She cringed. "What did Eliot say?"

"He denies everything, of course. Ready for this? McAlister found the contractor who finished painting the rear door on the pool house late Sunday. Eliot's print was on top of theirs."

"That's ridiculous. Eliot's the owner. He was probably looking over the job."

"When McAlister took his original statement the night Kerry died, Eliot denied walking around the building. Said he was too busy getting ready for the Sunday grand opening. He tried to change his story this morning but lost any credibility." He swallowed the last of his beer. "When Shawn asked me to take this case, he convinced me his friend couldn't be a killer."

"It's circumstantial."

"This much circumstantial evidence has tipped the scales. Eliot's retracted and changed his statements too many times." Ben tapped his fingers on the table. "Look, you're not the only fan who reads detective stories. Plenty of people get convicted on circumstantial evidence with a lot less. I read criminal cases for a living."

The restaurant's lunch crowd was getting more boisterous, and they weren't talking about murder. She turned again to Ben. "Did you know someone trashed my house two nights ago? It certainly wasn't Eliot."

"That's true. McAllister told me. On the other hand, your reputation for getting involved with criminal cases has spread. Not everyone's a fan. I'm sure there's a faction out there who would much rather you stick to real estate."

"If I told you I think Kerry Lightner was having a long-term affair with the CEO of Olsoff Marine Technology, would you believe me?"

"Should I care who she was sleeping with? That doesn't make either of them criminals."

"Hear me out." She took a deep breath. "Kerry was a pro at extorting money wherever she went. She accused an innocent travel agent at Howard Travel of stealing trip deposits in order to get herself a free luxury cruise. Lucky for Sarah Howard, the employee refused."

"Sounds like a chump change swindle." He chewed on his sandwich.

"She paid a local small-time con man to haunt the Davies B&B and stir up old rumors about Isaac. They even made the local papers. It worked. Eliot felt the pressure and paid her to keep quiet."

"According to your detective, she had proof Spencer and Isaac took bribes that helped companies keep poisoning the bay. Do I really think Eliot killed her to keep quiet? No, but the fact that he was out of money and couldn't keep paying her off makes him look bad. Very bad."

Helen shook her head. "Kerry's first job was with Olsoff. Later, she left to work political campaigns. I think she influenced politicians into helping OMT win contracts."

Ben leaned across the table, his voice a whisper. "Where's your proof?"

"Why would Kerry want to manage a campaign in little Kent County, Maryland? I'll tell you why. Every time she helped Craig win another contract, she got a nice big chunk."

"We're back to who killed her? Eliot's put himself in a hole. My job will be to prove state's evidence is not enough."

The attorney flagged their server. "We need our check, please." He studied Helen. "I know you like to defend people, and, God help me, if I ever need a friend as much as the Davies, I hope I have someone like you."

"I sense a big 'but.'"

"Did Spencer kill his partner? We may never know. Eliot was a fool not to contact the police the first time Kerry tried to extort money from him. If he had, she might be alive today, and he'd be running for office. But unless you can prove Craig was paying Kerry for getting him contracts, we're a long, long way from proving Eliot innocent."

"Darn it, Ben. You sound like a lawyer. I feel like I'm talking to my son."

He studied her. "I know. It's what we get paid for. I'm guessing your son would rather you stop your detecting, and I don't blame him. He loves you. As much as McAlister is a professional, I know he cares about you too. He wants you to stop."

She held up her palms in protest.

"Unfortunately, I'm selfish," Ben continued. "I'm hoping you keep on digging for the sake of my client. If this con is as big as you think, you're in real danger. Trashing your place is nothing. Next time, someone might burn down your house with you trapped inside. Be careful. Be very, very careful."

Ben stood up, covered her hands for a second, then headed towards the door.

* * *

Too exhausted to think, she sat in her car in front of Safe Harbor. What is happening? She locked her car and ran inside to pick up Rocky. He greeted her with a doggie grin and his paws on her chest.

"Unless you need me, I'll take this guy home and try to clean up my bedroom."

Tammi waved long purple-pink fingernails. "I've got this." Her phone rang, and she reached for it. She glanced up. "You look like you've lost your best friend. You okay?"

Helen nodded. "Let's go, boy."

He hopped into the front seat of her roadster. Helen opened the roof and the side window and watched him joyfully lean on the door.

They wound slowly along Osprey Point Road. She'd decided to take him for a run out to the lighthouse once they got home. They both needed the exercise. Six miles later, she nosed the little blue coupe around a sharp bend, passing old Lark's Church on the hillside. Half a mile later, she screeched to a halt and made a one-hundred-and-eighty-degree turn. She downshifted into the church driveway and up its steep hill.

"Come on, Rocky. Let's take a little walk."

He gleefully jumped out of the car and waited for her to clip on his leash. On the top of the grassy knoll, they reached the tiny cemetery. Headstones, some of them sunken and tilted, with names worn by the years, looked much like those at St. Cecilia's. Former slaves, landowners, and Civil War veterans all gathered on the same hill.

Helen stood at the crest and gazed down along the fields rolling toward the Chesapeake. The sun was bright, gracing the water with promises of warmer weather.

She inhaled. "Come, come." She walked to the far north corner of the graveyard and stopped to read a neat granite headstone with flowers carved into the surface. "This is my mother, Rocky. I miss her." A few steps farther, she kneeled down and rubbed her hands over the engraved name *Andrew Morrisey, Beloved Husband and Father*, stroking the letters. The Golden sat, turned his head to the side, and swished his tail across the grass. "No, my father isn't here. I don't know where he's buried."

Helen brushed the tears off her cheeks. "Let's go home. We've got work to do."

* * *

Lizzie walked in a little after ten. Helen had left three calls for Joe. No answer. She was sitting on the living room floor in her pajamas with stacks of yellow file folders, printouts, and sticky notes surrounding her. Trixie was perched on an armchair. Watson was curled up on a cushion. Rocky greeted her at the door.

"Whew! What a day." She tossed her stage clothes and makeup bag at the bottom of the stairs and threw herself on the couch. "What are you doing?"

"I cleaned up my bedroom, then started on Kerry and Eliot's files. I'm done." Her mother rubbed her eyes.

"Anything?"

"Utter waste of time. Couple articles on marine pilots and local scams."

"Did you eat? I'm starving." Lizzie dug around in her mother's freezer and pulled out a carton of vanilla ice cream. "Where else can you look?"

"Haven't a clue. I'll take Rocky for a walk down to the dock. What's happening with you and Jason?"

"Shawn's coming next weekend to help me clean out," said Lizzie, rinsing out her dish.

"I wish I could fix this for you."

"Mom, you can't fix everything. When are you going to accept it?"

"Maybe never. I have to admit, I do like having you home."

Three in the morning, Helen roamed the house again. Rocky lifted his head, blinked, and went back to sleep next to the fireplace.

Agatha whispered. 'You should try one of those online sleep apps.' 'Way ahead of you,' Helen replied. 'Six million subscribers, and they never work for me. Since when have you given up on a case, by the way? If you don't have a suggestion, keep quiet.'

Jane spoke up. 'Start over. I told you from the very beginning the most unlikely people can do the most surprising things. Are you listening?'

Helen's eyes roved over her bookcases. One by one, she started pulling out the Nancy Drews and returning them into their numbered order. Next, the Agatha Raisins and Nora Charles. It took another half hour to arrange the Jane Marples and Jessica Fletchers. Tomorrow night, I sort through my male detectives, starting with Jesse Stone, she thought. She turned off the last of the lights, then hesitated before running her hands across the Nancy Drews.

She pulled out *The Secret in the Old Attic* and tucked the book under her arm.

Chapter Twenty-Nine

E arly the next morning, Lizzie left for ShopTV before she was awake. A note next to the coffeemaker said she was meeting a friend for dinner and staying with her overnight.

Her cell rang. Shawn. "Good morning. Surprised to hear from you so early."

"I'm checking in on you. Have you heard from Joe?"

"Not yet. I did meet with Ben. Arraignment is this morning." Her voice broke.

"This is out of your hands. Give Ben some time. He's a great criminal attorney." Shawn hung up.

Her phone rang again. "Joe?"

"Hi. I'm sorry I couldn't call you last night. Haven't had a minute," he said.

"It's okay. I understand."

"How's Rocky?"

She smiled. "He's next to me now, looking for breakfast."

"I'm sorry about the news."

"I knew it was coming," she gulped. "Any more on Ronnie or Craig?"

Joe sighed. "The Sixers won the night Pam was killed, but contrary to Ronnie's statement, the score wasn't even close. The game was a blowout. I did check out Ronnie's sister. She does have M.S. Probably why he's driving around in an old car."

"Are you considering him a strong suspect?" Helen counted on her fingers. "One, he lost his job to Kerry. Two, he had access to contributions coming into Eliot's campaign and he buddied up to Craig Olsoff. Three, he knew

Captain's Watch, and it's floorplan because he and Eliot worked from that house until their office headquarters opened in Port Anne. Four, he has a degree in finance."

"How do you know?"

"I googled it. Now, you tell me he has a sick sister. Another reason why he could have gone ballistic with Kerry. He needed the better-paying job." Helen went silent.

Joe sighed. "We'll talk to him again, but I don't have anything at either murder scene to incriminate him."

"Craig?"

"Lives high, but nothing at either scene."

"I have another idea. It's a little outlandish, but it could be worthwhile."

"Helen, no."

"Listen, and don't get mad. Have you ever used a canine unit for a search?" She waited. "Joe?"

"Yes. Once for a kidnapping. Once for a missing cop. Why?"

"From what I've read, trained canines can scent a body through concrete. Is that true?"

"Yesss."

"We need a trained dog to search the pool house." She braced herself for his reaction.

"What in the world are you talking about? Why?"

"Kerry's murder has to be linked to her blackmailing Eliot for his grandfather's crimes. Her threats of exposure were based upon what happened to Isaac. Whether Spencer really killed him."

"Helen, I am up to my eyeballs with these two murders. I don't care about a man who's been missing for sixty years."

"Someone met Kerry at the pool house and killed her. Someone so afraid Pam saw them that night they killed her too. Maybe Pam approached them for money."

"We know Eliot was determined to protect his reputation and save his campaign. She blackmailed him, and he retaliated. We've got motive, opportunity, and physical evidence I can't ignore. Sometimes, it's not that

240

complicated."

"Joe, Kerry was an expert at working swindles. A master at sucking in people. Isn't arresting the right person the most important?"

"Of course it is," he retorted. "You think searching the pool house with a trained dog will provide a different answer?"

She cleared her throat. "I don't know. It's a flip of a coin. But Isaac's death still needs to be solved. This is our chance."

"Sorry. I'm not doing it. I don't care enough."

"Since when don't cops care about a cold case?"

"Not this cop."

* * *

Helen dialed Alison. "Hi, could I stay with you tonight?"

"Of course, but why?"

"This may sound strange, but I want to stay in Kerry's bedroom. Are you alone tonight?"

"Mom is staying with me. You're welcome to stay too."

"See you about six or so." She tossed a pair of jeans, sneakers, and a sweatshirt, along with her PJs in an overnight bag. An hour later, Helen was in her office.

* * *

"You've got a visitor," Tammi said, smiling.

"Knock, knock," Diane announced. "Can I interrupt?"

"Hello! I wasn't expecting you this morning." Helen came around her desk and gave her a hug. "What brings you here? Come sit down."

Diane settled into a chair.

Helen raised her eyebrows. "I see you're wearing your signature look. I wish you'd teach me how to tie a scarf. Mine always turn into a big messy lump."

Diane laughed. "I don't have your legs or Tammi's earring selection. How is Alison? I tried to call Sarah, but she didn't pick up. I wish I could help them more. It's awkward now that I'm running for senate."

"If you rehired Ronnie, I'm guessing you don't think he was involved."

"I don't know why he would be."

"His girlfriend could have driven him to get rid of Kerry. She was known for opening old wounds."

"Finding a new manager takes time. Right now, I don't have time to consider my options."

"Keep an eye on him. By the way, I talked with James Corcoran. He got very prickly when I questioned how the county awards contracts. Could he have any connection with Craig Olsoff and their testing?"

Diane shrugged. "James has a lot of influence with who gets grants. He likes to choose his favorite causes and connections. Don't forget, he paved the way for the Davies' restoration loan. Could they have offered him money to smooth their application process?"

"Are you suggesting James might accept bribes?" Helen frowned.

"Who knows? James likes his county fiefdom. But Sarah mortgaged her travel agency for them, and Eliot had to find funds to initiate his campaign. They're in over their heads. Kerry's demands for money to keep quiet could have been the tipping point."

Helen rubbed her temples. "So confusing." Her cell binged. "Eliot was charged this morning for Kerry and Pam's deaths, no bail." She blinked back tears.

"Heartbreaking. We think we know someone." Diane grimaced. "Remember, his attorney is paid to hide his client's misdeeds. I've got to hand it to you. You did all you could."

Helen nodded and cleared her throat.

"I hate to change the subject, but I thought we could narrow down your property suggestions for a few minutes. The landlord wants me out."

"Of course. I lent my laptop to another agent for the day. We could use Tammi's if you want."

"I just came from another meeting. Use mine. The search you sent me is open." Diane set her laptop in front of Helen, and they scrolled through the photos and information.

Diane's phone rang. "I have to take this." She picked it up and stepped outside.

Helen continued to build their list. A document tab titled 'State Library Speech' sat next to hers, dated today. She jerked to a stop. Is this the speech Diane claimed she wrote the night Pam died? Quickly, Helen opened Diane's Microsoft file folders. There were no previous versions of that speech.

Helen's stomach made a flip-flop. Desperately, she scrolled up and down. Nothing. She swallowed. How could that be?

"I'm back," Diane announced. "Did you decide which properties we should consider?"

Helen worked long after Diane left her office, struggling to concentrate on clients and not Diane's missing speech. A text popped up from Joe.

Meet me at the pool house today at four. I've notified Alison we're coming. Happy birthday and Merry Christmas.

"Step at a time," she said out loud. "Step at a time."

* * *

She pulled into the B&B's parking area at five of four. Two marked police cars, Joe's Explorer, a white van labeled 'K-9 Unit,' and another unmarked car, were lined up in a row.

Helen gulped. If this doesn't pay off, Joe will never speak to me. 'Love and justice don't always meet,' commented Jessica. 'Must you be so practical?' complained Helen.

Two uniformed deputies, one with a handsome German Shepard and the other with a long-eared bloodhound, stood at the entrance of the pool house. Joe was clenching his jaw. Rick gave a cursory nod and unlocked the cordoned-off pool house, gesturing them all inside.

The two handlers unhooked the leashes from the dogs' collars and let them wander. No one moved an inch. No one spoke. The canines circled along the perimeter, out the rear door, around the building, and back into the room through the front. Their intelligent eyes looked up at their deputies and returned to sit at their feet.

Joe stood to the side, his hands in his pockets, jiggling his keys. "Thank you. We appreciate your help."

The dogs circled around the blood stains.

"I'd expect them to react to our victim," Joe said. "She was removed two weeks ago."

One of the uniforms raised his hands. "Let's give them a little more time."

The bloodhound pawed over the floor before lifting his baleful eyes to his trainer. The deputy walked forward, leashing him up, and led him toward the door. The dog turned around and tugged on his lead, refusing to leave.

"He senses something. He's talking to me," said one handler. The group didn't move while the dog wound around the center of the room and began to whine. He pawed at the same spot on the floor. "We need to break through this concrete."

"Are you sure?" Rick asked in disbelief.

"I know my partner. He's trained to find cadavers forty feet underground. He's never been wrong."

Joe and Rick exchanged incredulous glances. "I'll call the head of County Works," Joe said. "We'll need a crew with jackhammers."

"I'll track down Ed at the Coroner's Office."

* * *

Ed paced along the edge of the broken floor as his forensic team cordoned off the area. Two jackhammers broke through the thin sheet of new bluestone then into old concrete by six pm. Two county members dug through a layer of dirt underneath. The forensic team took over. A skull, chest, and femur bones slowly appeared.

Helen breathed out loud. "It has to be Isaac."

The sun was melting into the bay as forensics finished extricating the body, leaving a deep hole in the shape of a grave. Silently, Joe walked Helen to her car as the coroner's van pulled away down the drive.

He rubbed his eyes. "You realize this doesn't change Eliot's charges."

"I know." Her face was pale in the fading light. "Rocky is inside with Alison. I'll go get him." Joe waited. She returned with a happy dog.

"Thanks." Helen handed Joe the leash and gave him a kiss. "I know you went out on a limb to arrange all this."

He kissed her back. "Your instincts were right. Call you tomorrow." He climbed into his car, then lowered his window. "Rick ordered another review of Kerry's financials. We put in a request to get access to Olsoff's. Do me a favor. Keep your mouth shut. No one is to know about this until I say so." Helen nodded.

After sharing dinner with Alison and Sarah, Helen crawled into Kerry's bed. It had not been a celebratory evening.

Diane called her. "Where are you? On your deck?"

"I wish. Believe it or not, I'm staying overnight with Alison in the guest room Kerry used."

"What in the world for?"

Helen chuckled. "I decided I needed to check out her room one more time. I wish I were psychic and could speak to the dead. After all, this house is supposed to be haunted."

"Is your Detection Club with you?" Diane asked.

"They're keeping me company."

"Can you meet me at my house tomorrow at ten?"

"Sure. See you there."

"Thanks. Get some sleep." Diane hung up.

Helen sipped a glass of water on the bed table. She lay in the quiet, listening to the waves hitting the docks far below.

Hours later, she sat up and felt around for her glass. The moon floated across the unfamiliar room, reflecting on the high plaster ceiling. She threw back her covers, pulled on her sweater and jeans, and reached in the dark for her sneakers. She pocketed her phone. Gently, she turned the knob on the bedroom door and peeked down the hall.

Chapter Thirty

The only sound from the house was the grandfather clock in the front hall, its pendulum a reassuring steady click. The chime began to count off the hour. It struck twelve. She tip-toed up to the third floor, opened the door to the attic, and slowly closed it behind her. She climbed up the narrow stairs to the attic. Skirting across, she climbed the last few steps to the widow's watch and peered out. The wind was picking up, lifting the dark water and creating white streaks as waves crested, rolling toward shore. Not a boat was in sight.

Helen closed her eyes, sensing the last time she was here with Joe. The crash of china and Alison's scream resounded inside her head. They'd charged down three flights of stairs, across the lawn, and out to the pool house. Alison, with her hands and shirt covered in blood, Kerry at her feet. Slowly, she mentally roved across the faces of the shocked guests standing at the edge of the pool. She tried to recall them all one by one.

She saw Diane, Calli, and a few others leave the party just before she and Joe went upstairs to the widow's watch. Shawn, Lizzie, and Lacey ran from the house when Alison screamed. She pictured Eliot and Sarah in the doorway, the pool lights behind them. The old man with the odd clothes and the overdressed woman with the Vuitton handbag were in the crowd. Craig Olsoff stood next to James Corcoran, a drink in his hand. We know Pam was in the woods smoking a cigarette. Owen was milling about with a few other business owners. Dustin never attended. Ronnie, where was he?

She opened her eyes and stared down at the pool house. A flicker of light between the building and the pool picked up the reflection of the yellow Do

Not Cross police tape. It went out.

Helen pressed her hands against the window glass. I'm tired, and I'm imagining things. I'm going back to bed.

She skirted along the stair edges, trying to avoid squeaking antique floorboards. At the second-floor landing, she listened again to the pendulum below. Tick, tick, tick, tick. 'You have to check out that light,' Nancy urged.

* * *

Alison and Sarah's rooms were quiet. She ducked into her room, grabbed her keys to the house, and continued down the stairs, through the dining room, and out the kitchen door. Running across the damp grass in the moonlight, she approached the pool house. She ducked under the yellow tape and moved to the front door. She slowly started to unlatch the handle. Locked, of course.

Standing alone in the dark with only her flashlight, Helen shivered. What in the world am I doing here? I've lost my mind. She stuck her hands into her jeans, tucking her arms tight in the midnight chill. She felt the silver gum wrapper in her right pocket and pulled it out. The sliver of blue was entwined, and she studied the fabric. She swallowed, realizing why it looked so familiar. Helen's feet felt glued to the pavers beneath her as she fingered the silk. Her fingers were stiff. It matched the scarf she gave Diane. The same one she wore to the party.

A hoot owl in the woods screeched. She jumped, her heart pounding out of her chest as she took off toward the house. She could barely breathe.

I've got to call Joe.

* * *

Back in Kerry's bedroom, Helen tucked herself in bed and dialed Joe's phone. He didn't pick up. She counted to five and hit his name again.

"Helen?" He said, his voice groggy. "It's one in the morning. What's the matter?"

"Joe, I think I know who killed Kerry," she whispered. "Or at least I'm close, very close."

"What?" he cried back. "What are you saying?"

"I think it's Diane."

"Tell me," he breathed. "That's a serious accusation. She's a commissioner. She's running for state senator."

"I know. She stopped at my office today because we're trying to find a new headquarters for her. She was wearing the scarf I gave her for her birthday. She calls it her signature scarf. Today, I noticed a tiny little tear on a corner."

"So?"

"Do you remember when we were in the woods, and I saw a piece of fabric caught on a vine near the back door of the pool house? I stuck it in my pocket because it reminded me of something. Tonight, I realized why. It came from that scarf."

"Helen, she could claim she brushed against it during a tour. It could have been anytime."

"Joe, she told me at the party she hadn't seen the pool house. I promised I'd show it to her, but she left early. Then Kerry was killed." She inhaled. "There's something else. When she came into my office, we used her laptop. Diane had a bunch of document tabs open. Joe, she never wrote a speech for the State Library Association the night Pam died. She didn't write it until today. Why would she lie about that other than to give herself an alibi?"

"I'd have to get a search warrant to check her laptop. If I had a dollar for every time someone thinks they worked on one document and it was a different one, I'd be a very rich man."

"Come on, Joe. Is it possible?"

"Yes, no doubt."

"When do you get your analysis back on OMT and Craig's income statements?"

"I expect a twenty-four-hour turnaround. Late tomorrow, maybe."

"Maggie sent me an article about a clean-up project on the West Coast. Olsoff's company conducted the tests, and the county questioned the results. I think Kerry and Craig were running a scam together. Every time she helped

Craig win another contract, she got a nice big chunk. She'd come into a new section of the country to run a campaign, and she'd find a disgruntled hard-working politician looking for either a leap in rank or a pay-off on the side."

"From day one, you and I wondered why Kerry wanted to manage a campaign in little Kent County, Maryland. I asked Ben the same question today. It's because we're on the Chesapeake, and every politician from Maryland to Virginia wants to look like they're saving the bay." She swallowed. "It breaks my heart to say this. Here in Kent County, I think the local politician is Diane. Either Craig or Diane had the fight with Kerry and killed her."

"We'd have to get financials for OMT before we could accuse Diane or Craig. He's already pushing my D.A.'s buttons because we requested his bank statements."

"One more thought. Calli at Tomes and Treasures told me she passed a dark car on one of the lanes that meets the Davies driveway. She was leaving to pick up her granddaughter about seven-thirty. Diane left the party at six-thirty. She said she had a Five Star meeting in Far Hill at seven. When I told Sarah Howard that Diane had to leave for a Five Star meeting, she was surprised. She's on the same committee and didn't know about the meeting. Can you check that out? Ten bucks, there was no such meeting. Diane was meeting with Kerry."

"We'll check first thing tomorrow. I'll also have that dirt road checked for tire marks against her sedan."

"Another thought. The day Eliot announced he was bowing out of the race, I was parked in the courthouse lot. Diane's car was parked in her assigned spot. It had a long scratch on the passenger side. Now I'm wondering if she scraped that side on the way through the woods."

"We'll take a look," he replied.

"What do we do now?"

"I want to talk this out with Rick in the morning. Let's meet tomorrow at your house, at noon. I rather you not come to the station. We need to flush out either Diane or Craig without accusing them first."

"Why'd one of them kill Kerry?" Helen whispered.

"Based on experience, I'd bet Kerry wanted more of the take, and one of them lost it. We might have motive and opportunity. We don't have much evidence to tie Diane to the pool house and nothing on Craig. Can you sit tight until then?"

"I'm supposed to meet Diane for a quick meeting about properties at her townhouse at ten. I want to keep it."

"How are you going to hide your suspicions?"

"I can do it. She's expecting me. Not showing up would be even more odd."

Joe let out a deep sigh. "Your appointment is at ten. If I don't hear from you by ten forty-five, I'm breaking in the door."

"I'll be fine. Talk to you at ten forty-five. Don't worry."

"Darn you." He hung up.

Chapter Thirty-One

Diane's townhouse had one of the best locations in Port Anne Isles, directly on the water with a view straight down the river to the bay. Helen found the unit for her when she divorced.

"Wow. It's been months since I've been here. You've turned this into a palace." She ran her hands across the gleaming black soapstone covering the island and the textured granite countertops."

Diane glowed. "I decided after everything I went through during my divorce, I deserved to make it nice."

"Agree. If you win your election, will you have to move to Annapolis?"

"Much too soon to think about that. We've a long way to go."

"You look like you're about to go out."

Diane gave a little tug on her spring jacket. "Thanks. I need to go into Hollings soon. Let's narrow down those properties we chose yesterday." Her cell rang. She frowned. "Do you mind if I take this? I've been trying to get this person for days now."

"Of course not. Mind if I take a look at your bedroom? I'd like to see what you did with it." Helen grinned.

Diane gave her a nod as she answered her call and stepped out onto her deck, pulling the door behind her.

In Diane's bedroom, Helen made a quick glance around, pushing open her closet sliders, eyeing her clothes. Everything looked like she'd expect. Neat rows of jackets, tops, skirts, and pants. Her shoes were aligned in shoe compartments on one side. Helen slid the doors back along their tracks, then stopped.

What's that weird smell? She took four steps and peeked into the kitchen. She could hear Diane's muffled voice from the deck. Back in the bedroom, she sniffed along the racks, then the shoes. 'Nancy, Trixie. This is your expertise. What is that scent? Is it my imagination?'

She grabbed a hand towel from the bathroom. Down on her knees, she wrapped the towel around her right hand and shuffled through handbags. Her nose caught another faint whiff. Shoe polish? She ran her hand down the cubbies, drawing out shoes one by one. The smell was stronger. She stopped at a set of low black heels.

Helen sat back. Oh, my God. Carefully, she nudged them out and sniffed. The heels were slightly tacky, and the odor was familiar. Boat varnish.

"Helen?"

She leaped up and shut the closet doors. "Coming! I needed to use your bathroom. You sure did a gorgeous job."

Diane walked in, smiling.

"When are you going to come over to my house and redo my bedroom?" Helen prayed Diane didn't see the sweat on her brow. She inhaled, glancing at her phone and trying to control the quake in her voice. "Let's finish your list before we're out of time. I need to be in the car by ten forty-five." It was ten twenty-eight.

* * *

Joe walked into Helen's house at three minutes after twelve.

"Hi, want some coffee?" Helen offered. "I picked up subs. Turkey or roast beef?"

He pulled out a kitchen stool. "You trying to soften me up with food?"

She forced a smile. "I thought we could use some staying power." Her hands shook as she poured his coffee into a white mug. She poured a mug for herself.

"I wanted Rick here, but he's interviewing Ronnie Mann." Joe rubbed his hands across his face. "You know this whole case could blow up in our faces, right?"

"I know," Helen said softly.

"You look upset. Tell me. How'd your meeting go with Diane?"

Helen's voice wobbled. "She had a phone call and stepped onto her deck. I searched her bedroom closet."

Joe narrowed his eyes. "Go on."

"She has a pair of black dress shoes. I think they're the ones she wore to the party. They have a couple drops of varnish stuck to the heels."

Joe choked on his sandwich. His eyes gleamed. "She *was* in the pool house. Please tell me you didn't touch them."

"I didn't touch them." Helen's eyes were dull, and her face pale. "I think she found the key kept over the doorframe outside the rear door, argued with Kerry, then killed her. She slipped back out and locked the door behind her. She probably tossed the key into the woods on the way to her car." Helen put her hands over her face and started to cry.

Joe took her in her arms. "I know. I know this is ugly."

"I can't believe it's her. She did so much good for this county all these years. How'd she go down this road?" She wept onto his shoulder.

"Here." Joe handed her a white handkerchief. Helen started to laugh.

"Why are you laughing?"

"You're the only man I've met in years who carries a handkerchief." She dabbed at her mascara.

He smiled. "Comes from having a mother with three daughters. Someone was always crying."

Helen sniffed. "What's next?"

"First, we put surveillance on Diane and Craig, so they don't slip away. Then, we set a trap. Whoever shows up is our killer. Most likely, it's Diane. Are you ready?"

Helen pulled back her shoulders. "I'm ready. As Nancy would say, I'm on the case."

Joe smiled and sat back down on his stool. "Do you mind if I eat my sandwich first, Nancy? It's really good."

* * *

253

At six that night, forensic reports came in to Joe.

Helen called Maggie.

"When's your next deadline for posting your 'Around Town' feature in *Kent Whig*?"… She glanced up at Joe. "Tomorrow night at five o'clock. Comes out Mondays and Fridays." She turned back to Maggie. "When do your readers see it online?"… "Seven pm tomorrow night?"… He gave a thumbs up. "Okay, here's what we'd like to do. There's a major story in it, and you get the scoop. You in?"

* * *

Their day of planning had been long and tedious. When the State's forensics paperwork analysis came in that afternoon, they'd hit the mother lode.

"Craig and OMT not only had the inside track on winning bids, they altered the test scores," Helen said. "When water quality keeps dropping and tax money goes down the drain, politicians look bad. When water tests show funding is working, politicians look good. Lots of happy faces in the press clapping each other on the back. Politicians praise OMT and take the credit for hiring them. They get re-elected and rehire OMT over and over. Craig keeps paying Kerry, and Kerry keeps plugging his company. They find a local politician to smooth the way for a piece of their pie. He tampers with test results, and they get the next job. It's one big vicious circle. And lucrative."

"It means none of them were concerned about water safety or people's health," Joe said. "They had no conscience. They acted from pure greed."

Helen nodded. "Now, we wait to find out who takes the bait and shows up at the pool house tonight."

* * *

Tucked back in the trees, her feet deep in decayed leaves, Helen perched on the little knoll with a clear view through the window into the pool house. The sun painted a pale orange-yellow band in the distance across the water.

It was misty, and a soft, light rain had started. Joe and Rick stood in silence, shadowed by Alison's striped canvas drapes inside the dark pool house. The worn green Eastern Shore Piloting Services sign still hung on the wall over Spencer's long wooden desk. With their squad positioned along the perimeter, they waited.

Friday night. Maggie Dyer's 'Around Town' feature posted in its usual spot, bottom right corner, first-page screen. The headline read in bold type, "Police close to break-through in Kerry Lightner murder case." It continued. "An off-the-record source says a forensics team is scheduled for a return visit early tomorrow to confirm a tip on new evidence." The rest of her features covered countywide events, including a speech scheduled for Commissioner Diane Gleason at the VFW.

Helen was afraid she'd cast a light if she checked her phone for the time. Her nerves were shot, and her muscles sore from lack of sleep. Her mind kept spinning. The articles from Todd Bowers about marine pilots and spotting scams on the bay had troubled her. Ever since their lunch at the yacht club, Lizzie's story about ShopTV's discovery of fake testing by one of their face cream providers had gnawed at her. She hadn't known why. She'd been fixated on OMT and how Craig consistently outbid his competitors. She'd been sidetracked by Spencer and Isaac's involvement in dumping waste in the 1960s. It was Todd and Lizzie who pointed her toward an even bigger scandal, fake test results that helped slow down the bay's recovery.

As much as she was relieved Eliot would be exonerated, her heart hurt. Craig Olsoff and Kerry Lightner were easy to shrug off. They built their lives around deception and greed. Diane Fischer invested years into helping her county. How she lost her will to do the right thing weighed on Helen. Accepting this truth cut to her core. She peered through the woods toward the bay, praying Diane wasn't the one who killed Kerry. 'Please, let it be Craig who comes to check the pool house,' she implored her sleuths.

Her cell made a low buzz. She jerked out of her trance and read Joe's text. **Someone sited walking dirt road. DON'T MOVE.**

Helen took in a careful breath, her eyes straining through the dim moonlight.

A dark, hooded figure made careful, soft crunching steps over the leaves and approached the pool house from the rear, slowly edging toward the door, glancing right and left. They turned the knob. Locked. Silently, they stared at the knob, tried again, then stood back. With a low, pin-holed flashlight, they reached up and felt along the inside of the gutter over the doorframe. A tiny glint reflected their light as they touched the missing silver key. Carefully, they slid the key into the lock and turned it, pushing the door open and stepping inside.

In seconds, an entire bank of Maglites flooded the pool house and the surrounding woods. Helen watched as Joe's squad swarmed out from hiding.

"Detective McAlister, Sheriff's Office! Stop right there. Hands above your head!"

The hood dropped, and Diane's stricken face was exposed. Rick put his cell to an ear and barked orders. Helen knew more detectives waited at Diane's townhouse, search warrant in hand.

Helen stepped into the pool house. One sight of her and Diane went wild. Cursing, she leaped at Helen, her hands outstretched, clawing the air. Two police deputies wrestled her to the ground. Joe snapped on cuffs.

Chapter Thirty-Two

Helen stood at the foot of Isaac's grave in St. Cecilia's Cemetery. The stone planks had been removed, and a mound of soft dirt covered in flowers filled the once-open grave. His memorial service was over. Eliot and Alison surrounded her in a bear hug and then headed back to Captain's Watch. They had overnight guests waiting and his local party was poised to endorse him for state senate again. Maggie Dyer's breaking story made front-page news across the country.

She turned to walk down the path and across the neatly mowed grass. Joe waited, hands in his pockets, at the entrance gate with Shawn and Lizzie. Tammi leaned against Helen's blue Mini, her dangling orange and silver earrings sparkling in the sunshine, with Britany and Todd next to her. They were holding hands.

"The coroner's report came in late last night," Joe said. "Isaac died from trauma to the back of his skull. There's no sign of any blunt instrument being used."

Helen nodded. "Safe to presume, Spencer Davies and Isaac argued. They fought, and Isaac fell back on the concrete. Eliot's grandmother overheard them arguing. Spencer never intended to kill his partner. Why he didn't call for help, we'll never really know."

"He panicked, afraid he'd be accused of deliberately killing his partner. Afraid he might be charged for covering crimes that polluted the bay."

"Spencer's grandson's pride got in his way too."

"It almost landed Eliot in jail. He's lucky he had you. You believed in him."

"Any more news on Diane? When she approached the door, I realized I'd tipped her off as to where to find a key the night she killed Kerry. She was so smart."

"Not smart enough. You were right. She let herself in through the rear door, killed Kerry, then locked the door behind her as she slipped out. She hid the key in the gutter. That was a fatal mistake. She should have tossed it into the woods. We searched her house, and found the shoes and scarf she'd worn the night Kerry died and the gloves she used when she killed Pam."

"She loved her fashion statements. She couldn't give them up." Helen blinked away her tears. "I still can't believe she was so desperate for money, and influence."

"She admitted she hired Dustin to raid your house. She hoped she'd get you to stop your sleuthing. She should have known better," Joe said. "By the way, Owen's got a help-wanted sign in his bait shop window."

She smiled. "Where's Craig?"

"Charged with fraud, political election tampering, and impeding a murder investigation. State and federal agencies are climbing all over him." Joe wrapped his arms around her. "Ready to go home? Lizzie is planning dinner on your deck."

"Thank goodness you're not waiting for my cooking."

"Not a chance." He laughed and stroked her back. "Shawn tells me you're leaving tomorrow morning on *Persuasion* for the week. Do you want a shipmate?"

Helen was still. Slowly, she shook her head. "I need some time to myself. I'm even leaving my Detection Club chums behind."

Joe set his chin on the top of her head and was quiet.

"You know you have a problem, don't you? You can't rescue everyone."

Her eyes locked with his. "It's a problem not likely to go away."

* * *

The early sun was warming the bay the next morning as she stowed away the last of her supplies. Her first stop was Still Pond, an easy sail south. She would throw anchor, uncork a bottle of Sauvignon Blanc, and study the stars. Shawn handed her a big duffel bag and a spare blanket.

Lizzie gave her a big kiss. "Have a good time. Make sure you check in every few hours, or Tammi will be texting us."

"Don't make me call out the Coast Guard," Shawn warned.

"My only worry is how I'll survive on my own cooking," Helen grinned.

"You can always survive on Twizzlers," Lizzie said.

"I left them behind. Thought it was time to cut back."

"Did you bring enough wine?" asked Shawn.

"Of course!" she shouted back. "And vodka. Let's not get obsessed with too many new healthy habits at once." Helen waved.

They released the lines and gave *Persuasion* a push off the dock.

* * *

About three hours down the bay, Helen gazed across the water at a blue and white powerboat with a large Coast Guard insignia on the bow charging straight toward her. She frowned and let out her sail to change course and let them pass.

One uniformed sailor was behind the wheel, another on starboard. A tall man, his cap pulled down over his eyes, gripped the rail near the bow. They slowed and cruised alongside her.

The man in the cap pulled off his sunglasses. His dark eyes gleamed.

"Permission to come aboard, Captain?"

Her eyes widened. She hesitated, then grinned. "Permission granted, Sailor."

Gently, the driver tapped up against her hull. Joe tossed a duffel onto *Persuasion*, grabbed her rail, and leaped onto her deck. He turned and saluted the sailors. They returned the salute and sped off.

"Why are you here?"

Joe smiled a slow, hesitant smile and studied her. His eyes traveled from the top of her head down to her chin. "I have a gift for you." He reached into his duffel and handed her a small, wrapped package.

Helen untied its coarse string and pulled back the brown paper. She smiled.

"A 1930s, first edition of *The Murder in the Vicarage* with Jane Marple and a 1940s copy of *The Gatehouse Mystery* with Trixie Belden. Heaven." She held them tight against her chest. "Can't imagine how you found them."

He grinned. "I'm a detective, remember?"

She studied his upside-down smile and the fine lines at his eyes. "You called out the Coast Guard to deliver these?"

His expression turned serious. "It's important, isn't it, to tell someone how you feel? The opportunity once gone may be gone forever."

Helen gazed across the bay, then back. Her eyes cleared. "That sounds very familiar. And, very wise."

He chuckled. "Jane Marple's advice. *The Body in the Library.*"

Acknowledgements

Life can be lonely for a writer. It's a lot of hours, days, weeks, months working alone. Fortunately, I have a lot of enthusiastic people keeping me energized. For all of you, I am so very grateful.

My quirky, clever Detection Club sleuths have strong opinions as to who to thank. My loyal readers are the very first to come to mind. Your encouraging words, enthusiastic reviews, and interest in my characters fuels my writing flame. Each time I read a review, an email, or a post that says you have embraced my characters and my storylines, my heart jumps in joy.

Thank you's go to all the local shop owners, history buffs, and friends up and down the Chesapeake for being a rich source of local history. I enjoy knowing there are readers discovering this special part of the country. Thank you to Kathy Malone Roff for your interest in helping local authors and spearheading my first book launch and promotion. To all the book clubs and organizations that invite me as their guest, thank you. You have opened your arms and become wonderful friends. Special thanks to the Cabin in the Woods and Girls Under Cover clubs. You are smart and kind. I am so happy to know you.

To the Cecil County Public Library staff who always find a quiet corner for me when I need a home away from home to write. My first job as a teenager was in a library. Libraries will always be a haven for me.

To my family, especially my children, Meghan and John, who are my biggest supporters. Your beta reading is invaluable. To John, my husband, who is resigned to being abandoned as I hide away in my study, thank you for believing in me.

A special thank you to Shawn Reilly Simmons of Level Best Books for your editing expertise and patience, Dawn Dowdle of Blue Ridge Literary

Agency, my representative for print and e-formats, and Cindy Bullard of Birch Literary Agency for audio publication through Blackstone Publishing. To Peter Senftleben, thank you for your wise advice on my storylines.

I so appreciate all the writers with the Sisters in Crime and Mystery Writers of America organizations. You are a daily resource as an encouraging sounding board. I could not write without your warm camaraderie.

A small black frame sits on my great grandfather's oak desk in my study and displays a quote by Neale Donald Walsch. He suggests, "Life begins at the end of your comfort zone." Nancy Drew would definitely agree. If this helps you embrace your future, I am happy to have passed it along.

Reach out to me through my website. I would love to hear from you.

About the Author

Judy L. Murray is winner of the Silver Falchion Award, Independent Publisher Gold and Silver Medals, two PenCraft International First Place Awards, and an Agatha Award Nominee. A former Philadelphia real estate broker and restoration addict, Judy has worked with enough delusional sellers, jittery buyers, testy contractors, and diva agents to fill her head with back-office insight and truth versus gossip. She began her professional writing career, after graduating in newspaper journalism from the S.I. Newhouse at Syracuse University. as a newspaper reporter and magazine columnist. She holds a Master's in Business from Penn State University. She lives atop a cliff on the Chesapeake Bay with her husband. They're buffeted by winds in winter and invaded by family and dogs in summer. Judy is a member of Sisters in Crime and Mystery Writers of America. Sign up for her newsletter at www.judylmurraymysteries.com.

SOCIAL MEDIA HANDLES:
  https://www.facebook.com/judymurray4
  https://twitter.com/judylmurray
  https://www.instagram.com/judylmurraymysterywriter/
  https://www.linkedin.com/in/murrayjudy/

AUTHOR WEBSITE:

www.judylmurraymysteries.com

Also by Judy L Murray

Murder in the Master – A Chesapeake Bay Mystery

Killer in the Kitchen – A Chesapeake Bay Mystery

Printed in the USA
CPSIA information can be obtained
at www.ICGtesting.com
LVHW041243301023
762543LV00004B/35